PRAISE FOR THE MIDNIGHT MAGIC MYSTERIES

Werewolf Sings the Blues

"[Vivian's] journey ends with a twist that will have readers rapidly flipping the pages." —*RT Book Reviews*

Witch Upon a Star

"This has it all! Suspense, mystery, fantasy, characters that are completely unforgettable, and a hot romance, as well as a truly strong and hysterical main character! What better way to praise this novel than to say: this is one WICKED story!"

—*Suspense Magazine*

"Hell's bells! Harlow's balanced blend of romance and intrigue makes this one a winner." —*Kirkus Reviews*

"An entertaining romp through a fantasy town where even murder has a little bit of magic involved." —*Library Journal*

Witch Upon a Star

Witch Upon a Star

A Midnight Magic Mystery

Jennifer Harlow

MIDNIGHT INK
WOODBURY, MINNESOTA

First Edition
First Printing, 2015

Book design and format by Donna Burch-Brown
Cover design by Ellen Lawson
Cover illustration: Mary Ann Lasher-Dodge
Editing by Connie Hill

Midnight Ink, an imprint of Llewellyn Worldwide Ltd.

Library of Congress Cataloging-in-Publication Data (Pending)

ISBN: 978-0-7387-3613-6

Midnight Ink
Llewellyn Worldwide Ltd.
2143 Wooddale Drive
Woodbury, MN 55125-2989
www.midnightinkbooks.com

Printed in the United States of America

DEDICATION

For Lydia, the brave

AUTHOR'S NOTE

The events in this book begin twenty years before the events in *Mind Over Monsters*, and twenty-one years before the events in *What's a Witch to Do?*

They are not long the days of wine and roses:
Out of the misty dream
Our path emerges for a while, then closes
within a dream.

—ERNEST DOWSON

AGE 29
GARLAND, TX

"Happy Birthday, Mommy! I love you!"

I stare down at the bouquet of three wilting dandelions, a rare sight for mid-February, even in Texas, my five-year-old holds out to me like a turn of the century courtier, complete with blush on his round apple cheeks. I shut my book, a biography of Eleanor of Aquitaine, and beam at my lovely Max. "Oh, my goodness, they're beautiful," I coo, taking his offering. "You have excellent taste in flowers, *mon cher.* I adore them. Thank you." I peck the top of his towhead. "Now go play. It's getting dark. We'll be heading home soon."

My baby glances at the smirking woman sitting beside me, shrinks in on himself, bows his head, and scurries back to the sandbox to play alone. Happiest in solitude with only his vast imagination as his companion. At least he'll never truly be lonely. I move my gaze to my oldest, pushing my benchmate's little girl on the swing. Seven and already showing a penchant for the ladies. From the girl's giggles and squeals, the feeling will be mutual. My little heartbreaker. He gets that from his father.

"It's your birthday?" the woman beside me queries.

She's been waiting for an opening to strike. Eleanor's kept her at bay for the ten minutes since she and her children pulled up to the park in a beat-up, rusting orange Camaro. The exhaust still saturates the air. This park is technically only for the members of the Valhalla Community, but I always found that rule rather fascist. I've said as much at the homeowners meetings but my protests fell on deaf ears. Letting in so-called "undesirables" such as this woman and her adorable offspring is my form of peaceful protest. Every little bit helps. And most days I'd be more than happy to chat with her, even invite her over for tea as the children played, just not today. Never today.

"Yes, it is," I say with a gracious smile.

"Doing anything special?"

"We're going to my in-laws for supper."

"In-laws." She fake shudders. "Sounds like hell."

"I've had worse birthdays," I say, picking up my book again.

The woman doesn't take the hint or if she does, she ignores it. Judging from the pink leopard-print plastic jacket and ripped tank-top showing off her cleavage, I have the distinct impression this woman does her level best never to be ignored whether the other person likes it or not. The last person did not like it one bit. The heavy make-up fails to hide her black eye.

"God, me too! Last month, when we were living with this guy Buck in Dallas, he took me to a bar to celebrate. Then the bastard spent the whole night flirting with his ex. Should have known then that he was a total loser. Took a smack before I finally wised up."

"Sometimes it takes seeing a person at their worst to learn our lessons and force us to change."

"Totally. Right on." After another gracious smile, I return to my book, getting all of a paragraph read before, "Your boys are adorable. How old are they?"

"Joe's seven and Max is five. Yours?"

"Eight and six, seven at the end of the month. Hope we're settled in by then. We're off to Nevada, maybe Arizona. Wherever I can find work."

Or a man. Hopefully one that doesn't dole out black eyes. Be it my birthday, the sudden chill in the February air, or the fact this woman reminds me far too much of my own mother, I have the sudden urge to flee. I only wish I could scoop up her children and take them with me. Let them disappear into a new life away from dysfunction masquerading as freedom. It was the best and worst event that happened to *me*. For the ninetieth time today, his phantasm visits me, overwhelming every sense to the point of suffocation. Literally. My stomach clenches, and I cease breathing. But only for a moment. I mastered the art of exorcising that particular ghost almost a decade ago. The veil is simply particularly thin today. So, though it goes against my breeding, I choose to be rude. After collecting my book and flowers, I rise from the bench. "It was lovely meeting you. Good luck in Nevada." I step away from the lost soul as I call, "Joe, Max, time to go!"

"But Moooom," Joe whines.

"Say good-bye to your new friends. Come on."

Joe sighs but steps away from the swing and his latest girl-friend. "Fine. Bye, Bea. Bye, Brian." The brown-haired boy on the monkey bars, Brian, nods as Joe passes him. I take Max's sandy hand, wrap my arm around Joe's shoulder, and usher them down Winchester Place to our home. "Mom, can't we stay a little longer? Bea *needs* me to push her. You're always telling me I should do more good deeds and stuff."

"You should. Just not right now. You still have homework, and we don't want to be late to Grandma and Grandpa's. Aunt Donna and your new baby cousin will be there. You can practice your good deeds with them. Maybe you can change a poopy diaper."

"Gross, Mom."

We live in what my father-in-law calls an eclectic neighbor-hood, but he just means the architecture of the houses, most of which he developed or sold himself. Our white two-story rests be-tween a ranch starter home and a gray-stone five-bedroom. We have the distinction of a white picket fence surrounding our pal-ace, with a stone path up to the door, lined with pristine holly bushes, thanks to my husband's green thumb. When I told Na-than I always dreamed of living a suburban, white-picket-fence lifestyle, he took me at my word.

The outside of the house is his domain, but inside is mine. In the blink of an eye I went from squalor to riches, and the décor reflects both experiences. Hardwood floors, ivory walls with prints from Van Gogh and Matisse in frames, bookcases filled to the brim in every room, but the furniture is all secondhand, from estate sales or auctions. The importance of preserving history and its stories was drummed into my consciousness beginning at age nine, and I carried the lesson with me even after I abandoned its teacher. Of course having boys makes the preserving almost impossible. I couldn't get the cleat marks out of my eighteenth-century end table when Joe tossed his shoes on it last week. Boys. I feel as if I spend half my time wiping mud and snot from everything. Good thing I adore my hellions more than life itself.

The phone rings in the kitchen when we walk in. "Joe, take your brother upstairs, then start your homework. I'll be up shortly to help you." As I make my way thought the living room, I hear their thumping footfalls on the steps. The machine is just about to engage when I grab the portable from the stand. "West residence."

"Hey there, birthday girl," my husband says in his usual Texas twang. My favorite accent ever, and I've heard quite a few. Our boys inherited that from him along with his long lips and pointed chin. Thank the universe the bushy eyebrows gene passed them by. "How are you doing?"

"Some moments are easier than others. I'm better now I've heard your voice."

"Naturally," he quips. "Are you still up for supper? We can always cancel."

"I can grin and bear it for a few hours. Besides, I mixed that pain potion for your mother's arthritis this morning."

"Is it any wonder why she likes you more than me?"

"Well, my stock will be plummeting considerably tonight. I'll be lucky if I can muster a smile, let alone mirth and elation. I keep … you know. He's everywhere."

"I know, Annie," Nathan says soothingly. "But hey, just remember: I met you on this day too. It's ours now, not his. I ain't sharing you with him, especially not today."

6

Oh my goodness, it's our ten-year anniversary. "I'm all yours, Mr. West," I say with a private grin.

"Damn right, Mrs. West. And you can prove it to me in a few minutes. I'm leaving the office right now. Need me to pick up anything from the store? Champagne? Edible panties?"

I laugh for the first time today. Without fail that man always brings a grin to my face. "No, just get your cute buns home fast."

"You got it, Mrs. West. Love you."

"Love you too."

We hang up. My smile slowly crumbles. I completely forgot today was the day we met. What kind of wife am I to forget a thing like that? A wretched one. I have officially spent as many birthdays with my husband as I did ... *him*, yet the father of my children has garnered only a momentary thought today. It's usually not this difficult to keep him at bay, even on this date. In the past year I've gone days, weeks even without conjuring his image or a memory, even with the usual triggers. A red rose, the color of his hair in soft light. A classical music piece he used to play on the piano as I pirouetted around him. Dvorak's Symphony #9 came on the radio last week, and I could actually listen to the very end. But today ...

My self-flagellation is cut short but the low creaking of the floor behind me in the laundry room. Oh, I hope the mice haven't returned. The banishing spell shouldn't have worn off yet. Of course there is another possibility. Once a Federal Agent, always one. I stand as still as the stone Galatea before Pygmalion's love brought her to life, even closing my eyes to listen for further disruptions. No breathing. No more movement. Still, I'm taking no chances. Not today. I grab a butcher knife from the wooden block before cautiously padding toward the open room. Nothing in the tiny cell but the pile of whites I've neglected. I lower the knife. Old age is making me batty. With a sigh, I put the knife on top of the washer, add the whites, and wipe down the kitchen counters before going to check on my little men. Homework, baths, and dinner attire next. They'll fight me all the way. They get their fighting spirit and stubbornness from me. Like with most things about motherhood, this makes me proud, terrified, and exhausted all at once.

I slog from the kitchen back into the living room. Be it the day or perhaps there's something in the air, my tension fails to wane with every slow step. No, this will not do. I cannot face my children when I'm amped like a live wire or I'll electrocute them. Their father does that more than enough. This must be how Nathan feels all the time. Our poor electronics incur his wrath on his off days. We just replaced the last television he fried after a shopping center development deal fell apart. A massage usually helps, though I receive static shocks every ten seconds until he calms. The things one endures for love.

I just need a few moments. The pictures on the fireplace mantel are slightly askance. In a fit of nervous energy I cleaned the house top to bottom earlier. Nothing should be out of place today. I move to the fireplace to line them up. My friend Audrey from next door once observed there was nary of photo of me from childhood on display anywhere—that it was as if I didn't exist until my wedding. I told her they were all destroyed in a fire. Not a total lie.

This. This is what matters.

I stare at the picture of me teaching Joe to walk in our backyard, my blond hair blowing in the breeze with a proud grin on my face. Then at the photo of Max's first Christmas with three generations of the West clan sitting around the tree ripping open gifts. Last year's trip to Niagara Falls. Me demonstrating at the *barre* the arabesque position to my ballet students. Joe receiving his soccer trophy. Me hugely pregnant with Max as both Joe and my husband kiss my belly. Our wedding…

That one brings the widest grin. I pick it up. I wear a simple off-the-shoulder cotton dress for a simple wedding thrown together in two weeks. I didn't want a big to-do and I found out later my fiancé was petrified I'd change my mind if we dawdled. As if I ever would. He was my best friend. The man who brought me back to life with patience, kindness, and love. Who gave me everything I never knew I wanted. He still is, and always will be. My gift from the universe. Okay, I'm ready—

In the glass's reflection, the man materializes from nothing. One moment I'm alone, the next a man in a black ski mask holding something in his hand is inches behind me. There isn't even a moment to be afraid. Long dormant instinct awakens like a roaring giant, ready in that millisecond it takes for me to spin around and catch the intruder's wrist before he lowers the object into my body. A needle. By the time that fact penetrates my consciousness, I'm already raising my knee to his groin. I hit nothing but air. As fast as he arrived, that's how quick he vanishes. I stare at the space he inhabited, hand curled around nothing and leg up. I take one second to think. Teleporter. Danger. The boys.

My babies.

I grab the nearest weapon, a fireplace poker, and dash toward the archway. I make it one step through the threshold to the foyer before he pops a foot in front of me. He's almost as tall as my 6'3" husband, but with a medium build and dressed in all black, the only flesh visible being his gray eyes. I also take in the gun holster with pistol on one side and pouch on the other. He lunges needle first, but I swat the hand away with the poker. With a grunt, he drops the syringe in my hallway. Momentary victory. As I raise the poker once more, he teleports away. Once again I lose a precious second to adjust my strategy. Less than. Just as I realize he's gone, strong arms wrap around mine from behind in a bear hug. My forearms cross my chest as if I were in a casket and very well could be soon.

"I don't want to hurt—" the man says in French.

The back of my head walloping his nose and jaw silences him, save for the groan of pain. He releases me. Poker first, I pivot around to find my assailant stumbling back into the living room just out of reach of my metal baton. He uses my missed attempt to his advantage, taking one step forward and kicking me square in the stomach hard enough to stun. For a few seconds there's nothing in the universe save for agony and suffocation. But he doesn't attack again. He simply stands there and in French says, "I don't want to hurt you."

"Mom?" Joe calls from upstairs.

Whatever pain, whatever terror I'm experiencing vanishes when I hear my son's concerned voice. The man's attention turns toward the voice. Through the pain, through the fear, one word shrieks through. *Fight!* As I raise my poker again, I charge him, bridging the ten-foot gap. This time his hand wraps around my wrist. With one quick movement, he jerks my arm downward, my elbow twisting unnaturally, almost 180 degrees. The shooting pain and violence of movement forces me to lose the poker. It clatters to the floor. My legs still function though. I pivot on my right foot to sidekick him in the stomach with all my might. He releases my arm and backs into the sofa. He's in a perfect position for the front snap kick, which I deliver right to his sternum. Thank you, F.R.E.A.K.S. training. The bastard flips over the couch but doesn't complete the trip. He teleports out of sight. *Merde.*

"Mom, you okay?" Joe asks.

"Get your brother and hide!"

"Mom!" Max shrieks in terror.

He's upstairs.

I'm about to reach for the poker but cannot make the journey. The man reappears to return my kick. His foot connects to my chest, and I collapse backward to the floor. My already sensitive cranium thumps against the hardwood, stunning me for a moment. My opponent uses my weakness to remove another syringe from his holster. At least it's not a gun. "You are making this more difficult than it has to be. He gave strict orders not to harm you or the children." He uncaps the needle. "Please do not—"

I raise my finger, pour all my fear, my anguish, and my power into its tip and shout, "*Lapsus!*"

A blast of magic siphons through my body, smashing into him with tidal wave force. As if shot from a cannon, the man lifts off the floor and flies backward fifteen feet into the bookcase. Even over the clattering and thumping of objects colliding, the distinct sound of snapping bone and tendons can be heard as his neck hits an oak shelf. The bastard's head snaps back as his throat arches forward at an unnatural angle. Broken. He collapses in a heap, books raining down and around on him. He's too dead to notice. Damn it.

"Mom?" Joe calls.

"I-I-I'm fine," I shout back. "Do-don't come down here. Stay with your brother."

"Is the mean man gone?" Max asks.

"He is. Are you two okay?"

"Yeah," Joe says.

"Just … stay up there with the door locked until either I or your dad gets you, okay?"

After a few deep breaths, I manage to stand, retrieve the poker in case I'm wrong, and walk over to the prostrate assassin. Those gray eyes remain open, unblinking as I lower myself to his level. Just in case, I exchange the poker for his gun, a Walther PPK with a silencer. The only other items on him are a car key and third syringe. Three syringes. Me and the boys. Then why … the gun weighs heavy in my hand. He didn't pull it once. A chill runs down my aching spine. Nathan. For Nathan. But when I peel off the dead man's mask, my legs literally fail me. I thump to the ground and a second later realize I'm trembling.

I don't know how long I sit here, shaking like a leaf on the wind, pointing a gun at a dead man. Minutes maybe. Feels like a blink of an eye until I hear my husband's voice. "Annie? Anna!" he shouts, panicked. I blink again, and he's by my side, brown eyes double their size as he stares at the man. "Who is—"

"His name is Didier Fournier. He's a Swiss National I met in Vienna when I was seventeen. Contract killer."

"Killer? The boys—"

That word snaps me out of my haze. "My boys!" I bound up like a spring and sprint out of the room and up the stairs with my husband a step behind. "Joe?" I ask, pounding on his bedroom door. The lock clicks a second later, and the moment the door opens, I'm through, scooping up my son and hugging him tight. Max dashes toward me from the bed, and I lift him too. I shower them with kisses. On a normal day, Joe would push me away but there's nothing normal about today. He clings to me as tight as I do him. "Are you okay?"

"We're okay," my son says. "He didn't hurt us."

I carry my boys to Joe's bed and lower us into the purple *Tiny Toon Adventures* bedspread. "I'm sorry. I'm so sorry."

"Was he a ghost, Mommy?" Max asks.

"No." He just worked for one.

"What did he want?" Joe asks.

I turn from my son's aquamarine eyes, so like mine, to my husband's brown ones hidden behind his glasses. Even still I can see the dread stretching them to unnatural proportions. Because he knows the answer. Because he knows what it means. *That he's alive.* He's finally come for me. The man who was my father, my mother, my friend, my savior, my mentor, my heart, my soul, my angel, and ultimately my devil.

My Asher.

PART I

NIGHTS OF BLOOD AND ROSES

AGE 9
ALBANY, NY

It was odd that the knock on the door woke me that night. There was nary an evening when my father, Sven, didn't have nocturnal visitors, be it old friends from Haight-Ashbury passing through to crash for a few days or clients looking to score his seemingly endless supply of pot and LSD. Through years of hard-won adaptation I could sleep through jam sessions and high-pitched laughter. I even once slumbered through a client's bad trip that ended with a broken table and split lip for Sven. I did wish I was able to have seen that last one. Would have been refreshing to witness someone turn the tables and beat my father for a change.

There was nothing out of the ordinary about that night or the knock, but it still pulled me from slumber like true love's kiss did Sleeping Beauty. My eyes fluttered open with the first rap but by the second, I'd never been more awake. Even before I met him he had the power to change the air around him, calling me to him. But that night all I knew was it was just past midnight, I had a history test in the morning, and the later the visit, the greater the chance the visitor would cause mischief. The perfect beginning of my birthday. I threw off my covers and tiptoed to my bedroom door, opening it just a crack. If there was to be a problem I wanted to be ready. My father stepped into view but not the stranger. I didn't dare open the door farther. I learned the hard way not to draw attention to myself when we had company. Once or twice I even had to use an invisibility charm to get to the bathroom.

"... something to drink?" Sven asked. "We have Tab or—"

"I am not thirsty, thank you," the mystery man replied in a lyrical voice, as if the words glided on air. I couldn't place the accent but knew it wasn't American.

"Right on, right on," Sven said, blond head bobbing. "We're both busy men. Straight down to business, I can dig it." My father gestured to the yellow linoleum card table in the kitchenette. "Sit down." No matter the angle I stretched, I could not catch a glimpse of the man even as he sat at our tiny table. "So, you didn't say much on the phone. How'd you get my name anyway?"

"A mutual friend. Gerard. He speaks most highly of your work." Gerard MacIntyre. Sven sometimes dealt in his nightclub, and on occasion he'd request a charm or potion I had to make.

"He's a good cat," Sven said. "So, what exactly can I help you with? I just got in some simsmilla and angel dust from Hawaii, or—"

"I am here for a spell," the man cut in.

"It's witchcraft, baby," Sven's girlfriend chuckled from her usual spot on the couch.

"Shut up, Andie," Sven snapped. If we didn't have company, a slap would have followed. Instead, Sven grinned at the man. Without a doubt my father was a handsome man, with long straight blond hair, aquamarine eyes, pretty face, and milky skin, all of which I inherited. All it took was a single grin, and he'd be out of trouble or in a woman's bed. No real magic required. "What kind of spell?"

There was silence for a few moments before the chair scraped against the tile. "This was a mistake. You cannot help me."

"Wait, what? No, I can. Whatever you need, man, I can deliver."

"You are no witch, sir. I do not know how you acquired the items for Gerard, but he will hear how you lied to him about your abilities and lineage. And he does not suffer liars well, Mr. Olmstead."

"No, wait!" Sven said, leaping up. "Okay, I never told him *I* was the witch, man. It's … It's my kid, *she's* the witch." My father looked my way, and I froze, not even blinking. I'd catch hell later, but he was all jolly smiles then. "Anna? Anna, sunshine, come on out. It's okay. He won't bite."

Having no real choice, I left the relative safety of my bedroom dressed in nothing but my ratty, faded blue nightie with more holes than not, hair a rat's nest of tangles, and eyes crusty from sleep. None of that mattered, though. Nothing mattered the moment I laid eyes on him. *Nothing.* My father, the apartment, the state, the whole world exploded into ashes save for the stranger twenty feet away. At the time I didn't know what it meant, that strange, frightening, glorious moment, but I did recognize it was important. That the universe had shifted, and my life had irrevocably changed. For better or worse.

It wasn't just because he was handsome. Compared to my father he was almost plain, with too rectangular a jaw, an asymmetrical nose, hollow cheeks, lips as thin as the rest of him, and piercing blue eyes a shade too far apart. I didn't notice any of that, and when I did, those flaws made me love him more. If possible. And though I did not glean it at the time, the man staring at me with his mouth slightly open as if he'd just taken a sudden, gasping breath, experienced the same shift.

My father's touch, an extremely rare loving squeeze to his side, jolted me back into my body. "Anna, this is Mr. Asher."

"Just ... Asher," he said, not removing his eyes from mine.

"Say hello, sunshine. Don't be rude."

"Hello, Asher," I mumbled.

"Hello. Anna."

We stared at one another, neither wishing to break the gaze first. Sven must have noticed because he stepped in front of me to block our line of sight. I was almost glad for it. I could breathe again.

"She may be young, but she is a bona fide genius. Got tested and everything. Even skipped two grades. My wife Astrid taught her some spells before she split. Forgot some spell books too. We collected a lot through the years. You want it, Anna can do it. *Whatever* you want. If the price is right, that is."

I peeked around my father to see Asher's reaction to that last proposition. The left side of his face twitched with displeasure. The sides of my mouth did the same in a momentary smile.

"I require a demonstration of her abilities."

"Easy peasy, man. Anna?" Sven stepped aside. "Show the gentleman your stuff."

"Yeah, dance for him, monkey," Andie chuckled. She sat up and peered over the back of the orange couch the same color as her hair. She would have been pretty if not for the plethora of freckles and bloodshot brown eyes from her chronic pot habit. "Dance."

She asked for it. Literally. I raised my hand, pointed my finger at her nose, channeled my magic through it, and said, "*Sanguine nox.*"

The second I lowered my finger, two streams of blood gushed from her nostrils. "Fuck! You little bitch!" She leapt off the couch and rushed to the bathroom for tissues.

Sven laughed, but Asher remained silent, staring at me with a tiny, proud smile. "Can she waltz as well?" he asked.

"Sorry?"

"Never mind. I shall give her an opportunity." He reached into his still-buttoned brown trench coat and removed a piece of paper. "This is the spell I wish performed. I simply need the girl to prepare the potion and perform the ritual. For her time, I shall pay five hundred dollars. Is that amenable?"

Five hundred was about what Sven made all month. He would have sold me to the devil himself for half that price. "Um, yeah," Sven said, taking the paper from our generous benefactor.

"*Bon.* I shall return tomorrow evening at eight sharp."

"With the money," Sven added.

"Of course." Those blue eyes met mine. "Until tomorrow, Anna," he said as if savoring the sensation of my name on his lips. He never pronounced it another way again. Asher bowed his head, glanced at my father, then showed himself to the door without looking back. The moment the door shut, the breath I held was finally released. I hardly drew in the fresh air when the slap my father administered to my cheek forced it out again. As if his palm was part jellyfish, the stinging began immediately with the aching to soon follow. I'd had worse, much worse, but this one caught me by surprise.

"What have I told you about spying? You know better. Go apologize to Andie, then get your ass back to bed. You got school tomorrow. Get!"

He shoved me toward my bedroom, and I ran the rest of the way, sealing the door in case Andie wanted a pound of flesh too. As I climbed back into my bed, my cheek throbbing as violently as the act that caused it, I did so with a smile on my face. Tomorrow. Tomorrow and tomorrow and tomorrow no longer creeping in this petty pace from day to day. Because of *him*.

"Asher."

———

For those grueling sixteen hours, time crept to a standstill. I couldn't concentrate on my schoolwork, my one friend Rachel gave up attempting to talk to me at lunch, and what little focus I possessed was channeled into learning the spell he needed performed. It was complex, far more powerful and dark than anything I'd attempted before. Potions and charms were easy, simply following a recipe, but this required more than adding burdock to sage. He wished me to master life and death. My life and someone else's death. I honestly did not believe I was up to the task. That I'd let Asher down. I wouldn't. *I couldn't*, the universe all but whispered to me during those sixteen hours.

At the stroke of eight, I was bundled in my thickest coat and bell bottoms perched on the edge of my bed staring at my closed door, willing that knock to come. My hands ached from the hundred times I'd balled them into fists. I would do this. I *would*. A minute past the deadline. Another. My bedroom suddenly felt as if the walls themselves were sucking the air from the enclosure. I couldn't stand it a moment longer. I voluntarily joined the others. Sven sat at the table parsing marijuana into dime bags as Andie maintained her spot on the couch, enjoying one such bag. If either recalled it was my birthday, they didn't let on. I didn't expect a pony or even a card, but a simple, "Happy birthday," would have been nice. Instead I got, "You damn well better be ready when he gets here, girl," from my father.

"I am," I said as I sat beside Andie. Maybe *Green Acres* would keep my mind off the tardy stranger.

"That guy gave me the creeps. You're really letting her go off alone with him?" Andie asked.

"Yeah. She can take care of herself," Sven replied.

She took a hit off the joint and shrugged. "She's your kid."

"He won't hurt me," I said with utter certainty.

"Take a knife just in case," Sven said. "If he even fucking shows."

"He'll be here," I said.

I barely got the third word out before there was a knock. A wide grin crossed my face at that beautiful noise. I leapt off the couch before even Sven rose to answer the door. "Come in," he told Asher.

He was as ethereal as my memory made him out to be. His snow-white skin almost glowed, and as he stepped under the light, his hair became the color of a red rose. Or blood. "Is she ready?" he asked without polite preamble.

"She is if you got my cash."

Asher removed the money from his trench coat pocket as my father salivated. "Groovy. Looks good. She's all yours. Anna, get your stuff. Time to go." I grabbed my bag and checked to make sure I had the potion, crystals, and other ritual items required. *I could do this.* "No refunds," Sven added as he pocketed the cash.

"Fine." His gaze moved to mine. "Shall we?"

"Yes, sir," I muttered as I hustled to his side so I could grab him and hold on for dear life in case he changed his mind. Luckily I didn't need to resort to embarrassing groveling. Asher placed his hand on my back to usher me from the apartment. That one touch loosened the strangling knot in my stomach. *I could do this.* I walked by his side down the hall and stairs with nary a word spoken. Though I kept my eyes forward, I sensed the stolen glances at the bruise on my cheek from the previous night's unwarranted discipline, yet he said nothing. I was grateful for it.

It was obvious which car was his, the only Porsche amid vans and Oldsmobiles. I climbed in without prompting. Asher got in as I clipped my seatbelt. He didn't turn on the engine. We just sat in that chilled car for a few seconds, staring at the dead trees dancing with the frigid air. Finally, he said, "You have nothing to fear this night. No harm will come to you at my hands."

"I know," I said after a pause.

Despite the freezing temperature, my body warmed when I saw him smile. It was only for a flash and the moment it vanished, he appeared almost guilty for the show. Still. I was proud to have earned it. More than proud. I was addicted. He started the car.

Our destination was twenty miles away. Twenty miles and the only words uttered were my request to swith on the heater. We didn't need to say anything. The few times I dared to gaze upon him, my companion was so deep in thought I was surprised he even noticed the other cars on the road. He put up a good front, his face almost unreadable, yet I could almost feel the nervousness, and the undercurrent of melancholy that grew with each passing mile prickling my skin. Even at the beginning I was so in tune with him I could glean his emotions before I'd even notice my own. I wanted to reach across squeeze his shoulder or hand to comfort him, but I didn't dare. Whatever was going on inside his mind, he didn't want me invading it, even to rescue him from himself.

I deduced our destination from the spell, but I was still a tad unnerved when we did in fact pull up beside a wooden fence surrounding a small cemetery. I'd never been to one before. I was no medium, but as a witch the veil between the dead and living was thinner than for normal people, especially during a full moon like that night. Even from that distance, I could faintly sense them, see them out of the corner of my eye. I avoid cemeteries to this day.

Asher shut off the engine and stared at the tombstones outlined by the bright moon. I lost him to his thoughts again, but this time he didn't bother to hide his trepidation. His mouth was as tight as a vice and jaw clenched hard enough every muscle and tendon poked out high enough his face could double as the Rocky Mountains.

"I can do this," I said with absolute certainty after a few seconds.

"I do not doubt it," he said, finally turning my way. "I am simply not sure I want you to anymore." He flashed me a sad smile before staring at the graveyard once more. This time I did tentatively reach to touch his arm. Halfway there those blue orbs jutted my way, almost in warning. I jerked my hand away. "Please retrieve your bag." He opened the car door and leapt out before he lost his nerve.

I trailed a few paces behind him through the headstones and overgrown grass to the back of the cemetery, stopping at the only plot with a fresh bouquet of white roses resting on it. Asher started at the half broken tombstone with his back to me, I guessed he was deep in thought once more. I stood attempting to cease trembling, both my body and soul chilled by the atmosphere. "Please begin your preparations."

It was time to pierce the veil and raise the dead.

I placed crystals in the four corners of the plot and rimmed the perimeter with salt to keep the magic centered and spirit inside. I was salting when Asher said, "You are shivering. Here." He removed his jacket.

"You won't be cold?" I asked, teeth practically chattering.

"No." He stepped toward me to hand me the jacket. "It would be far too ironic for you to catch your death in a graveyard."

My grateful smile garnered one from him. "Thank you." He wasn't a tall man, barely topping 5'9", so the jacket fit perfectly, though it did little to assist against the elements. Still, this act of kindness did wonders for my spirit. It was lovely—someone actually being concerned about my welfare. Foreign but lovely. "The spell says I need something of the person to add to the potion."

"Left pocket. The locket."

Sure enough I found the necklace with a lock of golden hair. A few strands went into the glass vial holding the potion I had mixed earlier. Next came the part I hated. The athame, or ritual knife, weighed heavy in my hand. After removing my glove, I pressed the blade to my finger but couldn't finish the job. It just hurt too much. "Allow me." My gaze whipped toward Asher, who was bridging the small gap between us. He took the athame from me and said, "Please look into my eyes." I obeyed without hesitation. My body began pleasantly prickling as if I were close to a Tesla coil. "You will feel no pain." He was right. I sensed the pressure of the blade, even my tender skin parting, but didn't register the sensations as pain. When he stepped away, breaking eye contact, the buzzing vanished. "See? No pain."

"Thank you."

Using my blood, I painted the spirit sigil in the center of the grave before pouring the potion in the center and touching a crystal with my bloody finger to energize the perimeter. Then came the hard part. "What was her name?"

"Jane. Jane Ann Jackson. She was born September 18, 1760, and died July 27, 1783."

Clutching the locket and touching the hair, I shut my eyes and called to the universe, to the magic all around—in the trees, in the ground, in the air, in every living cell and energy source in this world and the next. I was its vessel, a container expanding and contracting with every beat of my heart. The potion, the hair, the blood, the name Jane Ann Jackson, I funneled that power into piercing that fragile divide, slicing it open with my will alone. If before I was touching a Tesla coil, at that moment I was at the center of a nuclear power plant. It built and built and built until … critical mass. The burst of energy exploded out of me, propelling me backward from the force. Instead of crashing to the ground, arms caught me before I fell. Asher stared down, face contorted with worry, but I managed a reassuring smile. My hero grinned back. Oh yes, I was addicted to those smiles already.

"Where am I?"

Both our attentions turned toward the grave. My mouth dropped open a little at the sight of what I'd done. A tiny young woman dressed in American Colonial garb I'd only seen in history books, with a kerchief covering her head, hovered an inch off the ground. Through the majority of her features could be made out—large eyes and lips, straight nose, prominent cheekbones—she was still slightly out of focus with a glowing aura outlining her. I'd done it. I was staring at a real, undead ghost I'd yanked from another realm. My actions were too large, too grave for my nine-year-old mind to wrap around. All I wished to do was run shrieking back to the car and hide. I could have run too with nary a glance from my companion. My existence faded from Asher's mind the moment he saw her.

"Jane," he whispered in wonder.

"Asher?" she whispered in the same enchanted tone. "'Tis you? I...I can barely see you."

"I am here, my love," he said, taking a few uneasy steps toward her. "I am here."

"What...what witchcraft is this? Why...why can I not feel anything? Where am I?" she cried. "I...I do not know this place. Where are Mama and Papa? I...I think...I was just with them."

"All is well, my love. Please do not be afraid," he pleaded. "You...You...are safe. No harm can come to you. I'm sorry to frighten you so. I...I simply had to see you one last time before..."

The torment roaring inside that cut short his words also contorted his expression into a mask of sheer agony. I wanted to dash to his side to offer some comfort, but my legs stayed firmly planted. I had no place in this exchange.

"I waited for you."

"I know," he said.

"I waited as long as I could, but you never returned for me. You swore you would return."

"I did," he responded desperately, "but you had already … moved on."

"I waited," she said, voice cracking. "Three years, yet no letter. No word. I thought you had forsaken me. Forgotten me."

"*No*," he said with enough force to startle both the living and the dead. "I loved you with all I possessed, Jane. I have *never* forgotten you. *Never*. I had to flee. You know I did. There was no other course of action. They would have slaughtered us both. I would have sent for you, but with the war and price on my head, it would have been too dangerous for you. And when all was settled, you were already gone. You were gone, thinking I held no love for you. You were gone … hating me."

"I never hated you, my love. You were my sun, my moon, my stars. You showed me a beautiful, enchanting world few had seen. The year we spent together, the love we shared, brought such magic to my life it could sustain me for eternity. I could never hate you."

"For true?"

"Yes, love," she said with a sad smile. "For well and for true."

Asher stared at the phantasm in disbelief, jaw slowly dropping as the words sunk in. "I …" he said breathlessly. "I miss you. I still love you, and I miss you so. And I am sorry. I am so sorry for causing you a moment's pain."

"I forgive you," she whispered. "And I love you too. Forever and for always. Now go and love for the both of us." The specter looked straight at me. "Please send me back now. *Please*."

I glanced at Asher, but he was gone in all but body. He was more of a ghost than Jane, staring at nothing and trembling in a vain attempt to release the anguish evident all over his face. I could have set him on fire, and he wouldn't have noticed. Or cared. He would have welcomed an agonizing death. Any death. I stepped in front of him.

"Take care, my love," she whispered just before I raised my hand again and said, "*Quies quietis.*"

And she vanished with a serene smile on her face.

Five seconds. I gave him five seconds of privacy before spinning around. Just as I did, he turned his face away as he wiped his cheeks with his sleeve, leaving dark smudges on his beige sweater and face. I took one step. Two, before wrapping his hand in mine. One touch, just one touch and he crumbled, literally crumbled to the ground as he let out a wail to wake the rest of the dead. I offered no resistance as he collected me into his arms and sobbed against my tiny shoulder as I hugged him back as tight as I was capable. We stayed like that until all of his tears were spent. Until his heart was empty of her. And when he finally released me, and I stared into his blood-filled eyes, wiping the tears away from his red-streaked cheeks without fear or hesitation at the gruesome sight, that was the moment I officially took my place in that now-vacant spot inside him. That empty void that even death could never touch.

The place I was always fated to be.

———

"Are you hungry?"

These were the first words he'd spoken since we left the cemetery. I was sent back to the warm car as he cleaned up both himself and the scene. When he returned, the only remnants of what occurred were his ruined sweater and jacket, and the tang of blood that hung faintly on the air. Of course I had a thousand questions but kept my lips firmly shut tight. Not the time. Asher started the car, and for ten minutes only Mick Jagger and then Rodger Daltry uttered a word until we passed a Denny's sign for the next exit.

"Yes," I said. "Thank you."

Then not another syllable until we stepped into the restaurant. The hostess, a middle-aged woman with a beehive hairdo, gave us a toothy grin. If she thought it odd a customer was dressed only in a white undershirt, grass-stained pants, and sunglasses to cover the missed bloody smudges on the coldest night of the year, she didn't let on. "Hello. Two?"

"Yes. And where is your lavatory?" Asher asked.

"In the back by the payphones."

"Thank you. Please show her to our table. She may order whatever she desires." He nodded to us both before walking away to freshen up.

"This way, sweetie," the hostess said to me. I followed her to a booth. "Your daddy sure is proper."

"He is *not* my Daddy," I stated emphatically.

"Oh. Sorry. My mistake."

I scooted into the booth and after setting down two menus, the hostess departed. I hadn't eaten since lunch so I ordered a Grand Slam with extra bacon and hashbrowns, a chocolate malt, and water for Asher. He returned, now fresh faced and sans sunglasses as our waitress, an elderly woman with silver hair, strolled away.

"I got you water," I said as he slid across from me.

"Thank you." We stared at one another for a few seconds, neither sure what to say next. He took the reigns. "You must be ... confused by all you witnessed tonight."

"Not really. She was your girlfriend, you left her, and she died." I paused. "How did she die?"

"In childbirth. The baby as well."

"I'm sorry."

"As am I," he all but whispered.

"You must have loved her a whole lot."

"More than I thought myself ever capable of, yes," Asher said almost angrily. At himself, at her, at the fates, to this day I don't know.

"Then ... why did you leave her?"

"I had no choice. There was a price on my head. Had I remained, my enemies would have discovered our affiliation and brought harm to her and her family. I did what I believed was best at the time."

"Why were you in danger?" The sides of his mouth twitched with displeasure. "It's okay. You don't have to tell me."

"No, I ... simply do not wish to frighten you."

"You don't frighten me," I proclaimed.

"Perhaps I should," he said with the same certainty.

The waitress returned with my milkshake and his water, breaking the uneasy mood. So my mouth couldn't get me into more trouble, I sucked down my malt. "Here you go. And can I get you anything, mister?"

"I have already dined tonight, thank you." With a nod, she walked away. "Is your treat up to your standards?"

"It's really good," I said, mouth full. "Thank you."

After a pause, "No. Thank *you*."

"What for?"

"I shall admit I did not believe one so young would be up to my task. Witches three times your senior could not do what you did this evening. You shall be a force to be reckoned with when you fully come of age. You are a High Priestess without doubt."

"What's a High Priestess?"

His eyes narrowed. "Your mother never ... it is a witch who, in addition to performing spells, can control the elements: earth, air, fire, and water."

"And I'll be one of them?" I asked. "Groovy. When?"

"When you ... blossom into a woman."

"How will I know when that happens?" I asked, genuinely perplexed.

"One simply knows," he answered with a lopsided grin before nervously clearing his throat. "So, is it just you and your father now?"

"Yeah. Astrid ran away. She's been a Deadhead for almost two years."

"A Deadhead?"

"Yeah. She told Sven that when she heard Jerry Garcia sing at Woodstock, it was like the universe told her it was her mission to follow the band around and become his muse. So she split. I mean, she wrote us two letters, but that was over a year ago."

"I am sorry. That must be difficult."

I shrugged. "Sometimes one of Sven's girlfriends lives with us or he lets clients stay. They're even nice. Sometimes."

"And other times?" he asked with a hard edge.

I just stared down at my plate.

"That bastard," Asher whispered. "Your father should not sell you like chattel to the highest bidder."

I didn't say a word. I kept my eyes lowered and lips on my straw. I didn't like talking about Sven or the fact I was what Andie called "damaged goods." I didn't want one negative thought about me to cross Asher's mind. "So, there are really witches who couldn't do what I did? You're not just saying that to make me feel good?"

"I would not lie to you. What you accomplished took such focus, not to mention tremendous power. You have such potential," he said, almost wistful. "You are a true diamond in the rough. And what you did for me this evening, not simply the spell . . ." He paused. "No one has shown me such kindness in eons."

"I'm sorry."

"Why would you be sorry?"

"That no one's been nice to you. That you're so sad. And lonely."

He studied me for a few intense seconds, as if daring me to blurt out I was faking sincerity or to break down in tears. But I matched his expression, staring over my milkshake. A slow, sad smile crept across his face. "You are extraordinary, do you know that? Never allow anyone to make you feel otherwise. Not for a moment."

"Okay."

The waitress walked up with my meal and a grin for Asher. "Lotta food for such a little girl. Your daddy gonna help you with it all?"

"He's not my daddy. And I'm not little. I'm eigh—no, nine."

"My mistake. Just have a birthday, then?"

"Yes. Today."

"Oh! Happy birthday, hon! Nine is a big year, almost double digits!"

"Thank you."

The waitress departed again. I wasted no time in piling food into my mouth. Asher watched as I gorged myself on grease. "Is it truly your birthday?" I nodded as I chewed my eggs. "She is correct. Nine is a momentous year. When I reached your age, I was sent to the front as a messenger boy for the Plantagenet army."

"Were you scared?" I asked with my mouth full.

"Oh, yes. Especially after being captured by the Capetians. I was their prisoner for months until I liberated myself."

"So, how old are you now?"

"How old do I appear?" he asked with a raised eyebrow. I narrowed my eyes at him and scowled. I didn't enjoy being treated like a fool. My ire unleashed another of his grins. "When did you deduce my secret?"

"In the car. I could see my breath but not yours. Then you used magic with my finger, cried blood, and Jane was dressed like Thanksgiving. Astrid told me you guys existed."

"And yet you are not frightened of me."

"I told you. No. You promised you wouldn't hurt me. Why would I be?"

Judging from the half-open mouth and squinted eyes trained on me, my matter-of-fact delivery confounded him. "Even still, most are."

I shrugged. "I think it's groovy. Never getting sick. Hypnotizing people to do whatever you want. Being superstrong so no one picks on you. Getting to live forever."

"Never feeling the sun radiating against your face. Never tasting food or wine again. Standing by as all of those you love wither and die," he countered. "It is possible for one to exist for so long they forget what it is to truly live."

"Is that why you're so sad? Everyone you love is dead? Like Jane?"

"It is one of the reasons, yes."

My nine-year-old mind pondered his quandary. "When Astrid left, Sven was gone a lot. We'd just moved to Albany so I didn't know anyone. They skipped me two grades, so I'm younger than everyone else. People in school were mean. Still are. They call me a freak. I always say not even my own Mommy wants to be around me. I was sad all the time. I cried a lot. Then one day there was this noise at my bus stop. A meow. It was an orange kitten, real skinny and missing an eye too. She was going to die so I brought her home. Kirsten," I said with a sad smile. "She was my best friend. And I wasn't sad anymore. Until ..."

"Until?"

"She ate some of Sven's pills and died a month ago when I was at school." Remembering her soft fur, the way she curled up against my tummy at night purring away, me coming home and telling her about my day made me want to burst into tears right in that restaurant. I bit the inside of my mouth to stop the impulse. I didn't want Asher to think me weak crying over a silly cat.

"I am sorry, Anna," he said in a low tone.

I shrugged again. "'Don't cry because it's over, smile because it happened.'"

"Wise words."

"They're not mine. Dr. Seuss said it." Asher stared at me blankly. "*Green Eggs and Ham? The Cat in the Hat?*" He shook his head.

"Don't know many kids, huh?"

"Is it that obvious?"

"Well, you don't talk to me like I'm stupid, so yeah."

"I would not dare," he said playfully. "It would be a disservice to us both."

My cheeks flared as red as his tears. I wasn't used to people saying kind things to me, except that I was pretty. That compliment was usually followed by an inappropriate statement that sent worms wriggling in my abdomen. They never said much about my mind except they thought I was weird or too smart for my own good. Not sure what else to do, I stared down at my plate and ate more. I knew he was still watching me, making me even more uncomfortable if possible.

"You should learn to take a compliment, Anna. You shall receive more than your fair share through this life."

"If you say so," I said through my chewing.

"And you should not speak with your mouth full." His eyes zeroed in on my elbows. "Or place your elbows on the table. Both are considered quite rude."

I gulped down my food and immediately dropped my elbows. "Sorry."

"It is not your fault. It is a failing of your upbringing. Such as it is. You cannot know if you are not taught."

"Okay. What else?"

"I beg your pardon?"

"What else do I need to know? What else can you teach me? I'm a real fast learner. I like learning new stuff."

"And I am sure you are the most apt of pupils. However, I am an ill-suited instructor."

"No, you aren't. I learned more from you tonight than in a year of school," I insisted.

He stared at me with pity then, which turned my stomach. Even at that age I could withstand just about anything but pity. "You flatter me."

"It's true! And you said it yourself, how can I know things if I'm not told them? Someone has to, why not you?"

Asher chuckled and shook his head for several seconds, the silence growing crueler the longer it lasted. The worms began wriggling as those blue pools darted back my way. I had to glance down. "What do you want from me, little one? *Exactly*?"

I was aware of him staring, scrutinizing every inch of my face, but I was afraid to reciprocate. I was afraid my embarrassment, fear, and confusion would be evident on my face. Really, at nine years old, I couldn't quantify what I wanted from the man across from me except for him to simply stop looking at me.

"I am not a good man," he began, finally breaking the silence. "I am a vampire. A soulless monster. I am not even a man. I have stolen. I have lied. I have killed more than I can account for. Without a doubt, I am destined for hell and I … welcome the upcoming journey. I welcome the eternal atonement for my multitude of sins. My reckoning is past due." He paused. "I am not for you, Anna. I have nothing to teach but misery and nothing to offer but perpetual darkness."

As I gazed down at my lap, the worms burrowed through my whole body. Every one of those little bastards wanted me to start crying, to run away, to give up, and for a second I almost listened. But they hadn't reached my soul yet. My spirit forced my eyes to his as I asked, "How about what I can offer you?"

The snarl I was greeted by slowly dropped as he stared at my impassive face. Thank the universe our waitress showed up carrying a piece of chocolate cake with a candle in it. "Hope I'm not interrupting. Thought you might like this. Happy birthday, hon." She set it right in front of me. "Blow out your candle and make a wish, sweetie."

I gathered all my energy, all the magic I could muster, and blew the candle out.

"What did ya wish for, sweetie?" the waitress asked.

Without taking my eyes from Asher, I said, "I can't tell you or it won't come true."

————

He pulled up in front of my building without even bothering to shut off the engine as I sat in his car, strangled by the oppressive silence that had followed us from the restaurant. It became worse, *real* the moment the car stopped. He wouldn't speak. He wouldn't look at me. I was wrong. Everything I believed was wrong. This was it. I would never see him again, and there was nothing I could do about it. Anything I said or did would just make matters worse. We sat in that car for a full thirty seconds before I forced my hand to the door. "Bye," I whispered as I put one foot out of the car into the frozen night.

"Anna . . ." I looked over at him. "'The greatest thing you'll ever learn is just to love and be loved in return.' There is nothing else in this world worth knowing."

"Then I guess you're right. *You* probably can't teach me anything."

I slammed the car door as hard as I could and trudged back to my apartment without a single glance back. Sven and Andie lay on the couch watching TV when I walked in. "How'd it go? You do your thing?" Sven asked.

"Yes."

"He get fresh with you?" my father asked.

"No. He just took me out for a birthday dinner."

Both adults peeked over the couch. "Shit. It was your birthday today? Happy birthday."

"Thank you, Sven. I'm tired now. I'm going to bed."

"I can't believe you forgot your own kid's birthday," Andie whispered as I passed.

"She didn't remind me," Sven whispered back.

I shut my bedroom door, set down my bag, removed my coat, and flopped into bed. And that was that. I'd never see him again. Life would continue as it always had. There would be nothing but these four walls and the man in the next room until I could find a way to survive on my own. That is if I could survive him. I barely had so far.

That same horrendous oppression from the car followed me, all but suffocating me inside that tiny cell I called a bedroom. I threw open my curtains to gaze out the window at the full moon. I would never look at it the same ... my eyes instinctively moved down to the parking lot and all my gloom evaporated. Because he was there. *He* was still parked down there. He didn't leave me. He couldn't leave me. Because he knew. He *knew.* How could he not? A slow smile crept across my face as I pressed my palm to the icy glass. It was only then he drove away, returning once more into

38

the darkness. But he'd return. For me. I felt it down to my soul. He'd be back. And that was the moment I learned wishes could come true.

It would just take years for me to realize to be careful what you wish for.

———

I didn't have to keep the metaphorical candle in my window burning long. The next night, while I was lying in bed reading *Wuthering Heights,* the knock on the door came. We were expecting Sven's supplier, so I stayed on the moors with Heathcliff. He'd keep me company until…

"What are you doing back here?" my father asked.

"I have returned with a proposition," *he* said in that lyrical baritone.

He came. He came back for me. Never had a doubt.

I leapt from bed to the door, racing into the living room with book still in hand. Asher set eyes on me and smiled as if he'd just seen the sun rise for the first time in a millennia. I knew just how he felt.

"Look who came back," Sven said.

Andie poked her head over the couch. "You must have done *something* right."

"So what can I do you for, kemosabe?" Sven asked. "I'm getting some great hash in later or—"

"I have come for your daughter," he said, eyes still affixed to mine.

"Groovy. Got a repeat customer."

"*No*," Asher said, once tender gaze turning monstrous as it moved to Sven. "I said I have *come* for your daughter. I am taking her with me this night."

"What? I don't …"

"You mean, like, adopt her?" Andie chimed in.

"What? I'm not giving you my kid. You're fucking insane, man. What the hell do you even want with her?"

"As if you give a fig for her well-being," Asher snarled. "Striking her without cause. Selling her body and talents to anyone with a bit of coin in their pocket. You are a whoremonger, a blackguard, and are not fit to breathe the same air as her, let alone guide her though this life, you piece of excrement."

"Fuck you!" Sven cocked his fist back, but Asher grabbed it, gripped even tighter. He brought the whimpering Sven to his knees.

"Anna, please go wait down in my car," Asher uttered softly, as if he weren't in the process of breaking my father's fingers.

"Don't you—" Sven started, but Asher squeezed even tighter, strangling the words with further pain.

"What the fuck! Let him go!" Andie shouted, actually leaving the couch for once.

"Anna, please. Go," Asher said, calm as can be. "*Please.*"

I took one step. Then another. Then I bolted to the door, grabbing my coat along the way. As I quickly put it on, I took one quick glance at my father, the last look I ever would. That's how I remember him to this day. Helpless. Scared. Brought to his knees for all his considerable sins. That sight still reminds me there can be justice in this universe. I shut the door.

Over ten minutes later, Asher finally emerged from the building carrying a duffel bag filled with items from my room and blood smudged on the corner of his mouth. When I saw it as he climbed into the Porche, I was too nervous and excited to fully grasp what that smear meant. Even when I did, I did not mourn either of them. Never have and never will. Asher started the car, turned on the heat for me without me asking, and sped us off into the night just as flames ate the curtains in my former bedroom. My former self.

"I packed a few of your belongings. Whatever else you require, we shall purchase when we reach Toronto. I have friends there who will aid us in acquiring you a passport and false birth certificate. Though it may take several days."

"Okay."

We drove in silence for a few seconds. "After Toronto ... if you could see anything, go anywhere in the world, where would it be?"

"Egypt. I always wanted to see the pyramids."

"Cairo then. Excellent choice. I have not been in two centuries. My Arabic is a bit rusty though. It is a good language to learn. I shall do my best to teach it to you."

"Okay."

There was more silence save for the hum of the heater, before he said, "I warn you, I shall not be easy to live with. As with all of my species, I remain up all night and from sunup to sundown I am essentially dead. You will have to alter many of your habits, not simply your circadian cycle. I am an old man, quite set in my ways. Not to mention I have not cohabited with another soul in quite some time, and never one so young. I am what I am, and I enjoy what I enjoy. That will never change. *I* shall not change. You will have to acclimate to me, not the other way around."

"Okay."

"And should this experiment fail to work out for whatever reason, I shall not hesitate to drop you off at the nearest orphanage."

"Okay."

"I expect you to be quiet, polite, a good pupil, but first and foremost I expect obedience and loyalty."

"Okay."

"And stop bloody well agreeing with everything I say! You sound like a parrot."

"I agree," I said with a smirk.

He returned the gesture.

"Thank you."

"No, *mo chuisle* ... thank *you*."

And that was how Anna S. Olmstead died, and Anna Asher was reborn.

In love.

AGE 11
PARIS, FRANCE

"AGAIN!"

I attempted to get *en pointe*, but with the shooting pain from my big toe up to my hip, not to mention the pain I woke with in my stomach and lower back, the act was next to impossible. I groaned in frustration. "I can't," I shouted in French. "It hurts!"

"Then you may as well quit now, little one," my instructor Collette responded with a sneer. "Your form is terrible anyway."

"It is not," I spewed back. "Maybe you're a terrible teacher."

"Or you're not practicing enough because you're a spoilt, lazy, bratty *child*."

Oh, how I wished to hex her right then, mostly for that last word. I was no child. *Child*. I was a world traveler. I spoke Arabic, Spanish, and French. I was the most advanced pupil my magic tutor had ever encountered, or so she told Asher. I had a season pass to both the opera and the ballet, for goodness sake. How

43

many eleven-year-olds could claim that? How many adults? And how dare she insult me, and on my birthday no less?

"Better a child than a past my prime has-been like you."

Collette's pouty mouth dropped open, but no sound escaped. It was an easy jab, too easy but it completed the job. Oh, I loathed that woman. I loathed her gorgeous full lips, her decade on me, her talent, but especially her effortless flirting directed at *my* Asher. Every time I watched her demure smiles and the light touches of his chest whenever they spoke, I cringed. It was a dagger to my heart, especially when he matched her smile for smile, touch for saccharine touch. I could almost tolerate that, almost, but her quick temper, her cruel words whenever I failed, and the chip on her shoulder about my seeming wealth and privileged upbringing gave me a sense she had similar roots to mine. I'd thought of getting her fired, but with Asher's concerns of letting too many people into our inner circle and her credentials, I knew it'd be an all but impossible sell. The only other option was ceasing the lessons, and I just couldn't. Ballet was my favorite activity even before fencing and magic lessons. I loved how my body stretched, how I could interpret music into a physical entity with my body, how graceful I felt not only while dancing, but even as I walked.

I just *hated* Mademoiselle Collette. The only blight in my otherwise picture perfect new life. The only threat.

"You …" Her mouth shut and for a moment I believed I'd won the round, that is until a cruel grin formed. "Well, your *Papa* does not think me past my prime or pathetic. He proved as much last night. In my bed."

"He's not my—" I caught myself. I was under strict orders not to dispel the misconception Asher was my father. Fewer questions and prying eyes that way. I almost forgot in my anger. "You lie."

But I knew she hadn't. It was as plain as the bruise on her neck barely concealed by make-up. After our fencing lesson, Asher claimed he had to call on an old friend, which was odd, because Asher went out of his way to avoid his own kind those early years. It was dangerous for us both. I had to learn vampiric law in those first days in Toronto. While there was no law expressly against children, save for not turning them before age thirteen, I lacked the protection afforded consorts and familiars. The mere fact I even knew about the existence of vampires could result in a death sentence for us both in some territories. I was fair game. So if we ever did run into an old friend at the opera or theater, I'd be introduced as my governess Clifton's granddaughter. He'd been with us since Cairo when it was decided I needed a daytime guardian. I was expecting Sherlock's Mrs. Hudson or even an older Jane Eyre, and instead got a portly, dandy, fifty-something Englishman. Asher knew Clifton during his tenure with some vampire Lord, wrote the dandy, and a week later I had a new male governess. Not only did Clifton run the household, he instructed me in Latin and English, did all our shopping, escorted me around town, and taught Asher to cook. Having lived almost eight hundred years, Asher had mastered almost every skill imaginable but never cooking. It took almost a month before he created something edible, but by Paris he'd surpassed his tutor. If not for the dancing and fencing I'd have weighed two hundred pounds. As I stared at the usurper of my Asher's attention and love, I wondered if he cooked for her as well.

"We've been lovers for a week now," she said with a triumphant smirk. Asher was in love with *her*? This? He deserved better. So much better. I was so angered my stomach and lower back ached harder. "Once we made love in this very room. He took me against the *barre* you touch now." My hand involuntarily jerked from the abomination. "And we have no intention of stopping." The bitch took a step toward me. The agony in my back ratcheted up another notch. "And wouldn't it be wonderful if I became your new Mama? Of course we'd require some time alone to truly get to know one another. Years perhaps. A Catholic boarding school might be just what you need. They'd whip the brat right out of you. God how I wished to do it myself, but—"

My pain momentarily vanished as I sucked the magic into me, releasing it into the air like shrapnel. A gust of gale force wind knocked my tutor flat on her nonexistent derriére. She skidded on the hardwood floor for five feet until thwacking into the far wall hard enough to leave a dent. I watched all this, mouth agape, afraid to move or even blink in case it happened again. I knew I'd done it but didn't know how. I hadn't meant to. Truly. I always had to focus on the magic, the words, what I hoped to accomplish while casting. Control. I had control. But with Collette...

We stared across the room at one another with equally wide eyes, both sets growing with shock and fear. Neither of us moved or spoke for several seconds with the only sound coming from our panting. "What—ow!" she shrieked as she gripped her right wrist. The knot in my stomach tightened with her every howl of pain.

"What is going on?" Clifton asked before he opened the door.

"W ... we don't know. She ... she just fell," I managed to get out as he walked in.

"My wrist. I think it's broken," Collette sobbed.

"I'll take you to hospital," Clifton said as he helped her rise. "Anna, collect her things."

As I gathered her coat and purse, Clifton escorted her through our *pied-à-terre*. Asher purchased the whole building eons before my grandmother's grandmother was born and rented out the flats save for the one we inhabited, which on occasion a vampire friend might arrange to use. I discovered this was a standard arrangement in almost every major city worldwide. A port in every storm. So far I'd spent three months in his Cairo flat, nine in a Gaudi building he purchased in Barcelona before we laid down roots in France. The Paris flat was by far my favorite, with bay windows that overlooked the *Champs de Lyses,* antique furniture upholstered in real French silk, and a library of books no longer in print. The dance studio was the newest addition, something he built just before we moved in. The man fulfilled my wishes even before I knew I had them.

"I … I don't know what happened," Collette whimpered as Clifton helped her with her coat. "There was this gust of wind and … and …"

"Ghosts," I blurted out. "Maybe it was a ghost. This place is really old."

Clifton's small brown eyes narrowed at me, but Collette nodded. "Maybe."

"Let's go," Clifton barked. He all but pushed Collette out the door, kicking it closed behind them. I jerked when it slammed. He knew. He knew it was my fault, which meant when Asher rose, he would as well. I'd broken the cardinal rule: never use magic around non-supernaturals. It wouldn't matter if the act was intentional or not. If word got out, the infraction could be punishable by death.

Potentially both our deaths. Not that this fact scared me that much. No, I was petrified I'd be cast out for maiming his lover. That he'd hate me forever. That he'd finally realize I wasn't worth his effort. That I *was* damaged goods and no amount of love or guidance would ever change that. The anger, the melancholy, the anxiety that had been gnawing almost literally inside me for two days reached its climax.

I burst into tears, which shocked me further. I never cried, especially not these hard, wracking sobs I feared would never stop. I had to leave. I could not breathe in the flat. Still dressed in my pink leotard and ballet shoes, I simply threw on my pea coat and scarf before fleeing onto the streets of Paris. Away froom my crime.

The bitter cold wind sliced over my skin like razor blades as I ran down the *Champs*. I worried my tears would freeze to my cheeks. I had no plan, but after five minutes, I knew I had to get inside somewhere before hypothermia set in. With the one Franc in my pocket, I purchased a ticket to a double feature of *Harold & Maude* and *The Owl and The Pussycat*. Not that I could concentrate on the screen. My intestines still felt as if someone were twisting them in their fists, and ever-increasing anxiety kept me wound up like a clock. Or a time bomb.

He wouldn't really send me to an orphanage. After that first night the threat was never made again. Boarding school, on the other hand, was a real possibility. Clifton suggested it once or twice in passing when Asher expressed concern about my lack of friends. The finest education, being surrounded by girls my own age, making connections to the who's who of European society. Perhaps someday I could become a Duchess or even a Princess just like Grace Kelly. Wouldn't I like that? I just glared at my governess. But the idea was planted, and because of my one slip, there was a true threat of it sprouting. The thought of being shipped off brought fresh tears. Some birthday. Asher planned to prepare my favorite meal, chicken carbonara, then we'd go see the ballet *Sleeping Beauty*. Instead, I was alone in a smoky movie theater falling apart over an accident and terrified to go home.

Then I began to die.

Between films, I went to the lavatory. When I noticed the blood in my panties I almost fainted. I was bleeding internally. The three fold rule had struck with a vengeance. I'd broken Collette's wrist and as punishment my internal organs burst. There was only a little spot in my underwear, so maybe it wasn't that bad. Except for the aching in my back and I assumed intestines, I felt fine. Asher. He'd know what to do. He always knew what to do. Really I just wanted him to hold me and hug the fear away. I just wanted *him*.

The moment I stepped back into our flat, both he and Clifton pounced. "Where have you been?" Asher snapped. "We have been out of our minds with worry. You know to leave a note."

"I know. I didn't think. I'm sorry," I said, head bowed.

"You should be," Clifton said. "Not just for that. Your teacher has two broken bones."

"I'm sorry," I said again. "It was an accident."

"You do not accidently send a person flying across a room with enough force to break bones," Asher said.

"Well, I did!" I shouted back. "Okay? I didn't mean to, but I did. She was saying horrible things about marrying you and sending me away then the wind blew her across the room! I didn't mean to, okay? I'm sorry. I'm sorry."

I couldn't take those disappointed blue eyes of his a moment longer. I rammed past the men and ran to my room, slamming the door shut and falling face first onto my bed. I couldn't stop the tears then. I sobbed into my pillow like the pathetic little girl I felt like. That perhaps I was. I heard Sven's voice in my head. "Stop your sniveling, you little brat. You're descended from Vikings, act like it."

What was the matter with me?

He knocked before entering, but I couldn't look up. I was too ashamed and embarrassed. I'd never cried in front of him before. Never had cause to. Judging from the way he asked, "Are you alright?" he was as unnerved by my actions as I was.

"No," I cried into my pillow. The bed shifted as Asher sat beside me. "You ... you're going to send me away because I used magic, and I hurt your girlfriend. I didn't mean to. I really truly didn't, I swear."

"I believe you," he said, gently petting my hair. I loved when he did that. It was so soothing, like warm waves lapping against my bare feet. "And I am not sending you away."

I sat up to check for subterfuge, instead finding compassion and even a smile. Like an addict, that one fix made everything a little better. "Really?" I sniffled. "But wh ... what?"

"Truly. It would be like banishing my soul from my body, leaving naught but an empty shell. I existed like that for decades before I met you, I could not bear it again, *mo chuisle.* Never."

"Wh ... what if I died?"

His eyes narrowed. "What sort of question is that for one so young?" He studied my pitiful face as his nose twitched twice. A second later a tender smile crossed his face. "You are bleeding. Is it coming from between your legs?" I nodded and his smile grew. He pulled me into his arms as he chuckled. "Oh, Anna. You are not dying. Quite the opposite. You have blossomed."

"I've what?"

"You have become a woman. I believe the modern parlance is you have gotten your period. Surely your mother or someone must have told you …" I shook my head no against his chest. "It means you can now bear children and every month you do not, you shall bleed as you are now. It is the most natural occurrence there is." He began petting my hair again. "There are some unfortunate side effects, which is why you have been out of sorts the past few days. And it also explains what happened with Collette today. You are now a High Priestess. You commanded the wind to push her. I suppose she was lucky there was not a fire nearby. You might have burnt her to death."

"I didn't mean to. I just … she was being so cruel. It just happened."

"We shall begin working on gaining control right away."

"Okay. And the other stuff, the bleeding, can I get control of that too? Can I stop it?"

"I am afraid not. You will bleed every month until you are quite old or when you have a baby in your belly."

"Well, how do I do that? The baby thing?"

Asher was not anticipating that line of questioning. Though he did not exactly recoil, he did tense and shift around me. "You are not aware how babies are made?" I shook my head no. It never came up in the Olmstead house, at least not directly, and the one time I'd heard a discussion about it was at school when a classmate said she got her new baby brother from the hospital. I figured doctors made babies in the hospital and if you wanted one, you picked one out like a puppy in the pet store. The fact my body made them blew my mind.

"Well, when a man and woman find each other attractive, sometimes they desire to show that attraction by making love, and on occasion that coupling results in a child within the woman," he began. More nervous and uncomfortable than I had or would ever see him, Asher gave me the standard birds and bees talk.

"*That* makes babies? And women like doing it? It always hurt when Sven's friends touched me down there."

"Oh, Anna," Asher said, stroking my hair once more. We rarely spoke about my past, especially the uglier aspects. In fact, I tried to banish the life of Anna Olmstead from my every memory. The life of Anna Olmstead. It didn't matter. To me, I was born two years before. Everything before that was a mere bad dream Asher woke me from. "What those men did ... was for their pleasure, not yours. Do not allow them to poison you or your perspective of lovemaking. If your partner is skilled, patient, respects your body and its needs, and you love the person, then there is no more pleasurable experience on this earth."

"And ... that's what you were doing with Collette last night?"

His embrace tightened. "She should not have disclosed that to you. I am sorry."

"Do you love her?"

"No. Not in the least. She is comely, and on occasion a man's needs overwhelm him, like an itch in need of scratching."

"You're not going to marry her and give her a baby?"

"No," he chuckled. "No."

A grin stretched across my face. "Good." I hugged my Asher tighter. "Then since I'm a woman now, you don't need to see her anymore."

If Asher was tense before, he was close to granite after I said those words. "I beg your pardon?" he asked, his arms slowly lowering from my body.

"We can get married now."

His arms left me then, and he gently extracted me from his body. When I could see his face again a tumult of emotions were stacked on one another. Shock, discomfort, but above all concern. "That is...Anna, you are a child."

"But you just said I was a woman," I countered.

"Your body perhaps, and you are exceptionally mature for your years, but...you have only existed on this planet for eleven years. You are still so innocent in many ways. You have so much more growing, and so much more to experience before you even consider marriage and children. And out there in this wide, wonderful world is a man who will cross your path many, many years from now, who will adore you and give you all you wish from life."

"But that's you," I said with confusion.

"No, it is not."

"*Yes* it is," I said, my voice as hard as my eyes.

My utter conviction unnerved the veteran of three wars because a far from brief moment of pure fear filled his blue eyes. He even rose from the bed as if I were a bomb about to explode. "This has become a ridiculous conversation. You have had a trying day, I think you should rest while I go purchase you the necessary paraphernalia for your current condition. We have missed the ballet, but if you feel better later, we shall have cake and open your gifts. There will be no more talk of marriage and children. Understood?"

I had no choice but to nod. When Asher really put his foot down, it was over. Besides I'd well and truly upset him, and the few times I'd done that, it felt as if I'd plunged a dagger into my own heart. After a nod back, the vampire fled my bedroom. Fled from me. With a frown, I fell back into my pillows. My young mind could not wrap around why I'd upset him. I was officially a woman just like Collette. We loved each other. I wanted to kiss him and be with him forever. I would do anything for him. He was the Lancelot to my Guinevere. The Heathcliff to my Cathy. The Romeo to my Juliet. My one true love. Mine. He was all mine, and I was all his. Did he not feel the same? No, I knew he loved me, maybe I just loved him more. Patience. He always said I needed to learn patience. While I didn't think this was an intentional lesson on his part, it was a lesson none the less. One I'd master like all the others. I waited nine years for him to enter my life. I could wait for the rest to come in time.

I got my birthday wish two years ago. I would just have to do whatever was necessary to make sure I did again. *Whatever* was necessary. After all I was descended from Vikings, time to act like it. *We* were worth it.

———

A week later, I found myself back at the barre awaiting the broken ballerina's return. Life returned to normal the moment I stepped out of my bedroom and sat down to blow out my candles. Asher's tension waned with one sweet smile his way. I knew him well enough not to broach the topic again. At least not directly. Discretion is an effective weapon in a woman's arsenal. It worked too because if anything we spent more time together than ever. New abilities to harness and all. Of course, asking a pre-teen on her period to rein in her emotions proved as difficult as a man with no arms herding cats. Vampire patience came in quite handy those first nights.

Mademoiselle Collette proved braver than I had given her credit for. She walked right into our flat without visible hesitation or apprehension. I'm sure she'd convinced herself the incident was due to her tripping or that there was a draft. Most supernatural occurrences are explained away as such. After all what's more likely, your pupil is able to control the very air or you had a clutzy moment? As Collette strutted in, wan head held high and clutching her casted arm, I greeted her with my sweetest, most innocent grin. "Mademoiselle, watch!" On the first try, I lifted myself *en pointe* with all my weight on my big toe. "I learned it all on my own." By practicing hours upon hours and enduring intense pain through half my body just to view the ripple of displeasure that crossed her pretty face.

"Very good, *little one*," she said with emphasis on those last words.

Though my toes ached like mad, I remained *en pointe*. "How's your arm?"

"Fine."

"I'm glad you can still work."

"I'm sure you are."

"I am. Though I am surprised you came back here."

"Why?" she asked as she approached.

"Well, the ghost and all. I don't think she likes you."

"If you are trying to frighten me, little girl, it will not work. I don't believe in ghosts."

"You should. They're real. I've even met one."

"Have you now?" she sniggered.

"Yes. There's one in here right now. Can't you feel it?"

She moved to the barre to face me. "Alright, that is enough. Your childish attempts to—"

A stiff breeze wafted against her just as I commanded it to. Collette flinched and instinctively cradled her bad arm. She glanced around the room for the source. "See?" I asked. My tutor's immense eyes darted toward me. "You should watch what you say to me." A stronger draft knocked her hip against the barre. "Don't want to break your other arm."

"What … How …" she asked the air, voice trembling.

"I wouldn't recommend coming back here if I were you. Or contacting Asher. He's fininshed with you anyway. I mean, did he call you once this week? Visit you? No. I mean, I may just be a little girl but even I know that means he's bored with you. Not too bright, are you?"

"You lying little bitch," she hissed. "You—"

"Last chance to leave," I cut in. "I suggest you take it."

"Your parlor tricks don't scare me, you spoilt brat. I—"

"Fine. Don't take it. Can't say I didn't warn you." So much for the easy way. I grabbed my own wrist and squeezed as hard as I could, enough I had to grind my teeth to stop wincing.

"What are you doing?" she asked. I wouldn't let go, if anything I squeezed even harder. "What are you doing? Stop!" She grabbed my wrist to pull my hand away as I'd anticipated. Astrid often pulled this grift when she was caught shoplifting or a woman got too close to Sven. Worked more often than not. She may not have been much of a mother, but she knew her way around a con.

"Don't touch me! Get your hand off me!" I shrieked the moment she touched me. "You're hurting me! Clifton!"

By the time he rushed in, my bewildered instructor had released me, but I still clutched my wrist as if it were a wounded wing. "What is going on?" he asked.

"She hurt me!" I said as I rushed to his side for protection.

"What? I did not!"

"Sh … she said I tripped her, and she called me a bitch, then she grabbed my wrist and squeezed it really, really hard. Look." I presented my red wrist.

"Did you put your hands on her?" Clifton asked, voice hard.

"I was trying to stop her from—"

"I don't care. Your position here is terminated effective immediately. Please leave."

"She is lying! I want to speak to Asher. I am not leaving until I do. He'll believe—"

"Mr. Asher is out of town, and even still I very much doubt he will wish to listen to your excuses. Leave post haste, and you *may* still receive a favorable reference."

"I … She …" She glanced from him to me, confusion morphing into pure hatred. "You little monster! You bitch! I—"

"Leave," Clifton snapped.

Once again she looked at me, and I raised an eyebrow. I'd won the war, and we both knew it. Collette gathered what little dignity I hadn't sucked from her and walked past us with her chin up, out of our lives. Good bloody riddance.

"Are you alright?"

I forced a small pout to my lips. Collette taught me *that* at least. "I am now. Thanks to you." Flattery, perhaps a woman's greatest weapon. Works every time.

Did I feel guilty as I heard the front door slam? A little. Later a lot. I hated to fight dirty, but a woman handles threats any way she has to. And though I'd only officially been a woman for a week, I always was a quick study. In a few years, Asher wouldn't stand a chance against me.

I couldn't wait.

———

Any guilt I harbored evaporated the moment Asher draped his arm over my shoulders to comfort me. I snuggled closer against him on the sofa as he examined my bruised wrist. That one loving act made it all worthwhile.

"I am so sorry, *mo chuisle*," Asher said as he kissed the inside of my wrist over the freshly blossomed bruise. "I cannot believe I allowed this to happen. I should have seen how unstable she was."

"It wasn't your fault. You couldn't have known. It looks worse than it feels. I'm fine. Really. And she's gone now. That's all that matters." I nestled in closer. "But I was thinking. She still might say something about us. About what happened last week. I don't think she believed the ghost story. She does seem the type to spread rumors too. And we have been here a year. We've done everything in the city. Maybe we can go someplace quieter for a few months. Somewhere in the country." With fewer people and distractions. "I always wanted to see Ireland. We could live on the beach!"

"The beach?" he asked with a grin.

"Yeah. You can teach me to swim." Though I already knew. "And fish."

"You wish to learn to fish?" he chuckled.

"I've never tried. Maybe we can even get a boat. You can teach me to sail too. We can go around the world. Just the two of us."

My Asher stared down at me, lightly petting my hair and studying my face. He stared at me for seconds, and with each passing moment it became harder and harder to maintain my smile. It was as if he saw right through me. Right through the lie. He knew. And the moment I gazed away, he knew I knew. I sat there in his arms attempting to keep my face and body from tensing. I'd never lied to him before. I wasn't sure what he'd do. I could withstand his fury, even a slap, but not his disappointment. Even one little tap with that particular hammer would be enough to shatter my soul into a million tiny pieces.

Perhaps he gleaned this. He did know me better than anyone. Or perhaps he just didn't care about my dirty tricks. Hell, maybe he was a little proud and honored I'd go to such trouble, but I never found out. Instead he kissed my wrist again before saying, "Ireland *is* lovely this time of year. Whatever your heart desires, my Anna."

I already had that right in my arms, and I would do anything to keep him there.

Anything.

It just never occurred to me that it'd be a two-way street covered with blood, bodies, and soul-crushing darkness that only one of us could make off alive.

AGE 13
LONDON, ENGLAND

SWINGING LONDON IN THE 1970s. Glam rock, free love, wild drug filled nights, the perfect place for my official debut into the vampire world. My thirteenth birthday. I was legal, at least under vampiric law, which hadn't been changed from the days girls married as soon as they blossomed. Regardless, that night I could become a formal consort, taking my rightful place beside Asher's side until death. I was no longer a secret. I was no longer a child. I would now be part of every facet of his life. My dream came true.

"Anna?" Asher asked with a knock.

He stepped into my bedroom a second later. I ceased applying the glitter eye shadow at my white vanity table. Since moving to London the month before, I'd perfected the glam rock look so popular even taxi drivers embraced glitter and androgyny. Transitioning from Galway to London was quite a shock, tantamount to landing on a new planet. I could barely tell the men from the women. In our little Irish country cocoon there was no need for high fashion or even make-up. Most days I'd barely changed out of my leotard or peasant top and corduroys. The only way I knew to overcome the culture shock was to dive in with both feet. At my request, Asher purchased for me a whole new wardrobe from Biba, Chanel, even Bianca Jagger's boutique. Gone were the baggy peasant top and corduroy pants, replaced with miniskirts, halter tops, and boots. My transformation became complete with a trip to Vidal Sassoon. Good-bye to my lank, waist-long locks, hello to a glowing mane that barely passed my shoulders with my bangs swept to the side just like my favorite actresses, Liv Ullmann and Julie Christie. I'm still astonished by the power of an amazing haircut. It added almost a decade to my appearance, exactly what every thirteen-year-old desires. Asher's mouth flopped open when he saw me for the first time, which was just the cherry on top.

He wasn't the only one to appreciate the new me. Since we arrived in the big city a month before I'd been asked out on dates half a dozen times, five more than my entire two-year tenure in Galway. In Ireland I was that odd, homeschooled American with a fey grandfather and a hermit for a father, who only left her cottage for ballet lessons. Ralph Lang, the son of my instructor, worked up the courage to ask me to dinner, then grew even braver when he stole a kiss while escorting me home. I definitely preferred country boys to their city counterparts. I'd had my bottom pinched twice just walking the London streets. Both offenders sprouted boils by the time they reached home. They may blacken the soul, but hexes definitely brighten the day.

"I need a few more minutes," I told Asher.

"You are not wearing that," he said with a scowl.

"What?" I asked as I rose from my vanity. "What's wrong with it? You said I looked lovely the other day."

Asher took in my glittery blue crop top tied in a knot above my bare midriff and fringed miniskirt halfway up my thigh, scowl deepening with every inch he scrutinized. Puberty had so far been kind, rounding out my hips and breasts, though not to the Brigitte Bardot proportions I desired, and added three inches to my height with two more still to go.

"Beyond the fact it is freezing outside, we are about to enter a den of lions, and you are dressed as prime rib."

"But I'm your consort now. You'll protect me," I said with a seductive smile as visions of Asher fighting off three bloodthirsty vampires with swords flitted through my imagination.

"Then please make my task easier. Cover yourself."

"But—"

"*Please.*"

It was a miracle he agreed to let me accompany him at all. It took nights of pleading, of pouting, of making my case as if we were in the Old Bailey. Knowing my discovery was inevitable if we stayed in London, and the serendipity that the party was on my birthday, he gave in, but the ice I skated on was wafer thin.

"Of course," I said. "Whatever your heart desires."

"Thank you." After an uneven nod, he left the room so I could change.

He was nervous, about to leap from his own skin to escape the overwhelming oppression he was placing on himself. I'd never seen him in such a state before, save for the night of my eleventh birthday when I made my indecent proposal. That subject never arose again, at least not in such an overt manner. Kisses I once placed on his cheek now found their way to his lips, barely bordering on chaste. Instead of reading curled up in an arm chair, I read snuggled against him, my head resting in the crook of his shoulder. My hand always found his as if they were magnets. Doors were sometimes left open as I showered or changed. All perfectly innocent actions of an affectionate young lady, or I'm sure that's what he told himself. Just as he'd deluded himself to my reasons for wanting entrance to the vampire world. It was denied to me all our years together, this glamorous exciting underbelly, therefore I had to be part of it. I didn't assuage him of this misconception.

The truth was, given the choice between remaining at our cottage alone together for all eternity or in the exciting, seductive vampire world, the cottage won a million times over. Wagging tongues and vicious gossip, and growing suspicions about why Asher never apperared during the day, put an end to our country living. But Asher didn't seem to mind. I'd sensed he was ready to move on months before. His trips alone to visit friends went from yearly to monthly, the final one lasting two weeks. Two weeks away from me. Was it any wonder I gravitated to poxy Ralph then? The gossip just gave him an excuse to rejoin the vampire community he so desperately missed. A community with tempting distractions everywhere. Ones that had already begun working their wicked magic on him. Since we'd arrived in London he'd abandoned me for them every other night. There was only one option. No matter how frightening and literally bloodthirsty the world I was about to enter could be, I had to stay at his side as much as possible or someone would fill my spot. I had to remain vigilant. I cringe at the depth of my stupidity now. Is there anything more insecure than a teenage girl?

Asher was smoothing his auburn hair in the hallway mirror when I strolled out in my white knee-length dress, white tights, and red platform shoes that matched my lips and the roses printed on the white silk. If forcing me to change was so I appeared less enticing, the act failed. I went from looking as if I were pretending to appear mature to succeeding in the endeavor. Asher's mouth opened a fraction as he drank me in. The dress clung in all the right places and had a slight peek-a-boo slit in the middle to show a hint of cleavage. I'd witnessed a similar expression once or twice before when he "caught" me in nothing but my towel or even as I danced around in my skintight leotard. It grew harder and harder to hide my triumph through the years. Quickly, as always, embarrassment or scorn replaced his lust.

"Am I to your liking? I'm covered as requested."

"Yes," he said after a pause. "You look very pretty, *mo chuisle.*" My smile wavered a tad. Little girls were pretty, women are beautiful, sophisticated, or enchanting. My escort fit that bill in his white cashmere turtleneck, fitted brown blazer and trousers. "Now, you remember the story, correct?"

"We've been together eight months. We met in New York City, you snatched me up off the street, and brought me home with you to Galway. Tonight, for my fourteenth birthday present, you plan to name me as your consort. If anyone asks me about the past, keep it vague."

"Excellent. Also remember, do not meet their eyes, do not go anywhere alone, and do not attempt spells or magic. Your youth and … appearance will already make you a curiosity, do not add any gasoline to enflame them further."

"Okay."

He stared at me, tension constricting the corners of his eyes. "There are two more unpleasantries we must address before we can depart. There are certain conditions that must be met for consortship to be granted and legally binding. First, we must live under the same roof together."

"Okay."

"The other two, well ... the conditions have not yet been met."

"Then we should, right? Can we do them now?"

"It is not that simple. I have undergone much debate within myself and decided ... I should feed from you before we depart."

My back straightened. I was not expecting that. "Oh. Okay."

"If you bear my mark, there will be fewer queries regarding the third condition."

"Which is?"

The tension in his eyes spread like a virus across the rest of his face. "That we had made love."

The butterflies pirouetted inside my stomach. "Oh."

"So I shall feed now, leaving visual proof of the act, and should anyone query about our ... intimate relations, you are to smile and say, 'A lady never speaks of such matters,' then change the subject. Understood?"

Any number of replies filled my mind but considering that the ice beneath our feet was so wafer thin that even a smile would smash it, all I could say was, "Okay."

Some of the tension waned from the sides of his mouth. "Good. Now please roll up your sleeve."

"You're going to feed from my wrist?"

"Yes. It will not hurt, I promise you."

"It's not that. It's just wouldn't the neck be more ... intimate?"

His face twitched as if electrocuted. "I suppose you are correct. Very well."

Inside I was grinning from cheek to cheek, but outwardly I remained as neutral as Switzerland. I'd offered my blood dozens of times when his supply ran low, but he always refused. Wouldn't hear of it. He once went two days without when a snowstorm quarantined us. He fed from Clifton then. Not that night though. That night he was mine. All mine.

I swept my hair aside. Ralph had called my neck "swanlike." Pale, graceful, beautiful. Now Asher was finally claiming it. Me. The man I loved was centimeters from me. We'd been closer, I practically glued myself against him any chance I had, but never like this. My body was alive, in flux, all my cells breathing in the sensation of true lust. Anticipation. Love. I knew how much this act was costing him. How my nymphet routine had eroded his resolve not to cross that last, beguiling border he'd erected to protect me even though I didn't want that protection. This act, him tasting me, me nourishing him with my lifeforce, him invading my body and taking what he needed could very well crumble him, my noble love. *Finally.*

I met his eyes, his piercing blue eyes so filled with trepidation, and desired so badly to touch his face, caress the negativity away, but knew it'd make things worse. "This will not hurt."

"I trust you," I whispered.

As I stared into those turquoise pools, the pleasant prickle of magic trickled through me like gentle, warm rain. My neck tilted and eyes closed on their own, letting the pleasure overtake me, that I barely registered those fangs puncturing the flesh of my neck. My body jolted but my mind was too busy twirling in the rain in time to his lips and tongue caressing the flowing blood. Then those caresses ceased, as did the magic of the moment. When my eyes opened, Asher had already taken a giant step backward and was wiping my blood from his lips with a handkerchief as if it were poison. He wouldn't look at me, couldn't hide the disgusted scowl. Did I taste bad? Was my blood tainted somehow? I touched my neck where those two punctures still oozed blood. "What—"

"Go clean yourself up," Asher ordered. He gazed up, eyes now black as midnight, and bared his red fangs. "*Now.*"

Four years. I'd lived four years with that man, and for the first time ever, he frightened me. Truly terrified me. "O-okay."

I dashed to the bathroom, even locking the door behind me. I stared at myself in the mirror, breath ragged. It was easy to forget what he really was. A hunter. A predator. He subverted that side of himself around me. To protect me. I'd roused that beast, and though for the most part I was unnerved, a part of me was singing out in victory. One more hurdle vaulted, one more barrier down in my pursuit. And though his soul may be black, it would be mine. It was only fair. I gave him mine the moment we met.

———

The cab ride was a somber affair without a glance or word exchanged. When we finally pulled up to our host's townhouse in Kensington, the car was chillier inside than out. For the first time since the feeding, Asher touched me, giving me his hand to help me from the cab. He didn't release it when the act was complete, instead wrapping his fingers in mine. I gazed up with a grin but found apathy in return. That stone stare remained affixed as we walked up to the house. Judging from the loud music and laughter the party was in full swing inside the Georgian three-story townhouse. Asher rang the bell, and before his hand lowered, the door opened. A young man in black and white livery, perhaps a few years older than me, stood sentry.

"Asher and guest," my date said.

"You may enter."

We'd reached the official point of no return. There should have been a sign with, "Abandon hope all ye who enter here." I still would have walked right in and shook the hand of the Devil himself with a grin on my face.

We entered the foyer, which was far more modern than I'd anticipated. White walls, art deco end tables and lamps, even an orange shag carpet. The 70s. Ugh. As we handed our coats to the valet, a couple stumbled from one of the rooms, the woman toking a joint. She was pretty in a generic way with thick black hair, Mediterranean skin, wide brown eyes that would have given her an air of innocence if not for the layers of make-up and barely there silver minidress. I was grossly overdressed if she was an indication. The man was far more dapper in pressed black slacks and blue turtleneck, chestnut hair, and piercing brown eyes that instantly zeroed in on me.

"Hello, gorgeous-es," the woman chuckled in a horrible Barbara Streisand imitation. Both had trouble walking, one hanging on the other for support, though the man's problem had less to do with an altered state. He dragged his right foot slightly as they approached. "I am Minnie, your hostess with the mostest tonight. Thank you for coming to my abo-de. Abode," she corrected a second later before more cackling. I suddenly felt as if I were back with Sven and Astrid. "That's a funny word."

"I often have difficulty with it myself," her companion said in a clipped British accent. He momentarily lifted his eyes from me to my companion. "Hello, Asher."

"George. Glad to see you are looking well."

"Never been a problem of mine, old thing," George said, eyes once again undressing me. "And who is this delectable creature?"

I had the strongest urge to hide behind Asher, but he beat me to it, stepping forward to shield me. "*Mine*," Asher growled. His head swiveled to Minnie as he reached for my hand once more. "We have business with Lord Richard. Will you please show us to him?"

"Sure man. Right this way. "

Minnie led us through the foyer and upstairs. Over the psychedelic music and revelry I could still hear the groans and squeals of passion as we passed closed doors. Two men channeling Ziggy Stardust meandered out of one, both zipping their flies. Asher's grip on my hand tightened. Minnie knocked on the last door in the hallway.

"Yes?" a man asked on the other side.

"Someone's demanding to see you. Your old new best friend."

"Enter."

We entered a small, dark office a far cry from the rest of the house. It was as if we stepped back a century with oil paintings, antique furniture, and only one Tiffany lamp on his desk. The man himself matched the surroundings with burgundy smoking jacket, Von Hapsburg beard, and sandy brown hair.

"Baby, you're not even dressed!" Minnie admonished.

"I have a few more odds and ends to tie up. I shall be down shortly. Please leave us." Minnie blew him a kiss before literally skipping back to the party. "Please have a seat."

"I see you and Byron have reconciled," Asher said as he sat.

"A recent occurrence. When Minnie learned of our acquaintanceship, she insisted on an introduction. I have failed to shake him since. He has his charms, I suppose. And he keeps Minnie happy and distracted." I imagined that wouldn't take much. "Alain is here as well."

The corner's of Asher's mouth twitched involuntarily. "Thank you for warning me."

"I trust you both will be on your best behavior," Richard said.

"Of course. *I* have no quarrel with *him*."

"And on the subject of family," Richard said before turning his attention to me. "This must be the Anna you have been speaking of so highly. A pleasure to meet you. Finally."

"You as well, sir," I said with a gracious smile. "It's an honor. Thank you for having me in your beautiful home."

Lord Richard returned my smile. "Beauty and manners. You have chosen you latest consort well."

"Without question," Asher said proudly. "We simply need to fill out the required paperwork."

Richard contemplated this for a moment. "How old are you, dear?"

"Fourteen tonight, sir," I lied.

He looked to Asher, eyes narrowing. "In all the centuries I have known you, my friend, you have never taken a lover so young."

"I had never met Anna. There is not an older soul on this green earth than her."

"Be that as it may," Richard said, swinging his attention back to me, "I feel it necessary to warn you, girl. This is a large, lifelong commitment. From the moment you sign this contract, you are forever bound by vampiric law. If you break one such law, you and Asher shall both face the consequences. This world of ours that you desire to enter ... it is dangerous, amoral, and bloody. There are very few true happy endings. You are all but signing away your soul, dear."

"I've already done that, sir. I did the second I laid eyes on Asher. It, like my heart, is his. I trust him with my everything. There is nothing I wouldn't do to stay by his side forever and always."

"You say that now, but what of ten years from now? Twenty?"

"It's ... hard to explain, sir. I don't know if it's magic, or just fate but ... the moment I met him, I just *knew* no matter what, time, space, even death, I knew that I would always love him. We could be separated for decades and with one look or word, we would be right back where we are now. Devoted. In love. Meant to be. We're soul mates, sir. Nothing can ever change that, certainly not a piece of paper. It doesn't matter. We know what we are to one another, and what we will be until death."

"Such devotion."

"He's earned it."

"And when he does not?" Richard asked with a raised eyebrow.

"That'll never happen," I said with absolute certainty. "Never."

"I hope for your sake, little one, your faith is not misplaced."

I reached beside me for Asher's hand. "It isn't."

"Then who am I to stand in the way of true love?" He removed a stack of papers. "You must both read and sign these. One copy is for me, the other for you to keep. Present it if asked."

"Thank you," I said, scanning the document. It didn't matter what it included, if it literally required my immortal soul, I would have signed it. Asher took as little time as I did. We scribbled our names, and that was that. I was his consort. As I slid my copy back to Richard, I realized this whole event was rather anticlimactic. At the end of the night, nothing *had* changed. It was just a stupid piece of paper.

"Now, if you'll excuse me," Richard said, rising, "I must dress. Please enjoy yourselves." He grinned at me. "And welcome to the family."

He ushered us out to the hallway before disappearing into a bedroom. "That was easy," I said.

"Yes."

I took his hand again, but he didn't squeeze back. "This is the best birthday ever." I pecked his stiff lips. "Thank you."

"You are welcome, *mo chuisle*." The moans of ecstasy nearby momentarily drew his attention and a scowl. "We should go downstairs. Join the others."

"Whatever you desire."

His mouth twitched again. "Stay close."

"Always." I started down the hall, leading him by the clasped hand. "So, who is Alain? Why did you need warning?"

"We did not part on good terms when we last met. If he approaches you, simply excuse yourself and find me."

"Okay."

My nerves began to knot my stomach as we descended the stairs. I had no idea what to expect. I was so excited about the consortship, I didn't dwell on what came after. That I would be surrounded by creatures who wished to literally bathe in my blood. I'd endured my parents' constant parties with free-flowing drugs, fights, and even sex, not that I knew what it was at the time. If hippies were that wild, who knew what havoc vampires could wreak? I clutched Asher's hand tighter as we strolled into the parlor. Thirteen and swimming with sharks. Be careful what you ask for.

Shock almost stopped me dead. Most people just stood around chatting and drinking, but quite a few were half a base from rounding home or gang fanging near comatose half-naked models on the sofas or against the walls. One couple engaged in both. It was as if Caligula were the party planner. Asher pulled me closer to his side. "We *can* leave," he whispered.

I'd wanted this. This was his world. My world now. "No. Let's mingle."

Asher ushered me toward the buffet. I picked at the crab puffs as Asher poured me a glass of water. As I stuffed my face, I noticed Minnie and George whispering and stealing glances at me from the only non-X-rated loveseat. I flashed them a smile, and Minnie blew me a kiss. Asher handed me the goblet as he glared at the pair. He was too busy with his ire to notice the glam rocker wannabe approach. "It is you! Asher! I had heard you had finally returned to the land of the undead. We all missed you!"

"Tobias! It has been far too long!"

The men began catching up, and I was all but forgotten past the intro. As they covered a hundred years of the past, I stood like a lump shoveling appetizers into my mouth. At some point around the 1930s, our hostess meandered over, body bopping in time to the Rolling Stones playing on the record player. She filled her wine glass to the brim, then as she reached for a crab puff, accidently tipped her goblet on Asher.

"Bloody hell! I'm so sorry!"

"It is fine," Asher said as we all grabbed napkins to wipe his shirt.

"That's going to stain. Let me show you to the loo to wash it out," Minnie suggested.

"Very well. Anna?"

I took a step to follow, but Minnie said, "Oh, come on, Ashy. She'll be fine, ticky mo. She's among friends. Come on."

"Stay here," Asher ordered before he walked away.

The glammer Tobias and I exchanged an uncomfortable half smile. "So, how long have you and Asher been together?" he asked, not hiding his apathy.

"Almost a year."

"Fascinating," Tobias muttered as his eyes scanned behind me. "Oh. Please excuse me. I must say hello to someone." And he walked away as fast as his glittering platform boots would allow. What a wonderful party.

After one more crab puff, I decided to wait for my date in an empty corner. Keep my back against the wall. I barely made it a step before George flanked me. Quite quick on his feet for a man with a limp. "Now, this is a crime against nature."

"What is?" I asked.

"A beauty such as yourself should never be left alone. Not for one moment. You should be worshiped and adored every second of every day. Asher should be whipped."

"He'll be right back."

"Oh, perhaps he would also enjoy meeting David."

"Who's David?"

"Bowie. He is in the sitting room holding court."

My eyes bugged out of my head. Bowie? *The* David Bowie? "I-I-I love him! I have all his records!"

"Then I shall introduce you." George held out his arm like a gentleman. "Shall we?"

We found Bowie in full Ziggy make-up costume sitting on the sofa, vampires and companions three deep around him as he re-galed them with tales of antics in the recording studio. It took all my resolve not to fall on my knees and gush like a groupie at the sight of him. "David," George said when we were mere inches from the legend, "I bring you another adoring disciple. May I present Anna..."

"Asher," I finished. He held out his hand, and I actually shook it. I actually touched David Bowie. The memory still brings a smile to my face. "This is beyond an honor, sir."

My new escort glared at the couple to Bowie's left, and they im-mediately rose to give us their coveted spots. I spent the next hour holding a conversation, an actual back and forth conversation, with a legend about music and about his life on the road. He was funny too. Wonderful man. About ten minutes in, Asher appeared through the door, scanning the room with concern. I flashed him a smile, which he reciprocated. Lord Richard tapped his shoulder, and, convinced I was safe, they left once more. I was on such a high I barely cared about George's occasional caress of my hand or odd leer inside my dress's slit, complete with seductive grin when I glanced his way. I also chose to ignore the gentleman in the corner who stared at me for a full minute before wandering off, only to re-turn every five minutes to repeat the behavior. *That* is the power of Bowie.

Eventually some man came behind and whispered in the star's ear that it was time to leave. I almost swooned when the rocker hugged me before departing. It remains a highlight of my life. "He was so nice!" I said to George as we rose from the sofa as well.

"Yes. And he enjoyed you as well, pet," he replied.

"Really? You think so? I was so nervous. I've never met a famous person before."

"You wound me," George said with a pout.

"I'm sorry. Why?"

George chuckled. "'She walks in beauty, like the night, of cloudless climes and starry skies, and all that's best of dark and bright meet in her aspect and her eyes.' I may as well have written it with you in mind, pet."

"I don't ..."

Not sure why he was quoting Lord Byron, I peered at the strange man, but as his grin grew it slowly dawned upon me. When my jaw literally dropped, he chuckled again. "It is nice to know they still teach the classics to impressionable young minds."

"You're not ..."

He held his finger to his mouth to shush me. "Dare not speak it, pet. The walls have ears. I could be lashed simply for telling you. Though I do enjoy a good whipping on occasion." His eyes moved to the slit in my dress again. "Especially if one as beautiful as you were touting the whip." A flush crept from my chest to my face, which pleased Lord Byron to no end. "But pet, you are blushing like a virgin bride. Surely your Asher has indoctrinated you into the pleasures of the flesh."

"A lady never speaks of such things," I said as instructed.

76

Byron's brown eyes narrowed. After several seconds of uncomfortable silence he said, "You know it is a gift of mine, spotting virgins. I had it even before my turn. You are as pure as you look pet. I could stake my soul on it." He moved in closer. Too close. Closer than Asher had ever dared get. I could barely breathe. "Well, if your consort is not willing to relieve you of your burden, may I offer my assistance?"

"I am not a virgin," I protested far too harshly.

"Pet, you must learn to lie better if you wish to survive among us monsters," he chuckled. "But do not fret, your secret is safe with me. For a price."

My stomach knotted three times. "What?"

"A kiss."

"No. I need to find Asher. Excuse me." I tried to move, but he grabbed my arm. Hard. "Get your hand off me," I ordered, my heart beating out of my chest in fright. I'd never felt so young, at least not since Sven's clients snuck into my room, and there was nothing I could do to stop what came next. I wanted to shriek for help, but knew if I did it'd just prove Asher right. That I couldn't survive in his world. He'd disappear every night, he'd find someone else, and he'd ... *no.* "Please let me go. Plea—"

"Would you care to dance?"

Thank the universe for that man. I spun around to find the staring man who stood in the corner staring during Bowie time, stepping beside me. He was even more handsome up close, with Mediterranean skin and wide-set dark brown eyes the same color as his long wavy hair, but with a scar that cut through his eyebrow and cheek. This imperfection did nothing to mar his beauty, if anything it added to his roguish air. He didn't wait for my response, he just took my arm and guided me away.

"Pardon me, but we were in the middle of—" Byron called.

"And now it is concluded," my rescuer called back in French.

The rogue led me out into the hallway where a man and woman were having sex on an end table, which garnered a disgusted scowl from my companion. I just blushed. "Where is your coat?"

"I don't know. I gave it to the valet. Why?" I responded in French.

The man headed toward the stairs, past the rutting couple, dragging me beside him. He opened a closet. "Which is yours?"

"Why?" I asked, yanking my arm from his grasp.

"Because it is past time for you to leave. *He* should never have brought you in the first place."

"Look ... thank you for stepping in back there, but I really had it under control—"

"If you truly believe that, Anna Asher, then your head is not simply underwater, you have already drowned." He shook his head. "Asher has either grown crueler or stupider with old age."

"He has not. And who are you to say such nasty things about him?"

"A cautionary tale. One of the countless victims affected by his selfishness and spite."

"Alain?" I asked, finally able to recall the name.

"He has spoken of me?" Alain asked, surprised.

"Just to tell me I should avoid you. Excuse me." I attempted to step past him, but he moved to block me. "Please let me pass, or I'll scream."

"Scream all you desire. None here will come to your rescue. If anything, they will join in the torment."

"Asher will—"

"Asher is far too distracted by our host and hostess to give you a momentary thought. But I have no intention of harming you. Quite the opposite. Now retrieve your coat, and I shall escort you to a cab."

"I am not going anywhere with you. I do not need your help, and I am *not* leaving. Not without Asher."

The vampire glared, nostrils flaring. "Foolish girl. He has you mesmerized. You see an angel where only a devil lurks. Did he save you? Pluck you from a life of misery? From some deep loneliness only he can fill? Made you his whole world as you did him?" I was about to ask how he knew but stopped myself. Alain read my face like a book though. A cruel smile crossed his face. "I have known him for seven centuries, ever since he forced this life upon me. And do you know why he did? Why he damned my eternal soul to hell against my very will? Because I bested him on the battlefield. I did naught but wound his pride, and he made me pay the ultimate price. You believe you are special. That he loves you above all others, and at present perhaps he does. But love wanes. Time is a cruel mistress, eroding the luster and excitement of new love and revealing what lies under the surface. It shall reveal who he truly is. Who *you* truly are. You are young. Your desires will change. *He* will not. And should you cross him, or betray him, or even wound his pride as I did, he will make you rue the day you ever set eyes on him. I have witnessed it before, Anna Asher, many a time. I would not wish their fates on anyone. So go home. Go anywhere, but get away from him. Before it is too late."

I stared at the crazed vampire, attempting to find some artifice but only saw belief. Pure, total belief in every word he uttered. This stranger was genuinely frightened for me but *I* refused to believe.

He hated Asher. Alain would say anything to harm him, would even make *himself* believe to sell the lies. And whatever Asher did in the past, no matter how horrendous, he would never hurt me. Not a hair on my head. And regardless I would never give him a reason to.

"You don't know me," I said in a low voice, "and you certainly don't know *us*. Now, please excuse me."

That time he let me pass. Eyes downcast, I hurried past the still wildly shagging couple toward the parlor. He wasn't there. I checked the sitting room and still no sign. Where was he? Did he leave? There was one room remaining on the first floor where the music, Elton John, played. My own yellow brick road ended in the library, but I couldn't enter. When I saw him and … *them* on the sofa, I couldn't move. I couldn't blink. I couldn't turn away from the horror show.

Minnie straddled and writhed on my Asher's lap, his hands kneading her exposed breasts as their lips embraced with abandon all while Lord Richard suckled her neck in a now familiar way. They broke apart and Minnie's lips found Richard's, tasting her own blood in his mouth just as Asher sank his fangs into the pristine side of her neck while his hand roamed under her skirt. My own tender wound pulsed in time to his suckling. I was so angered, so embarrassed, so wounded it proved difficult to breathe. I fled before the tears began.

The wine helped. After chugging one goblet, the embarrassment waned. After two, the fire inside came not from fury but the alcohol working its magic. I still have no tolerance for alcohol but that night with little food in my belly and the blood loss, I was three sheets before that second glass lost its last drop. That still wasn't good enough. The world was hazy, but the wound still gaped and bled, and every second he continued to spend with them was like a shard of glass reopening it. Why wasn't he checking on me? Didn't he care? Had he already gone upstairs with *them*?

I wanted the thoughts to stop. A few hits on a joint I found helped too. I'd smoked marijuana before. More than twice Sven and his friends insisted I do it just so they could all laugh their stoned asses off as I hacked and gagged. Such was the price of being able to go to bed in the Olmstead household.

It was as if I were floating above myself, watching as this pretty girl stared into space for a full minute before taking another hit. Had I really been astral projecting, I would have noticed my shadow stalking me. When I left the loo, he was leaning against the wall with a sly grin across that cherubic face. The scourge of Regency London. The man who, without his existence, there would be no Heathcliff. No Rhett Butler. No Sam Spade. And the notorious lover was waiting for little old rejected, vulnerable me.

"Well, hello, pet. You—"

I silenced him with a kiss. A rough, savage kiss so hard our teeth collided. I'd only been kissed once by Ralph, which only lasted a few seconds and where I received more saliva than pleasure, so I had no idea what I was doing. Of course, who better than one of the most renowned playboys in history to teach me? At least that's what I kept telling myself while we continued the lesson. And he did help. Within twenty seconds I'd gotten the hang of it, even learned what to do with my tongue. I might have derived some pleasure in this act save for the fact I was so damn numb and out of it. I could barely physically feel his lips let alone forge a spiritual connection. Any connection. Not even imagining they were Asher's lips, Asher's tongue massaging mine helped.

Whenever I tried all I could do was call up the image of him and Minnie. When my head started spinning, I broke away first.

"My, my, my, you are full of surprises, my little Lolita," Byron said before kissing me again. He went a step farther this round, hands moving under my dress. Asher did this to *her* too. Did she enjoy it? All I felt were hands squeezing me. Not painful like with Sven's friends, just nothing. The groping went on for about ten seconds before Byron decided to double down. Without a word, he ceased fondling, took my hand, and led me upstairs. If I were in my right mind, I might have understood what this meant, or done more than glance at the pensive Alain as we passed him, but I was too busy concentrating on not toppling in my platforms. It wasn't until I saw the already rumpled bed I realized his intentions.

Not that I had much time to react before he flung me onto that bed. The weight of him against me a moment later brought back enough sense that I grew frightened. I wasn't sure if I was ready to go all the way. I wasn't sure I wanted to. Byron was handsome, but I didn't love him. I didn't even *like* him. But rage brushed aside common sense. Anything he could do, I could do better. So I said nothing, did nothing, as he kissed me and began taking off my shoes. My tights. I floated up again, watching as he pawed me, as my body did its best to mimic the love scenes I'd seen on film. That's all it was to me, something happening to another person. I didn't want to watch anymore. I shut my eyes.

He had his finger on the waistband of my panties, about to pull my last line of defense away, when I heard the creak of the door opening. Before I could connect cause and effect, or even open my eyes, the weight and hands vanished. My eyes opened just in time to watch Asher slam my would-be lover into the far wall hard enough to dent it and him. Even in an unaltered state I wouldn't have kept track of Asher. One moment he was by the bed, and the next he had traveled five feet to lift Byron from the floor to punch him repeatedly in the face, Asher's hand coming back bloodier by the second. I was too shocked to call out. Five punches that matched the savage expression on my Asher's face since he entered this room. Rage satiated, that snarl gravitated my way, along with the rest of its owner. Like a panther, he stalked toward me, grabbed my wrist with his bloody mangled hand, yanked me off the bed, and dragged me from the room without giving me a chance to even put on my shoes. The only time he spoke until we reached home was as we passed Alain, who earned a begrudging, "Thank you," from Asher before we continued my march of shame.

The five-minute cab ride home was excruciating. The anger radiating from him and my adrenaline shock finally got to be too much for me. I ordered the driver to pull over before vomiting all over Dorchester Avenue. "Sorry." I muttered as he began driving again. My pathetic state lessened Asher's rage. Unfortunately it was replaced with something worse. Apathy. His face was just blank. He wouldn't touch me, wouldn't even look at me, not even as we walked up to our flat.

"Hello," Clifton said as we stepped in. "How was—"

"Clifton, please bring Anna a ginger ale. She is feeling ill."

My governess glanced from my grimy, shoeless feet up to my greenish face to Asher's bloody hand and knew not to ask further questions. "Of course," Clifton said, before departing with our coats.

For once I dreaded being alone with Asher. I was afraid to glance at him, let alone speak. I bowed my head, waiting for the barrage of recriminations. None came. "Take a bath. You shall feel better afterward."

When I found the courage to raise my head, he was gone. I was alone. He'd given up on me. And it was all my fault.

———

The bath helped, at least with the physical consciousness. But when I noticed the red welts on my outer thighs that Byron's fingernails had left in their wake, I grew nauseous all over again. What I'd almost let him do ... to this day it still makes me grimace. I was ashamed, so ashamed I hugged my knees to my chest and silently wept against them. I'd never be able to forgive myself, and neither would Asher. I felt it. The shift. Things had irrevocably changed between us. A boulder dropped into our tranquil pond, rippling through every facet of our lives, enough to drain the whole thing, leaving nothing but an empty hole. And it was all my fault.

After changing into my flannel pajamas, I slid into my bed with the covers over my head. I attempted to sleep, but though I was exhausted my mind wouldn't let oblivion take me. There was something that needed doing first. I found Asher out on the balcony peering into space with his back to me.

"I'm sorry."

The man I adored was so deep inside himself, he didn't hear me approach. Startled, he spun around and stared at me as if I were a stranger. Another knife to the belly. "I'm sorry," I said again, chin trembling. "I'm so sorry. I was so stupid. I just saw you with them, and I drank too much, and he was there and ... I'm sorry. Please don't hate me. Please."

"Oh, Anna," he began, face falling with sadness to match mine. "Oh, *mo chuisle*. There is not a thing, not an act, not a word you could utter that could ever make me hate you, have you not learned that after all these years? Tonight was my fault and mine alone. *I* beg *your* forgiveness. I sometimes forget how young you truly are."

"I am not that young," I argued.

"But you are, *mo chuisle*," he said desperately, stepping toward me. "You *are* still a child with stardust clouding your eyes, an innocent in so many respects. And that is not something to rally against. It is a gift. What occurred tonight should never have even crossed your mind, let alone been put into practice. That was *my* failing, not yours. You should never have been put into that position. I swore, I *swore*," he said, forcefully, "to myself all those years ago, I would provide you the best life possible. That I would guide you, teach you, set you on the right path. And for my own selfish, pitiable reasons, I have been failing."

"No, you haven't," I insisted just as forcefully as I stepped onto the freezing balcony.

"I have. I have compelled you to grow up far too fast. I have coddled you, praised you when I should have punished because I was afraid ... *you* would hate *me* and abandon me once more to my loneliness," he said, voice cracking. He took a second to compose himself. "What happened tonight was not acceptable. How you have been behaving toward me since Paris is not acceptable. I am beginning to believe ... *I* and my world are not acceptable. Your youth is so special, so precious, and you only ever get the one. Yet most of yours has been tarnished by the selfishness of others. I have been no better than the man I stole you from. I may want you forever and always by my side, I truly, madly, deeply do, but that place is in the darkness. You need light to blossom into the beautiful, intelligent, astonishing woman I know you can be."

My knees were about to give out. "What?" I whispered. "What do you mean?"

"Clifton was right. You need stability. You need to be around people your own age. You need to explore the world. Discover who you truly are, and what you are capable of. Boarding school would—"

"No. No," I said, so panicked I barely choked the words out. "Don't send me away. Please don't—"

"You shall have the finest education. Meet the most influential people in the world. Children of diplomats and royalty. You could become a princess one day. Your children could rule Europe if—"

"I don't want to be a princess, I don't want children, I only want you!" I screamed back. "I don't want anything or anyone else in this whole wide world but you!"

He stared back at me, red tears forming in the corners of his eyes, as the heartbreak spilled onto his face. "And the fact those words passed your lips simply proves just how much I have failed you." He slowly stepped toward me, hovered for a second, then kissed the top of my head before whispering, "I shall love you until the sun rises in the west, until all the stars have burnt out and the bedrock beneath our feet is no more. And I love you enough to do this."

And my whole world walked away, leaving me alone out in the frozen darkness. I stared at the place where my soul mate once stood, my Asher, in total shock. He was sending me away. Discarding me like a used tissue—all in the name of doing the right thing. Didn't he know the only pure utter certainty in this entire universe was that we were meant to be together? How did he lose faith in us? I lost him. But as I stood shivering in the arctic winter night, with the whole of London swinging below me and the Sword of Damocles above, I swore to whoever, whatever was listening I would do anything, *anything* to restore his faith. To prove this universal truth. To gain his love again. Even if it killed me.

He was worth it.

AGE 15
ROME, ITALY

"Oh, Mr. Enrico Gorga, what a lovely birthday present you gifted me without your knowledge. *Molto bene.*"

Two hundred Lira. Not bad for a few seconds work. Astrid may have been a terrible mother, but she was a damn fine pickpocket who at least taught me that one useful skill. Not that I needed the precision of a surgeon in Mr. Gorga's case. In a crowded discotheque it was like shooting fish in a barrel. Most times I'd sneezing hex the mark then swoop in with a handkerchief and flirty smile. While he was distracted by my womanly ways, I'd swipe his billfold. Easy peasy. Purses proved more difficult, just because women weren't as dazzled by my fluttering baby blues, so I mostly preyed on men while my partner Dario targeted the ladies. We were a match made in hell. A week and a half before, he saw me fleece a mark at the Vatican, recognized a kindred petty criminal spirit, and suggested we team up. He was only a couple years older than me, gorgeous as sin, and immediately offered to let me stay at his place strings free. I was lonely. I didn't have a damn friend in the world, so I followed him to his squat. To his credit, he didn't start adding strings for a few days. Still. It beat boarding school.

In less than a week, I had found myself in a Swiss prison masquerading as a school. Once again, based on my test scores, I was skipped two grades, which just compounded my misery. Not only was I the youngest in my grade, therefore the dorm, but the girls knew each other for years and did not like outsiders, especially an American outsider. Prisoners of war received better treatment than I did at that school. The girls stole my clothes, spread heinous yet not wholly inaccurate rumors that I was a slut, that I spent time in a sanitarium, they even attempted to frame me for cheating from the moment I arrived. Every day, every *hour* brought some fresh new hell. They even found ways to torment me in my sleep, making me pee my bed or putting grease in my hair. Every. Day. And the teachers were no help. No one wanted to inconvenience a Duke or Ambassador daddy. I was in such a deep depression already I barely wanted to get out of my urine-soaked bed, let alone fight back. For a whole week I refused to leave my bed or eat. Even then they wouldn't leave me alone. One even tossed me a razor blade as she giggled, "To help things along."

I lasted all of a month before I ran away the first time. I found my way back to London, to him, but my pleas, my literal begging on my hands and knees fell on deaf ears. The next morning, Clifton escorted me back to school. I lost all privileges and couldn't even leave the grounds. Of course that didn't stop escapes two through five. My Houdini routine continued four more times, each with the same result. That last escape Asher refused to even see me. A week after my final return to hell, I received a letter with no return address, simply a short paragraph with a telephone number for emergencies and a heartfelt request for me to make the best of things. To try. He may as well have plunged a literal blade into my heart.

Then *nothing*.

Not a single word, not a single visit, from him in almost a year. Not even at Christmas. Asher arranged for me to spend summers and holidays with the High Priestess of Athens to continue my neglected magical tutoring. My Greek oasis. YaYa was sweet, and her grandson Costas even sweeter if not clumsy those first few times, but after Christmas instead of returning to school, I made my final disappearing act. I had saved about two hundred marks from my allowance and selling some jewelry, so I hopped a boat to Italy and worked my way up to Rome. Two days in the city and the money ran out. Hence my life of crime.

After fleecing Mr. Gorga, I spotted Dario chatting up a middle-aged woman at the bar. Judging from the sloppy caresses he tried on his mark, in the hour I'd been on the hunt, my partner apparently had drunk his weight in liquor. The mark scowled and tried to leave, but he grabbed her wrist to stop her. I hated when he drank. The night before not only were we bounced from a club, I had to practically carry him home. So unprofessional.

Before the woman could slap him, I threw my arm over his shoulders and sighed. "I'm bored. Can we go now?" I asked in broken Italian. I was nowhere near fluent but the language was close enough to Spanish, I got the gist of what people were saying.

"*Scusi*," the woman said before hustling away.

"No wait," Dario called after her. His face contorted into a snarl as he turned to me. "Why the fuck did you do that?"

"Sorry. Come on. We made five hundred. Time to go."

"We just got here."

"Well, I'm leaving. See you later."

As I meandered the few blocks to the squat be it the frigid air, the strolling lovebirds I passed with their inside jokes and eyes for one another, or the fact that all that waited at me at the end of the frozen trek were four water-stained walls and dirty furniture, the depression I'd attempted to keep at bay wheedled through the mortar. It was my birthday and the only gift I received was a canoli and a kiss from Dario. *Dario.* I thought moving in with him would alleviate my loneliness, not compound it. Another in a long line of bad choices. I'd believed it'd be an adventure breaking out on my own, tramping around Italy and surviving by my wits. Finding out who I truly was, and what I was capable of just as he'd wanted for me. Well, Asher achieved his objective, just not with the results he anticipated. Apparently I was a thief capable of nickel and dime crimes. Sven and Astrid would be proud I was carrying on the Olmstead family tradition at least. My real family would be ashamed. Or worse, as I believed that night, he wouldn't care.

There were a few moments through those lonely two years of exile where I hated that man. I begged, got down on my hands and knees with pleas and tears more than twice, but to no avail. Asher offered to send me to another school, but never to let me come home. He wouldn't even entertain the idea of my attending a school in London. No matter what spin he attempted to give it, the fact was that sending me away had precious little to do with education. It was all about banishing me from his side. "For my own good." He refused to tell me where he moved "for my own good." He even stopped taking my phone calls on the emergency line "for my own good." One envelope a month stuffed with cash, that was all I meant to him. He kicked me to the curb so he could play with his old friends. Left me alone to be picked on and terrorized by creatures worse than even vampires, miserable privileged teenage girls.

Right before Christmas vacation some of the girls started a rumor that I was a Satanist, that I recruited several boys in town into my coven with sexual favors, and the whole school ran with it. They drew pentagrams and goats inside all my books and clothes. Whenever I passed someone in the hall they'd whisper "Hail Satan" or ask if I'd sacrificed any babies or virgins. It was constant from the moment I woke to even while I slept. Finally when the entire school began calling me Rosemary's Baby and the local priest came to interrogate me, I made the decision never to return. Of course I left a few parting gifts with the ringleaders, boils and warts medicine could not cure. Far less than they deserved.

Did he even search for me in that past month? Had he simply moved on? Forgotten me? I'd tortured myself with every heinous scenario for a year, but once I struck out on my own, my self-inflicted misery was almost constant. If he were missing I'd scour the world until I drew my last breath. For all he knew I had drawn my last breath. Did he even care? With hindsight, I realize now the reason for my liberation was so he would chase after me, and every day he didn't ride up on a white horse to save me from myself, my depression grew. The night of my fifteenth birthday, my internal crisis reached its apex. I flopped down on Dario's mildew covered couch, stared at the black stain on the ceiling, and immediately burst into tears. What the hell had I done? Was this the life I wanted for myself? To be like my parents? To take advantage of people for a little bit of money? To all but prostitute myself just for companionship and a roof over my head? I couldn't continue. I didn't have another month left in me, but what choice did I have? Boarding school was worse than prison; I wouldn't go back. YaYa would just send me back to school. I was trapped. Completely, utterly alone. Why had he stopped loving me?

Dario stumbled into my pity party, and though I tried to quell the tears, the dike was demolished, and there was no reassembling it. Through my tears, I could still see the disgust written on his face.

"What the hell is the matter with you? Stop crying," he ordered. "Stop it."

I just sobbed harder, coming close to hyperventilating, and actually curling into a ball. About ten seconds later, the couch shifted as Dario sat beside me. "It … it's okay," he said, lifting me so he could hug me. I rested my head on his shoulder. He reeked of tobacco and sweat, but I didn't care. "It'll be okay."

It was lovely having someone just hold me. The sobs lessened as he kissed the top of my head, then down my forehead. He lifted my head to kiss my lips. He tasted of liquor and cigarettes, neither of which were appetizing. Neither was the tongue he shoved in my mouth. I pulled away.

"Stop."

He kissed me again. I tried to squirm away, but he held on tight. "I said stop!"

"Come on," he muttered.

"No!" I said as I pinched his side.

"Ow!"

He released me enough so I could literally shove him down on the couch and spring up. "I said no!"

"Bitch!"

"I may be a bitch, but at least I'm not a shitty thief like you. I'm outta here." I started collecting my meager belongings, mostly clothes strewn around.

"Good. Saves me the trouble of kicking you out. Just leave me the money from tonight, and get the fuck out."

I scoffed. "Hell no. *I* earned this money while you were drinking your weight in booze and getting turned down by someone's grandmother. It's mine."

He leapt up, face contorting in fury. "Give me that money, Anna."

"No way. I need it, I earned it, it's mine." I zipped up my suitcase and hoisted it from the kitchen table. "Nice knowing you."

I made it one step past him before his hand clamped on my forearm, and he spun me around. "Give me the damn money, Anna," he growled.

"Go to h—"

Merde. I'd asked him not to bring the switchblade to the club, but of course he had. The moment that blade popped in his hand, my blood ran cold. Not good. Not good not at all. "Give me the money, *putana.*"

My first instinct was to hand him the cash and run. But aside from the fact that without it I'd have to sleep on the street that night, I just didn't want to. The scared little boy bullying me had no right to it. He had no right to threaten me. Who the hell did this bastard think he was? I glanced down at his hand, then at his an-

94

gered expression. Mine went deeper. "You have three seconds to let go of my arm, or you'll lose yours."

"What the fu—"

He reacted to my knee going for his groin, releasing me but turning to deflect the blow. With only a split second for us to both adjust our tactics, he was almost faster than me, slashing the knife toward my chest. Just as it was about to make contact, I raised my palm and shouted, "*Lapsus!*" as YaYa taught me. I'd never used the spell on a person before, so I gasped as Dario literally flew across the room, whacking his head against the corner of the cabinet then collapsing to the floor. His eyes remained shut the ten seconds I stood stock still, just staring as the blood began to pool around his head.

I'd killed him.

No, his chest slowly moved up and down but not in a steady pace. My mind ran so fast, a thousand miles a second, I couldn't focus on a singular thought. So my body took control. While my brain remained screaming in that squat, my body ran me down the block to the first pay phone I spotted and punched in the emergency phone number. I almost fainted with relief when he accepted the collect call.

"Anna?" Asher asked, that beautiful baritone shaky and desperate. "Anna? Is it really you?"

"Asher," I cried. The second wave of relief almost overtook me that time. I consciously had to will my knees from buckling. "I-I-I've done something really bad. He-he came at me with a knife. I-I think he's dying."

"Are you injured? Are you safe?"

"I-I'm fine. I-I used a spell, and he hit his head. There was so-so-so much blood. I didn't know what—"

"Anna, love, where are you?" he cut in. "Tell me where you are."

"A st-street corner in Rome."

"Rome? Then I want you to go to 27 Paradiso Piazza. Someone will be waiting to let you into my flat there. I shall arrive in about two hours. Do not leave. Repeat the address back to me." I did. "And what is the address where this man is?"

I rattled it off. "He-he was alive when I left. Should I call the ambulance or—"

"No. I will take care of everything. Simply go to the flat and wait for me. I will be there as soon as possible, my love."

"Please hurry. I love you."

"I love you too. Now go, *mo chuisle*. I shall be with you soon. Go."

I hung up but couldn't move. He'd take care of everything. Like he had with Sven and Andie. That thought tied a knot in my already fragile stomach. Despite the fact he tried to stab me, I didn't want Dario dead. So despite Asher's orders, I picked up the phone and called emergency services for him without leaving my name. He'd live to grift another day.

The elderly woman in a housecoat at Asher's building grumbled at me for waking her as she showed me up to the flat. It was stuffy, dusty, and sparsely furnished, but to me it was the Taj Mahal. The adrenaline rush I was surviving on ended the moment the woman shut the door. I could barely keep my eyes open as I took a quick shower to warm up with no luck. It did nothing to stop my quaking limbs. I was so uncoordinated I could barely tie the knot on my robe. Ten seconds after I climbed into that four-poster antique bed, I was asleep.

The creak of wood drew me from dreamless slumber. He was outlined against the dim light I'd left on in the living room like a specter. Or an angel. "Asher," I whispered breathlessly.

"You seem so different. So frail. So old," he said, shock and melancholy dripping from every syllable. "I-I am so sorry, *mo chuisle*. I thought it was the right ... I am so sorry. I am so—"

I threw off the covers and rushed to him, throwing my arms around him and holding him as if I were about to plummet off the edge of the earth into hell itself. Without hesitation, Asher clung to me with the same passion and desperation. With this one embrace, two years of misery and doubt melted from my weary soul. He hadn't forgotten me. He missed me. He loved me. Truly loved me. Of course. Of course.

"I love you," I whispered against his neck before kissing that spot. "I love you." The kiss moved up. "I've missed you so much." To his cheek. "I love you so much." To the corner of his mouth. "Never leave me again." A gentle kiss upon his lips. "I'm nothing without you." Another kiss on his still lips. "I love you so much. *So* much." Another kiss, but that time his lips quaked against mine. "I'm nothing." I gazed into those blue pools, now tinged red from his tears. I kissed the first drop away. Then the second on the other side before meeting his eyes once more. I licked my lips, taking a part of him inside me, the tang of his blood invigorating us both.

His face, his body, every inch was trembling, crumbling along with his resolve. "Anna, this is no—"

He wasn't getting away from me. From us. Not again. I kissed the rest of the sentence away. His mouth parted as I invaded it, with my now expert tongue but once his began to play with mine I tore away to whisper, "I need you. I *need* you, my Asher. Please. *Please.*" And with those words and one more kiss, he was mine. All mine. I possessed him mind, soul, and after I lowered us onto that bed finally in body.

Mine.

———

We lay in bed afterward with my head resting on his bare chest as he played with a strand of my hair. It was something out of a dream. A perfect moment. Well, almost perfect. "Stop it," I said.

"Stop what?" Asher asked.

"Feeling guilty about making love to me. There's no reason for it. As of yesterday, I am legally an adult in Italy. Besides, let's face it, *I* seduced *you.* If anything, I took advantage of you. I'm the one who should feel guilty, but I don't because there is nothing to feel guilty about. I love you. You love me. Nothing else matters. It never did. I just feel so damn lucky I found you so young that I didn't have to wait an entire lifetime to meet my soulmate like some people have to." I stared up at him. "Do you feel lucky to have found me?"

His eyes grew cloudy with sadness and love. "Oh, *mo chuisle,* how can you not know what a miracle you are to me?"

"A miracle?" I chuckled.

Asher didn't smile back, he just gazed down at me with his usual intensity. Oh, how I'd missed that gaze. The one where it was as if a thousand years had passed since he'd last laid eyes on me, and was afraid I would vanish once more. "Before we met, I…" He trailed off into his own head for a few seconds. "I have been in existence for more than eight hundred years. I have circumnavigated this earth so many times I lost count eons ago. There was nothing I had not seen, nothing I had not done or experienced. And because of that there was simply nothing. Purgatory. For over a year I arose each night wishing I had not. Life was naught but a vacuum of darkness. Then one night I decided hell was preferable to the abyss. It was then I made up my mind to feel the warmth of the sun one last time. To leave this wretched world. I just could not depart without seeing her once more. My Jane. To apologize. To cleanse my soul of at least one of its sins before the devil claimed his rightful due." Asher gave me a rare, brief smile. "Then I met you," he whispered, caressing my cheek. "This beautiful, fierce, intelligent, damaged almost to the point of no return wonder. You stepped into view, and I sparked back to life. I knew, I *knew* I was meant to help you. To shape you. To guide you to your fullest potential. To love you even though I had forgotten how.

"And I fought, oh how I fought to carry out my plan in spite of the gift presented before me. I left you with those monsters and drove to the lake where Jane and I consummated our love the first time, waiting for the light to take me. But you followed me there. Haunting me with your need. Your love. Every time I attempted to push you from my thoughts, you returned with the force of an exploding star. You called me back to you. *Mo chuisle*, you saved me. You brought me back to life. And these last two years without you … I began craving the sun once more."

I leaned up to kiss the lips that gave me those beautiful words. I didn't think it possible, but I loved him more after this confession than ever before. He kissed me back, cupping my face with the tenderness he'd always showed me. I broke the seal first, resting my forehead against his. "Then don't ever do that to me again, okay? Don't ever, *ever* send me away again. Not for any reason, especially not if it's only for my own good. It isn't, not for either of us. You need me just as much as I need you. You are mine and I am yours until the end of time, and I don't want a single night squandered; I don't want to spend a single night where I am not by your side. I've experienced this world without you, and you're right. It is hell. Don't send me back into hell. Promise me. Promise me, no matter what, *no matter what,* you will never leave me. *Never.*"

My Asher smiled. "Never. You have bested me. I have finished fighting a battle I honestly never desired to win. I lay my sword down at your feet, my love. My blood. My Anna. I am yours 'til the close of the dream. 'Til death, I am yours."

"And I'm yours."

We sealed our covenant with a kiss.

Most pacts with the devil are.

AGE 17
VIENNA, AUSTRIA

WHAT ON EARTH WAS I thinking? White was never my color.

All the other debutantes were visions in their white ball gowns and gloves, but with my snow-white skin thanks to my nocturnal habits and pale blond hair, I was Casper the Friendly Ghost haunting the opulent, gilded Vienna Opera Ball. My blood red lips were the only factor that kept me from being completely washed away. Asher loved that color on me. Practically all I owned was red lipstick. The color matched the ruby and diamond necklace Asher presented me before we left for the night. Part one of my birthday present. I was dancing away at my second.

The year before we'd been invited to the ball by an old friend of Asher's, the Lord of Vienna, but had to cancel because I fell ill with the flu. Given the choice of staying home watching the event on TV, while wrapped in Asher's arms as he nursed me back to health or actually attending was a no-brainer. But in the grips of fever I made the offhand comment about how it might be fun to debut. To wear the white dress, dance all night with the man I loved. Why, it would be like a fairy tale come alive. Or a wedding. A few months later my excited paramour surprised me with the application, the name of my partner, another consort, and a left waltz dance lesson. He was so excited and proud of himself for setting it all up, I couldn't say no. So the night of my seventeenth birthday I found myself waltzing around the massive oval dance floor under centuries-old fresco murals in front of five thousand socialites, politicians, royalty, and a large percentage of the European vampire community. Not bad for the daughter of petty thieves.

The waltz ended, and I curtsied to my angered partner Gerhardt before the announcer called everyone to dance. I was officially out in European society. Bully for me. Stupid fever. One of the other boys I met at rehearsal, who came with a harpy from my former boarding school, asked me to dance, but I declined. Prince Albert of Monaco or John Travolta could have queried and received the same response. My dance card was full with one name.

"You were astonishing," Asher said after a quick kiss. "I would swear you were literally gliding on air."

"Where is Heinrich?" Gerhardt asked of his real escort.

"Catronia dragged him to the dance floor," Asher said, sliding his arm around my waist. "She shall return him relatively intact, I am sure." He pecked my temple. "There are more people I wish for you to meet, my love," Asher whispered. "Excuse us, son."

Asher led me toward the foyer where we passed Grace Kelly and her Prince husband chatting with Princess Anne. I still regret not meeting them. "Are you enjoying yourself?" I asked halfway up the red carpeted stairs to our box on the third level.

"Are you?" Asher asked, nodding to yet another vampire as we passed.

"I'd be having more fun at a private party for two back at our suite," I teased with a seductive smile.

"As would I," he replied with the same grin, "but we must not be rude to our host. He has not forgiven us for last year's abandonment. My kind are legendary for nurturing even the most minor of grudges into a murderous rage. This is one night, I am afraid, you cannot have me all to yourself."

"I am counting the seconds."

I learned my lesson after London. We were happiest just he and I alone in our country oasis. Or at least I was. Asher agreed to leave Milan where he'd been hiding from me, and we settled into domestic bliss in a small, two bedroom cottage in Holland. On the evenings I didn't have ballet class, I'd wake with enough time to heat his blood from the butcher shop and tidy a little. After his warm meal, he'd attempt a new recipe from Julia Child's cookbook for my supper, then keep me company as I ate, followed by television, reading together, my studies, or simply talking until dawn. Really it was just as before in Galway except we now shared a bed. Old married couples would be bored around us. And I *loved* every millisecond of it. The nights of blood and roses.

Asher did not share my enthusiasm for domesticity. Eventually, after a few months, he grew restless in the constraints of our dark paradise, and insisted we spend a few weeks in a new city. Rio, Moscow, Tokyo, among others. On occasion we'd meet his old friends there and attend a concert or play, but I put my foot down with the private parties like those in London. He swore he didn't care, he didn't want even a moment where my attention wasn't solely directed his way, but I could read his face when the invitation came. Just a momentary flash of light at the prospect, quickly snuffed out by my reluctance. I'd also learned in London to pick my battles, so when his wanderlust grew almost constant, I suggested we attend a party or two with strict rules applied. An introvert can only constrain an extrovert for so long.

Augustus's entourage had expanded in size as I made my debut, spilling into the hall, one person more pale and gorgeous than the last. I clung tight to my Asher as we joined the undead bacchanalia. The compliments on my debut bombarded me as we made our way inside through the pit of vipers. Lord Augustus of Vienna held court by the balustrade to watch the twirling dancers three stories below like ballerinas in a music box. He was one of only a handful of vampires I'd ever met who would never turn heads. Short, plump, with thinning brown hair and chubby cheeks.

"There she is, our very own debutante," our large host said as I curtsied. "You know what that means, do you not? It is now acceptable for Asher to make an honest woman of you, as they say nowadays. Bring you into the family. I was only a year older than you when I was turned. You do not want to wait too long, old friend. The bloom only remains on the rose for so long."

"I shall keep that in mind," said Asher graciously.

"And if he will not give you the gift, I am more than willing," Augustus said, brown eyes undressing me. "And it would solve problems like missing balls due to illness."

"You are most kind, Lord Augustus. And I do apologize for last year. I so wanted to meet you all."

Augustus's eyes jutted to Asher. "You have trained her well, old friend. Just one of her many tricks, no doubt."

The group tittered at his asinine joke. It took a lot not to slap his lecherous face. I just took it with a smile on my face. Give a vampire an inch, and they will begin flaying you right there. "Yes, sir."

"Well, be sure to save me a dance."

"I shall save you two, your lordship."

"Speaking of dances," Asher said, stepping beside me to hold out his hand. "I claimed the next. Excuse us. We shall return."

When we were far enough away near the stairs, I sighed. "Why do they always do that? Treat me like a literal piece of meat after a three-second conversation?"

"Well, you are most appetizing," he said before kissing my neck. "I should know." He squeezed my hand. "And you handled him masterfully. As always."

"I hate vampires," I muttered. "Present company excluded, of course."

"Do not say such things," he chided.

"But I do! I'm sorry, but I *really* do. Your friends either ignore me, try to bed me, or threaten me. They don't talk to me or try to engage with me unless the topic is fashion, our sex life, or gossip. They're all just so ... shallow and selfish. Will that happen when you turn me? I'll become a vapid, entitled monster? Because if it is, I may reconsider."

After working up the courage for a week, I broached the topic one night. Even as a child I always assumed he'd eventually turn me. We decided to wait until my twenty-first birthday at the earliest, later if I desired to have a child. He brought that subject up all on his own. Vampires are sterile. Once I turned, I could never conceive. But at seventeen it didn't matter to me one way or another. Nothing mattered but him. I could be swayed either way. If he wanted a child for us to raise then I would have one, and if it kept us at home as a family more's the better.

"You do not give them a chance, Anna," he snapped harshly. He was so incensed he stopped in the middle of the hallway walking to and fro, and frowned. "As much as I love you, as much as I wish to cater to your every whim, and more often than not do, on occasion I do crave the pleasure of other people's company. I crave an evening spent not bored to tears in front of a television or performing menial chores but out in the world among laughter, and music, and the chattering of old friends and new. It is not an affront to you, it is simply … what I need. I have spent close to a millennia a certain way, with certain people, whom I happen to miss. I adore you. I love you above all others, but you are smothering me. Whether it be that you fear I shall leave you or simply pure selfishness, you must push it aside and allow me to breathe. You must trust me." Asher leaned forward and kissed me. "And, if given half a chance, you may find yourself actually enjoying yourself. Will you try? For me?"

He *was* right. I wasn't giving them a chance. I never had. Vampires were nothing more than competition. The image of him on that couch in London sprang to mind whenever a pretty pale face approached him. My imagination and insecurity ran rampant with one smile not directed my way. It wasn't fair to him to be so distrustful or to bring his mood down when he wished to enjoy himself. He sacrificed a great deal for me, I could do this one thing for him. I could *try*. For him.

I grabbed the back of my lover to draw him toward me, kissing him deeply before pushing him away. "As you wish, my Asher." I slipped my hand in his. "But it will cost you a dance."

He gave me three, which were three more than expected. He enjoyed watching me dance more than the act itself. I practically had to give my paramour a command ballet performance in our home studio every other night. Not that I minded as it often led to another enjoyable physical activity. That night he handed me off to another vampire for the polka as he watched from the sidelines with a proud smile affixed. I lost sight of him during the waltz, and after that Lord Augustus claimed his two dances and my undivided attention. When I did spy Asher during the second dance, a dark-haired woman in a bright red gown had her arms binding Asher's neck while she kissed his cheek.

My first instinct was to rush over there and pry him from her clutches, but I managed to suppress the urge. However, when the dance ended, I convinced Augustus to escort me over to the now threesome. As I walked closer, I was struck by how young and innocent the girl appeared. The pale skin gave her away as vampire but she looked about my age, if not younger, with full, pouty lips, perfect elfin nose, and the largest brown eyes I'd ever encountered. And now this enchanting girl was sitting in my lover's lap laughing her beautiful head off with Asher guffawing loudly as well. The last time I'd made him laugh that hard was when I overloaded the dishwashing detergent and the machine exploded bubbles all over our kitchen. That laugh riot had an X-Rated ending. *Trust,* I thought. *Trust.*

The girl caught sight of me first but instead of rising, she threw her arm over Asher's shoulders. To most a perfectly innocent gesture, but I recognized the move for what it was: a claim of ownership. I'd enlisted the same maneuver every time we were out. Asher at least had the decency to appear a tad guilty when he noticed me, blue eyes diverting to the floor before rising to extract the pretty interloper.

"Hello again," Augustus said. "Didier. Christine. So glad you both could make it."

"I finished the job earlier than anticipated," the third man, Didier, replied in French. Even then I was struck by how tall he was.

"I was informed. Excellent work as always."

"And what exactly do you do?" I asked politely.

"He murders people for money," Christine said as if informing me he were a barrister. Did it with a smile too.

"Christine!" Didier hissed.

"What? We are among friends. Between the five of us he probably has the lowest body count. Unless lovely here is not as angelic as she appears."

"You have no idea, *dear*," I said with a knife's edge.

Not missing a beat, she said, "Yes, I do believe Byron mentioned something to me along those lines." I turned as red as her dress and glanced at Asher, who'd gone stony still. "Your reputation does precede you, Anna, is it?" She extended her gloved hand. "I am Christine. Lovely to finally make your acquaintance."

Having no real choice, I shook it. Her grip was so tight I wanted to flinch but kept my expression neutral. "Likewise, I'm sure."

Christine released my hand. "You are a fetching creature, little one." She turned to Asher and smirked. Even that was seductive. "You always did have a penchant for us nubile, pretty faces."

My stomach knotted twice. I knew it. They'd been lovers. One glance at Asher's shifty eyes that wouldn't focus on me confirmed it. She was *that* Christine. And he wondered why I hated attending social events. "Really? You two were an item? He's never mentioned you before," I lied innocently. "How odd."

Her name had come up once or twice in our long conversations. If memory served they had the same sire, Marcellus. Where Asher marked the first of his line, Christine marked the last. Asher slayed their maker when he'd discovered Christine's mistreatment, among other personal atrocities commited against his spawn that spanned over four hundred years. That was the trouble that separated him from Jane, him killing his maker then fleeing to the Americas only to be found once more. He spoke of his "sister" with tenderness, but he did finally admit to their on and off again carnal couplings through the centuries. I recognized the pattern. She'd get in trouble, he'd go running, they'd fall into bed. No matter the age, we are creatures of pattern. I hadn't consciously exploited his savior complex while in Rome, but my subconscious can be a real bitch at times.

My rival's smile faltered, and with that lie, in that instant I made a new enemy. Now how I wish I'd just kept my fucking mouth shut.

Asher, sensing the impending cat fight, cleared his throat. "I am parched."

"As am I," I said before holding out my arm to my lover. "Shall we, my love?"

He took it, though after a glimpse at Christine. I could sense the daggers on my back as I led us all back to our box. I took my place on Asher's lap and Christine did the same across from us on Didier's. She did make sure her foot touched Asher's, but I knew to pick my battles. It would be a long war. "So, how long have you and Didier been together?" I asked.

"We are not exactly together," Christine answered. "I mean, we fuck on occasion. Asher knows how that is."

"Not anymore," I said, wrapping his arm around my waist.

"Oh, domesticated him, have you? I attempted it once, though doing the same thing, the same person over and over, night after night, was so very ... dull." She sipped her blood then grinned. "Well, I suppose it is good for some."

"It has been absolute bliss for us," I said.

"Has it now?"

"Absolutely," Asher said with certainty.

The corners of Christine's mouth twitched a little. "Then who are you and what have you done with my Asher?" She chuckled before looking my way. "Unless Angel here is a witch and has you under a love spell."

"I am actually," I said, "a witch. But unlike some, I have never had to resort to tricks or spells when dealing with love. The universe saw fit not only for our paths to cross, but for both Asher and I to recognize the other for what we were. Soul mates."

Christine chuckled again. "So, you finally found that elusive of all the magics: true love." She sipped her blood again. "And here I thought it only existed in fairy stories. And as we all know, only children believe in those."

"Oh, true love is most real," Asher chimed in. "And there is nothing like it on this earth."

Christine sipped again. "Actually, if memory serves, you *have* been lucky enough to find it on more than one occasion, have you not my Asher? There was Cordelia. Jane. That barmaid in White-chapel. Olivia, was it? Terrible what happened to her once she left you, but Lord Richard had no choice I suppose. Did anyone ever find out who turned her in after she left you?"

Asher's grip on me tightened. "No."

"Shame. Out of all your true loves, her I rather liked." Christine took another dainty sip. "I only hope this one does not disappoint as the others eventually did."

"Oh, I'm sure you do," I said snidely. "But there's no cause to worry." I gazed at Asher, smiled, then leaned down to give him a deep, probing kiss usually reserved for behind closed doors. He returned my ardor and grinned back when I finally pulled away. "Is there?"

"No," he whispered.

"We shall see," Christine said in singsong, ruining the mood.

Both Asher and I glared at the bitch, who just smiled sweetly as she finished her blood.

Thank the universe Asher finally changed the subject, focusing on the hitman in our midst. I'd never met an assassin before, let alone one who could teleport. As Christine could not stand to have the spotlight off herself for more than five minutes that conversation was cut short. The first available opening, she steered us back down Memory Lane in a car built for two. I didn't speak seven words the entire hour as the old friends guffawed and reminisced about Victorian London and parties at Versailles. Usually I adored these stories, learning about Asher's life before me, but not when every avenue led to sex. Didier grew bored half an hour in and excused himself, but no matter how much I wanted to, I held my ground with a smile for every smutty anecdote. I could put up with her for a night. It was *me* he would return home with.

This was what I told myself when I could no longer hold off the urge to use the bathroom and left them to powder my nose. Trust. I trusted him. I trusted him enough to get something to eat and even dance a few times, though my partners only received a quarter of my attention as my eyes rarely left the entrance in anticipation of his arrival. Which never happened. He didn't come looking. Didn't chase after me. When I slogged back upstairs an hour later, they were huddled together laughing while she rested her head against his shoulder.

"Anna," a familiar voice said behind me.

I spun around to find Alain hanging over my right shoulder like an angel. Or devil. "I thought I saw you haunting the opera house."

"I would have requested a dance but was unsure if you would accept or hex me," Alain said.

"Four years ago, neither would I."

"And now?"

I took a deep breath and sighed. "Thank you," I said reluctantly. "Truly. You stopped me from making a horrible mistake. I don't know what the hell I was thinking that night."

"Thinking never factored into it. But all's well that ends well. At least from your perspective."

"Oh, don't start that again. A hex is still in the cards." We both smiled. "Your fears were unfounded though. He treats me like a princess. We're blissfully, madly in love."

"Are you now?" He nodded behind me. I glanced back to see that slag laughing so hard she doubled over, resting her forehead on Asher's legs as he just sniggered back at her theatrics. "She was always an amazing hunter, our Christine. She instinctively knows the perfect time and the perfect bait with which to strike. Ruthless. Manipulative. Patient. She is a credit to our kind." He gazed into my eyes. "You do not stand a chance, little girl."

"She's no threat. Let her have her fun tonight. We're going home tomorrow."

Alain chuckled. "Do not underestimate the power of shared history, long-term affection, and good old-fashioned ego stroking hero worship, Anna. Remember, she claimed him first. No matter how long the lifespan, habit is habit. She is his worst. Like a dormant disease, she rears her ugly head and wreaks havoc, leaving naught but death and misery in her wake. Though if it makes you feel better, if she has chosen now to resurface, she must view you as a true threat for his long-term affection. She is 3 for 0 though. Cordelia, Jane, and Olivia all stood where you are now and proclaimed the same. That he only loved them. That the love they shared was enough to conquer all, including Asher's corrupted soul itself. But Christine, she brings out the true Asher and she knows it. It may take a week, it may take a decade, but that woman will find a way to ingratiate herself into your lives and decay it from the inside out."

"Well, I won't let her," I said with utter certainty.

"I admire your spirit. I do. But at the end of the night, Anna, it may have precious little to do with *you*. You cannot change him, or what he is at his core. Despite what the fairy tales may want you to believe, love does not move mountains. It does not magically change a person into something they are not. And no matter how much two people love one another, sometimes that is not enough. Nowhere near enough. And the sooner one realizes that, the sooner their life can truly begin. I only hope for your sake when the revelation comes, our Asher can accept it as well. Otherwise, may you find the strength to survive all the hell he throws at you. And it will be nothing short of hell. I do not envy your odds, though. So please listen to my words this night. Run far. Run fast. And never look back." He took my hand and kissed the top of it like a gentleman. "It was lovely to see you again. Truly. Though I hope for your sake it is the last time."

Alain gave me a reverent nod before strolling away. Like four years before, he left fear and uncertainty in his wake. Sometimes that's all it takes. One bad seed planted to ruin the entire crop— one conversation with an almost total stranger to completely change your outlook on all you believed you knew. I stared at my soul mate with *her*. The casual way they touched. The loose posture. The ease of his smile completely in line with hers. Their intimacy as if there was no one else in the room. It sickened me. Worse, it scared the hell out of me.

"There you are," Asher said only when I moved right in front of him.

"Yes, we had given you up for lost," Christine added with a faux sweet grin.

"No such luck. Sorry," I said, matching her expression. I turned to Asher. "I'm exhausted. It's time to go home."

"No," Christine whined. "The night is still so young, and we haven't finished catching up. She is a big girl. I am sure she can get herself home. Or we can continue this back at your suite."

"No," I snapped. I really was exhausted. "If you want, you can stay here with your … *friend*. I'll be fine alone. I won't wait up." With one final glare for the interloper, I stalked away before I accidently set her on fire with a nearby candle. I should have.

"Anna, wait!" Asher called after me. He caught me halfway down the stairs, grabbing my arm and spinning me around. "What is the matter now? You are acting like a spoilt child and embarrassing me. We spoke about this."

"We did, but that was before you spent all night ignoring me and fawning over a woman who clearly hates me and wants to return to your already occupied bed. And from where I was standing, you were all but pulling back the sheets for her. Hell, maybe you two already found some corner and made up for lost time. Maybe that whole speech about me giving you space was planned because you knew she was coming and wanted me out of the way."

"Now you are purposely being cruel," he sneered back.

"Well, you didn't seem to mind when she was doing the same to me," I countered.

"Christine is one of my oldest, dearest friends. My sister. She has been by my side at my worst moments, and I have not seen or spoken to her in close to a decade. I have sacrificed a great deal for you, Anna. You can survive one night where you are not my sole bloody focus!"

"Is all well?" Christine called as she descended the stairs.

"Of course," I scoffed and rolled my eyes.

"Everything is fine," Asher said none-too-convincingly.

"No, it is not. Asher, I fear this is all my doing. The last thing I desire is to be the cause of any strife between you two."

"Oh, I'll bet," I said with a scowl.

"Anna," Asher snapped.

"Perhaps we got off on the wrong foot," Christine said, batting those gorgeous eyelashes of hers. "I *was* being a bit cheeky with you, and for that I do apologize. I simply could not help myself. I am incredibly protective of those I love, as I am sure you are. I do not wish to see our Asher hurt again. He barely survived his past losses." *Without her that is.* "But I see now there is deep, abiding love between you both. He spent the entire night speaking of barely any topic other than you. It is as if I know you already," she chuckled. "So I hope you will forgive tonight's bad behavior, and we can begin anew. It would mean a lot to me, and I know it would mean the world to our Asher." She extended her hand. "Friends?"

Alain was right. She was good. *Damn* good. And Asher bought every word. Every single one. What other choice did I have? I plastered a smile on my face and shook her hand. "Friends."

And just like that the dream was over. The nights of blood and roses had come to an end. I never could have foretold where the new path would take me. Or that I would lose everything along the way. Including myself.

AGE 19
WASHINGTON, DC

UGH. THE RINGING TELEPHONE drew me out of my only oasis in the world, the sweet nothingness of slumber. Oh, how I wished I could stay in the nothing instead of waking beside an equally naked man, my body covered in bruises and dried blood. Sadly a common occurrence in recent months. How on earth did I end up naked in Oliver's bed? I managed to extract myself from the beautiful, cold almost corpse to answer the phone on the nightstand.

"Hello," I asked groggily.

"Ms. Asher, this is the front desk. There is a Special Agent Nathan West of the F.R.E.A.K.S. here to interview you."

"Who? What?"

"It's about last night's murders. Lord Peter has ordered all within his territory to cooperate fully with the investigation. I'm sending the agent up now."

"Uh, okay." I hung up the phone with a sigh. I was in no shape for company, let alone one with questions, but the law was the law. Peter said jump, we weren't even allowed to ask how high. There was barely time to brush my teeth and slip on a robe before the knock on my suite door. It was near pitch black with the special shutters drawn so I added to my bruise collection before I found a light. "Coming!"

When I opened the door to the agent, I literally took his breath away. Just not in the usual, romantic way. Oh how I wished I'd at least taken the time to wash off the blood on my neck or brushed my hair. Not that I really cared a fig what the agent in the hallway thought. He was cute in a disheveled professor way, all spindly legs and arms in a rumpled too-short suit. His medium brown hair was as unruly with bangs in need of a cut, round rosy cheeks, and bushy thick eyebrows. Even his silver-framed glasses were crooked. "A-Anna Asher?" he asked with a Texas drawl.

"You the freak?"

"Um, yes. Sp-special Agent Nathan West," he said, pulling out his badge and an envelope. "May I come in?"

"Okay." I stepped aside to let him in.

"Oh, uh, this was left for you at the front desk," Nathan said, handing me the envelope. Our skin lightly brushed, and I got a huge shock. Literally. It was as if I'd stuck my finger in a light socket. "Ow!"

"Oh, sorry," Nathan said. "Sorry."

"It's fine." My hand still tingled though. At least I was awake now. "Um, do you want coffee? I can phone room service."

"No, no I'm fine. Thank you." He tried to turn on another light but the bulb flashed, then exploded. "Shit! Sorry. Sorry. I don't…"

The agent cringed. "I'm just gonna…" He pointed to the sofa before sitting. Clothes from the previous night, including my red lace panties, lay at his feet. He kept glancing down at them.

"Sorry about the mess," I said as I sat across from my guest. "We, uh, got back late last night."

"It's … fine." He removed a pad and pen from inside his ill-fitting coat. "So, uh, I'm sure you're aware of recent events between the vampires and werewolves, including last night's murders. Two vamps and their companions were killed just a block from Club Vertigo."

"Yeah, of course I do. Vampires killing werewolves, werewolves killing vampires, war all but declared. It's all anyone's talking about. I'm just not sure what it has to do with me."

"I understand you were friends with one of the victims, Dana Carver?"

"Well, I wouldn't say friends," I corrected. "We partied with her three nights ago and went lingerie shopping yesterday, but that's all."

"Did she mention anyone following her? Did you see anyone suspicious hanging around?"

"No. Not that I noticed, sorry."

"Did she mention having any dealings with werewolves, either her or her boyfriend?"

"No, at least I don't think so. All we spoke about were clothes and living with vampires. You really should talk to Oliver. He was friends with Jerome, one of the vampires who died. He'd be better able to answer these questions than me."

"And Oliver's your boyfriend?"

"Not real—no. I've only known him about two weeks since we got here. He's asleep now, but he'll be up after sundown. There's really nothing I can tell you. Sorry."

The young agent frowned and put away his notebook. "Well, thank you for your time, ma'am." He placed his card on the coffee table. "If you could have Oliver call me, or if you think of anything, no matter how minute, please contact me." He rose from the sofa, as did I. "And be careful. Don't go out alone."

I chuckled as I escorted him to the door. "What? Don't I look like a girl who can take care of herself?" I asked flirtatiously.

"No," he scoffed. "*God* no."

The moment those words passed his lips, I had a physical sensation to those three words as if he had literally slapped me in the face. I'd been one big, raw nerve for months and this stranger just sucker punched that nerve with brass knuckles. My face fell, and I even began to tremble a little. "Get out."

"I'm sorry," he said. "I—"

"Get out," I hissed.

"I didn't mean—"

"Get the fuck out of my suite. Who the hell are you to judge me? You don't know me. You don't know my life."

"I-I wasn't judging, I swear."

I threw the door to the hall open. "Bullshit. Get out. Now!"

The agent quickly walked through the door. "I'm sorry if I offended—"

The door slammed in his face. My breath didn't equalize until his footsteps receded down the hall. The moment silence hit, so did my mortification. That man didn't deserve the tongue lashing I'd given him. Besides, he was right. All the partying and feeding, not to mention the Quaalude from the night before, had left me as weak as a newborn. I couldn't fight off a mosquito let alone a malicious werewolf. I suddenly saw myself through the stranger's eyes, and it made me nauseous. I stared down at my wrist, the entire circumference more purple than peach where Christine and others fed almost every night. My neck and inner thigh no doubt matched. There wasn't an inch of me that didn't feel like a land-fill, even on the inside. My guts churned, and I rushed into the master bedroom for the nearest bathroom, passing a naked Asher and Christine in our bed with only a glance. "No. No," I moaned when I saw the blood between my legs. My period. Another fail-ure. At least I'd discovered the source of my outburst. I was always a nightmare right before. Cold comfort. The shower and Advil for the cramps didn't help at all. Nothing ever did. Not the alcohol, not the hard drugs, nothing worked. I was in a constant state of ache from the soul out. How had I let it get so far? I couldn't even place all the blame at Christine's feet.

She *was* good. Better even than Alain had warned me. She in-filtrated our lives so gradually even I failed to notice its demise until it was too late. It began with phone calls a few times a month, then invites on vacations with her and her various lovers. Then the occasional day or so at our house where she almost had *me* believing we were friends. No jokes, no flirting with Asher, she even helped with the dishes. With the baseline established, she pushed further and further, getting in fights with her boyfriends and needing rescuing or a place to stay until she got on her feet. Next thing I knew they were out hunting every other night be-cause the blood from the butcher's shop had spoiled or wasn't good enough for our Asher. Of course then the rumors started in town, and we had to leave. Asher didn't even attempt to hide his joy.

Asher loved our "grand tour," one endless party around the world led by Christine, the latest stop being Washington, DC. to look up Oliver, an old lover of hers, and coincidentally Asher's grandson via Alain. Just one big fucked-up family. Oliver wasn't as bad as some of the other vampires, he knew when to stop feeding on me at least, but it still felt as if my soul had departed my body whenever he touched me. The things I agreed to, the things I did … wasn't I a liberated woman? A risk taker? Didn't I want to embrace the lifestyle I'd soon be initiated into? Didn't I trust Asher as he trusted me? Every night the man I adored slipped further and further away, and I was beginning to think I should let him. Or cut Christine's head off while she slept.

Even my act of true desperation failed for the third month in a row as my trip to the bathroom showed. A baby would definitely banish the bitch. He'd have no choice but to settle down again. It had been six months since I brought the topic up right before our tour began, and though he'd been less than joyous about the idea, I *knew* he'd be thrilled when it actually happened. When he held the baby in his arms. He was the one who invited the men into our bed and fine physical specimens they all were. If I could just get my stupid body on board.

At least I had a distraction for the day. I'd volunteered my magical services to Lord Peter the previous night when word reached us about the murders. Things had been tense between the vampires and Eastern Werewolf Pack since our arrival, but within a week the animosity escalated when two werewolves were found dead with fang marks on their bodies. After the second murder,

Pack Alpha Bobby Conlon and his wolves stormed into Club Vertigo the night before and threatened Lord Peter. Conlon and Ivan, Peter's giant of a bodyguard, even came to blows. It was intense. Oliver had to yank me from the line of fire when Ivan threw a redheaded werewolf across the club. The pack left, but not even two hours later Dana, Jerome, and two others were coming to the club to meet us, and were jumped in an alley. Killed. We were still with Peter when we heard the news. Knowing I was a witch, and total war was on the horizon, his lordship more or less ordered me to drive down to Goodnight, Virginia, and create potions to stop the werewolf transform, basically rendering them human and therefore easier to kill. All's fair in love and war. Peter had me at Goodnight. Everyone in the supernatural world knew the town was witch central. Astrid was always proud to boast she was descended from the coven. Even YaYa in Athens sung their praises.

I found the envelope the Texan agent gave me and sure enough, inside were directions to the Midnight Magic Shop and a hefty check for Sally McGregor, High Priestess. What with our traveling, I'd fallen behind in my magical studies. Maybe the most powerful witch in America could give me what I needed: a banishment spell. As I stood beside their bed, *our* bed, Christine curled against Asher with a smile frozen on her dead face, I frowned. The bitch had to go. She wouldn't win. He was mine. He was all I had. And if I lost him … who the hell was I?

———

"You look like you can use some help."

"So everyone keeps telling me."

The boy behind the counter at the magic shop walked over to me. I say boy, but he was only three years younger than me, with hazel eyes and curly brown hair. "Well, what exactly are you looking for?"

"I'm not quite sure. I—"

"Mona Leigh, get back here!" a woman shouted from the back of the store.

A little girl no more than four came running from behind the counter, white curly hair bouncing in time to her chubby legs' pace. The cherub stopped right between the clerk and me, but the moment she gazed up at me, she all but recoiled and dashed behind the boy's legs. I *was* a fright, certainly enough to scare small children like that one. The make-up I'd caked on could barely conceal the bruises on my neck and wrists or the black circles under my eyes made worse by the whiteness of my skin. They were literally sucking the life from me night after night. The short, squat middle-aged woman with curly graying hair, who came out of the back carrying a toddler, had a similar reaction when she saw me. Grimacing even. "Um, hello," she said with a Southern accent just like the boy.

"Hi," I whispered. I didn't like them all staring at me. "I'm, um, looking for High Priestess McGregor?"

"Oh! You must be Anna," the woman said. Her eyes darted to my bruises as the baby in her arms began to wiggle from her grip. "Should have guessed. Welcome to Midnight Magic of Goodnight, Virginia. We'd given you up for lost."

"Yeah. I-I'm sorry I'm late."

"Well, better late than never," McGregor said.

"Yeah. Oh," I said, pulling out the check. "Lord Peter said if it's not enough, to let him know."

She took the check with a grin. "Say what you want about vampires, but stingy they ain't." She switched the squirming toddler to her other arm. "So, I gather things still aren't good between Peter and the pack? What's the death toll now? Six? Seven? Even heard the F.R.E.A.K.S. are in town. Hopefully George can sit those two pig-headed, no-goodnicks down and knock some sense into them before things get worse."

"Yeah. Well, Lord Peter appreciates your help in this matter."

"And I appreciate being able to pay my tax bill." The baby girl began howling. "Oh, hell's bells, Ivy. Quit squirming. This one missed her nap. I gotta run them back over to Leigh's. Tommy, everything's setup in the back for her. I'll return when I can. Hold down the fort until then." She turned to me. "Sweetie, anything you need, don't you hesitate to ask, okay? I mean it. Anything."

"Thank you."

Mrs. McGregor took Mona's hand and extracted her from Tommy's leg. The shy thing clutched her grandmother's leg instead until they left the store. I could now add terrorizing young girls to my list of crimes. I was running out of room on the page.

"So, um, come on back," Tom said, gesturing that way. The back room was as cluttered as the front. There was barely any room to maneuver to the altar with the iron cauldron, sigiled charms, and various herbs scattered around. "Yeah, here is everything including the potion recipe. Blocking magic, right? It seems kind of advanced. Are you sure you can—"

"Yeah." I shrugged off my coat. My late birthday present on my fifteenth birthday. A thousand-dollar black wool coat with mink collar and cuffs. My most prized possession. "I've done far more powerful spells than this."

"Like what?" the boy asked.

"When I was nine, I raised a ghost. On this very day actually." That realization knocked the wind from my sails. Ten years. A damn lifetime ago.

"Damn. I don't think even Aunt Sally's done that."

"I had a lot of incentive," I said, mustering a small smile.

I'd often thought what would have happened had I failed that night. Would Asher have been less inclined to take me away? What would my life have looked like had I remained Anna Olmstead? Would I have been a college coed rushing a sorority? In jail? Drugged out in some motel somewhere with a man I'd met the previous night? Any of those seemed preferable to my current reality.

"Are you okay?"

Tom's voice shut down my pity party. "I'm sorry?"

"Are you alright? Do you want something to eat? A chair?"

"I'm fine." I started grinding up the hyssop and rosemary in the mortar and pestle bowl. "Thank you."

"So," he said, sitting down himself, "the werewolves and vampires are really going to war? How'd it start? Who do you think will win? Does Lord Peter have a werewolf hostage yet or—"

"You ask a lot of questions," I cut in.

"I know. I'm just naturally curious. That's why I want to be a reporter for the *Washington Post* or *New York Times*, either one. Everyone agrees I'd make a good one. I just had an exposé published in the school newspaper about the cafeteria using expired canned goods. I almost got suspended, but my parents were real proud."

"Sounds like they had good reason to be," I said with a small smile.

The boy blushed. "So, are the F.R.E.A.K.S. really in DC? I've always wanted to meet one."

"Well, I have, and if the one I met is any indication, you are not missing much."

"Still. If I can't be a reporter, my next choice is F.R.E.A.K. Traveling all over the country, saving people? That is so Batman."

"I don't know," I said, adding the hyssop. "This town seems nice. Moving around isn't all it's cracked up to be."

"Neither is staying in one place. It's so boring here," Tom insisted. "Same old people, same old stuff day after day. Nothing *ever* happens here." The boy paused. "So, really, what's going on in D.C.? Don't spare a gory detail. I can take them."

"I can't really talk about what's going on because I don't really know. I just volunteered to help because Peter and my boyfriend are old friends. Well, among other reasons."

"Oh." He paused. "What other reasons?"

"My, uh, mother told people we were descended from this coven. I figured since it was nearby I'd see what I could find out. If anything."

Tom's eyes lit up. "Holy double serendipity, Batman! My dad is the unofficial town genealogist."

"Really?"

"Yeah! If you want to trace your roots, he's the one to dig them up. What's your mom's name?"

"Well, she called herself 'Astrid' but I think her real name was Mary-Ann Maxwell. Or that's the name on the marriage license I saw once."

"And your grandparents?"

"I don't know. I've never met them. I do know they lived around San Francisco twenty years ago. He was a car salesman ... wait. His name was Buford."

"Not ringing a bell, but I'm sure Dad would know. You can come over and talk to him if you want. He loves long-lost relatives."

"Oh, I wouldn't want to impose."

Tom scoffed. "You're family, right? Family can't impose on family. It's the law. My shift's almost over. When you finish, I'll take you over to meet Dad. How long do you think the potion will take?"

"Um, an hour?"

"Perfect." The bell on the front door tinkled. Tom frowned. "Crap. Customer." He rose. "Be right back. I have a ton more questions for you, cuz."

"Okay. Cuz."

Tom bounced out to help the customer, leaving me with my grin. He'd just met me and already welcomed me into the family with open arms and a warm smile. No good deed goes unpunished.

I'd been inside palaces. Yachts. Castles. I'd even toured Versailles, but I had never seen any home more beautiful to my eyes than the Harmon home in Goodnight, VA—a hundred-year-old three-story white Victorian with a wrap-around, blue painted porch coomplete with white picket fence. A little pink plastic playhouse in the front with dolls sitting around a tiny table and a flapping American flag. Hell, when I stepped inside, it even smelled of cinnamon. I'd walked onto the set of *Father Knows Best*, only with more clutter and toys strewn around. A true home.

"Tommy, that you?" a woman called from another room.

"Yeah," he shouted back as he shook off his coat. "And I brought a friend! She might be staying for dinner!"

"I-I can't stay for dinner. I have to be back in DC by seven."

"Nix that last one, Mama! Where's Dad?"

A big-boned woman resembling Sally McGregor, curly gray-ing brown hair, glasses, wearing a red apron, walked from the living room into the foyer. Her mouth dropped open a tad when she saw me. I was growing tired of that reaction. "Um, hello."

"Mama, this is Anna. She's here to see Dad. Genealogy stuff."

"Oh, well, he's run to the store. Should be back anytime. Hon, would you like something to eat or drink? I just made cookies. Snickerdoodles."

"Thank you. Uh, may I use your bathroom?"

"Upstairs, last door to the right," Tom said.

"Thank you."

I scurried upstairs, away from prying eyes. When I caught sight of myself in the mirror, my mouth opened a tad as if I were silently screaming. If possible I was whiter than before, and the make-up had rubbed off, revealing the bruises again. What Mrs. Harmon must have thought. I'm surprised the woman didn't shove me out the door right there and then. She should have. I did my best to fix myself up, but there wasn't enough concealer in the world to restore me. I stared at the stranger in the mirror wearing my face. What was I doing there? Even if I did trace my family, uncles and cousins and whatnot, then what? I show up on their doorstep with my vampire lover for Christmas? Have to tell lie after lie about my situation. My past? I was wasting these people's time. And there'd be hell to pay if I was late back to DC.

I found Tom in the bedroom next door sitting Indian-style at a tiny pink table with two stuffed animals and a pretty, brown-haired girl with pigtails pouring them tea, which was just milk. "Not so much there, squirt," Tom told the girl. Her blue eyes bugged from her head when she spied me in the doorway. Yeah, not enough concealer. Tom spun around and smiled. "Hey! You're just in time for tea and cookies."

"Oh, I don't think—"

He picked up the stuffed alligator to make room for me. "Come on. Bethany here makes the best darn tea in Goodnight."

"Well, in that case…" Not wishing to be rude, I entered the bedroom and sat on the carpet. I had zero experience with children, so I was as nervous as she was. My crooked smile seemed to quell her fright enough. She poured me milk. "Thank you very much, Bethany. And thank you for inviting me. I haven't been to a tea party in ages."

"You're welcome," she whispered.

I sipped the milk. "Oh, that is delicious. Fit for the Queen of England."

Bethany blushed. "Thank you."

"Oh. Don't want to be rude." I picked up the alligator and touched his snout to the cup. "I think he likes it too."

"She," Tom corrected. "Mrs. Florrie. And that's her husband, Mr. Boo Bear," Tom said, gesturing to the teddy bear across from me.

"My apologies to the table. Lovely to meet you all."

The little girl began babbling, I think to tell me a story, but she didn't have the vocabulary yet. I understood every fifth word but smiled and nodded regardless. With the story complete, she grabbed my hand and led me toward her toy box, pulling out Barbies and shoving them at me. "Be right back," Tom said, taking the chance to escape. Not that I minded. I spent the next ten minutes brushing doll hair and preparing them for a doll wedding. While

Bethany focused on Barbie, she tasked me with choosing the brides-maids dresses and hairdos. I hadn't had so much fun in years. And every time that little girl giggled all the bad thoughts floated into the ether.

I wanted a child. I did. I wanted to feel it grow inside me. To nourish it with my body. To sing it to sleep. Read it bedtime stories about brave knights conquering evil. Watch it grow into a decent human being through my guidance and love. To have someone that was mine, *really* mine to love and receive love in return, no strings attached. But as I sat across from that little girl, so joyful and brimming with the light that only happiness and security can bring, I suddenly grew sick to my stomach. What if I had succeeded in getting pregnant by one of those nameless men? What kind of life could I offer my child? Being carted around the world, constantly surrounded by vampires who thought of it as nothing more than an hors d'oeuvre? That is if Auntie Christine didn't smother it in its sleep. And Asher ... even if I did convince him to settle down again, how long would it last that time? Shame almost brought tears to my eyes. What the hell had I been thinking? Did my selfishness know no bounds? I was no better than Christine in that regard. Bethany must have sensed my misery because she frowned. I shook away the negativity and smiled to reassure her. "I'm okay, sweetie. I'm okay."

A door downstairs slammed shut, and Bethany immediately jumped up. "Daddy!" She rushed from the room with me a few paces behind. From the landing, I viewed Mr. and Mrs. Harmon kiss in the foyer below. "Hope I got the right kind," he said as he passed her a grocery bag. He was in his late thirties like her, but short like his son with a receding hairline and a paunch over his jeans. Suburban Dad chic.

"I'm sure it's fine," from Mrs. Harmon.

Tom joined me on the landing as Bethany scurried down the steps to her father's awaiting arms. "There's my girl!" Mr. Harmon scooped her up and planted several kisses on her chubby cheeks. That brought a smile to my face.

"Hey, Dad," Tom called.

Mr. Harmon glanced up and noticed me. After the initial sadly familiar shock, he grinned. "Well, hello."

"Dad, this is Anna. She's here to trace her family. Thinks she might be one of us."

Mr. Harmon's face lit up. "Oh," he said, placing Bethany down.

"If-if you have the time," I said nervously.

"Oh, he'll make time for it," Mrs. Harmon said with a cheeky grin.

"Heck yeah! Come on down," Mr. Harmon said.

I followed the Harmon men downstairs to the study across from the amazing smelling kitchen. The study was even more disorganized than the rest of the house with stacks of books and stray papers everywhere. Above the messy desk was a family tree with easily a hundred branches. "Impressive."

"My pride and joy," Mr. Harmon said, gesturing to the empty chair.

"Hey," Tom said.

"Besides you and your sister, son." He got out a fresh notebook and pen. "So, what makes you think you're a Goodnighter?" I gave him what little I knew of Astrid's past, which he scribbled down with a growing smile. The Harmons *really* liked to smile. When I finished, he said, "This is great."

"It is?" I asked.

"I think ..." Mr. Harmon said, rising. He scanned the elaborate tree then grinned again. "Found you. Here you are, Miss Anna. Buford Maxwell married his second cousin Willa Scott and had five children, the third being Mary-Ann, your mama. And your mama's sister Ruth actually moved back here and married Emma's brother, so you have an aunt *and* first cousins in town."

"So, she's my what? Third cousin?" Tom asked.

"Sounds about right. Our family tree's more of a tangled vine what with all the cousins marrying. Hang on." Mr. Harmon dug around his ledgers on the floor. "Here. I need to add Mary-Ann to the notes. Your daddy's name is Sven Olmstead, you said?" asked, writing it down. "Do you have any brothers or sisters?"

"Not that I'm aware of. Astrid could have a new family by now, I don't know. I haven't seen her in over a decade."

"All I got was that she ran away to San Fran at seventeen. Maybe Ruth'll know more. Now, you said your dad passed. How?"

"Um, fire. I think. Ten years ago tomorrow," I said, nervously playing with my hair.

Mr. Harmon's eyes narrowed. "So, who's been taking care of you, darlin'?"

"Um, I was adopted. Sort of. By a Mr. Asher."

"Wait, you said he was your boyfriend earlier," Tom cut in.

I turned as red as a tomato. "I ... it-it's complicated."

Tom's nose curled up as if he smelled rotting trash, and I flushed even more. I knew I should have lied. Whenever I attempted to explain our relationship it always came across so sordid. Mr. Harmon cleared his throat. "Tommy, why don't you go help your mom in the kitchen?"

"But I want to—"

"Go on, son. Now."

Tom rose and after an eye roll he walked out. The sharp sting of shame lessened when he shut the door. "It-it's not as illicit as it sounds. I'm the one who ... he didn't—"

"Anna, you don't have to tell me anything you're not comfortable to, and it's not my place to judge regardless." He patted my hand. "I'm sure he took real good care of you. You seem like a lovely young woman. And now you have us too. Your Aunt Ruth will be over the moon. Really. She always wondered what happened to Mary-Ann. I should call—" He reached for the phone.

"No," I cut in, even leaning in to block him. "I-I'm-I'm ... I-I don't know why I came or what I want or ..." I chuckled sadly. "I don't know what I'm doing here, Mr. Harmon. I-I-I have to get going anyway. I have to go or I'll be late," I said, rising. "This was a mistake. I think. Yeah. I'm sorry I wasted your time."

"You didn't, sweetie. Really. Just," he said, rising as well, "just know if you need anything, *anything* we'll be right here, okay? Don't hesitate to call or come visit. We even have a spare bedroom. Our door's always open."

"You're nice. You've been *so* nice. Thank you," I said, voice cracking. A few kind words, and I was on the verge of tears. "I-I-I have to go. I have to go." I rushed out of the small room only to be greeted by Mrs. Harmon and Tom in the kitchen. Eyes down to the floor, I muttered, "Th-thank you for your hospitality. It was nice meeting you all." And I hurried down the hall, past the smiling family photos, and out into the cold light of day. I sat in my car and willed myself to calm down, closing my eyes and breathing deeply. What was the matter with me? I—

134

The knock on my car window jolted my eyes open. Tom stood next to it, looking more than a little contrite. I got out of the car.

"I'm sorry," he said. "I—"

"No, *I'm* sorry. I'm so sorry. You have all been so nice, I just... have a lot going on. This is all me, it has nothing to do with you. You've all been amazing. Especially you. I swear."

"Okay. Uh, Mama wanted you to have these for the road." He lifted up a Tupperware container filled with Snickerdoodle cookies. "She said you could keep the container." He paused and began to blush. "Or you can come back. If you want."

Guess my revelation didn't completely quash his growing crush. With a smile, I leaned up and kissed his cheek. "You're one of the good ones, Tom Harmon." I kissed his cheek again and got back in the car. The teen stared at me, slack-jawed. "Too damn good for me, that's for sure." I started the car. "Stay sweet, Batman. Bye." And I drove away, leaving him in my rearview.

I wanted to stay. I wanted to get a hotel room, spend a few days exploring the town and playing magic and having tea parties with my cousins. I wanted to flirt with Tom until his self-esteem skyrocketed. I wanted to not be me for a few days. But I just kept driving. Back to my life. Back to my Asher who ten years before chose me to be his. Who knew, maybe that night he would again. Hope springs eternal.

———

A wreck on Route 29 slowed traffic to a crawl, so I didn't pull up to the hotel until after dark with only an hour left until curtain time. We had plans to see *Henry V* at the Kennedy Center, just

Asher and I. I'd even bought a rose red dres, with a plunging neckline and matching lingerie for the occasion. "Sorry I'm late," I shouted as I entered our suite. "Traffic was—"

When I stepped into our bedroom, my mouth snapped shut. Empty. Water ran in Oliver's bathroom but I found him alone, lounging in bubbles. Considering how the previous night ended, and the one two nights before that, I had no problem entering without knocking. Nothing I had not seen far too many times before. Without question he was gorgeous, with thick brown hair with blond highlights, gray eyes, and the reddest lips I'd ever seen, but I could not say I was overly attracted to him. We simply gravitated to each other as the odd men out in our supposed quartet. He didn't even bother to cover himself or remove the washcloth from his eyes when I stepped in.

"Knocking is still considered good manners, even in this day and age," he chided.

"Where's Asher?"

"Have they not returned yet? Shocking," Oliver answered sarcastically. "I have not the faintest notion where they went. They slipped out whilst I was being interviewed by that Texan." He pulled the cloth from his eyes. "Thank you for that, by the way. I just adore finding myself on the F.R.E.A.K.S. watchlist."

"So Asher didn't say when he'd be back? The play begins in an hour."

Oliver's face softened. "I am sure he is returning to you as we speak."

"Yeah," I said halfheartedly. "I'll, uh, let you get back to your bath."

"You are more than free to join me," the vampire said with that panty-dropping grin of his. "I can give you your birthday present."

"Tempting, but no thanks. I have to get ready. Have a nice night."

I returned to my bedroom and put on my new dress, a tight, bright-red number with next to no neckline, even curled my hair, but with each passing minute the anger and sadness festered. There was a brief glimmer of hope when I heard the front door shut forty-five minutes later, but it was only Oliver leaving for the night. I bit my lip to stop the tears before they began. I finally gave up my pathetic vigil on the couch, just staring at the door, when the clock struck nine. The curtain rose, not just at the Kennedy Center, it lifted from my eyes.

"Asshole," I whispered. "Selfish...fucking...asshole." Shaking my head, I kicked off my heels and returned to my bedroom. Christine's clothes were strewn around, with her panties lying on the unmade bed. *My* bed. I ripped off the sheets, the comforter, even the pillowcases, everything they touched, before lying flat on the bare mattress to stare up at the ceiling. I could still smell her everywhere.

He'd forgotten. Hell, maybe he hadn't and simply didn't care. He was bored with me, that much was certain. I'd done all within my power in the past six months, things I never believed I would, and still it wasn't enough. *I* wasn't enough. That bedroom felt like a coffin slowly losing air. My life was suffocating me. I had to get out. I barreled out of the room, grabbed my coat and purse, slid on my heels, and fled that decadent hellscape.

I was in such a hurry, and concentrating on not falling to pieces, I wasn't paying attention to my surroundings. I rounded the hallway corner and ran smack into the second-to-last person I wished to encounter. Agent West was in his own head too, reviewing his notebook from his last interview, so he was equally to blame for our collision. But the moment our bodies connected, another electrical shock jolted through me, frying my already jangled nerves to the breaking point. My purse and his notebook fell to the ground as I gasped. When I glanced up and realized who it was, my mortification from our earlier encounter somehow doubled. My mouth flopped open, as did his. "I-I am so sorry," Agent West said.

We both bent down to retrieve our belongings. All the contents of my purse spilled out, including my tampons. "It-It's okay," I muttered.

"Oh, uh, something's leaking," the Agent pointed out.

Brackish brown liquid from one of the potions flowed over the play tickets. I reached inside my purse and instantly glass sliced my finger. I just stared at the tiny shard as blood seeped down my hand and pain pulsed with every heartbeat.

That was it.

That was all it took. One tiny shard, and I burst into a million pieces. A sputtering sob escaped, then another. They wouldn't stop. I didn't have the strength anymore to stop them. The misery won. "Hey, hey," Agent West whispered. Without a moment's hesitation this stranger showed me a great kindness. He wrapped his arms around me, pulled me against him, and just held me. He didn't attempt to kiss me, there was nothing in it for him, yet he knelt with me in that hallway until both our knees ached. Until I was empty of tears, of sorrow, of any illusions about my life. My birthday gift from the universe, the kindness of a stranger.

Best gift I ever received.

———

And he even bought me dinner.

Nathan hadn't eaten, and I had no idea where else to go, so we walked around the corner to a small burger joint with vinyl booths, a checkered floor, and Buddy Holly playing on the juke-box. What the waitress must have thought. Him with a wet spot on the shoulder of his rumpled suit, and me with splotchy make-up and red cocktail dress with a neckline almost to my naval. Not that I cared. I was past caring about anything. I could have been hit by a car and would barely have noticed. We each ordered burgers and fries, and she quickly walked away from the crazy people.

"How's your finger?" Nathan asked.

I held up my bandaged finger. "Stopped bleeding. Still hurts. Had worse."

"I'll bet," he said, nodding toward my bruised neck. Embarrassed, I covered that spot with my hand. He didn't take the hint. "Doesn't that hurt? When they ... you know?"

"Only when they don't use glamour. And even then ..." I shook my head.

"Sorry. Too personal?"

"A little. I *have* just met you," I point out.

"Sorry. I tend to interrogate people within an inch of their lives. Even my family's complained about it. My baby sister's boy-friend won't even be in the same room as me. Hazard of the job."

"And how goes the case? Oliver told me you interviewed him. Hope he was more helpful than I was."

"Not a lick. Seems like last night's attack was random. Just some wolves looking for retribution. Your friends were just in the wrong place at the wrong time. I think we're really here just to make sure things don't escalate further. Keep both factions on their best behaviors."

"Yeah. Mrs. McGregor said your boss should just lock Peter and the wolf in a room and let them hash everything out. Or kill each other."

"Mrs. McGregor?"

"She's the High Priestess of the Goodnight coven. I was down there today mixing some potions for Lord Peter."

"You're a witch?"

"A High Priestess even," I said with a touch of pride. The waitress returned with our cokes then left again. I sipped mine. "And you have to be something too, right? To be a F.R.E.A.K.?"

"Electricity," he said, almost ashamed by it. "I can control it. Well, on a good day."

"Here I thought we had something special. So, it's not just me. You have a spark with all the girls," I said with a smile. "You cad, you." My new friend smiled back. "So, how long have you been an agent?"

"Since I was twenty. Two years. George, that's our boss, recruited me after the newspaper did a story on me."

"What happened?"

"I was struck by lightning four times in one week, twice in the same day. It was finals week and I'd just found out my girl since middle school was cheating, with my best friend no less. I was stressed out to hell. I was clinically dead the third strike for two whole minutes. The fourth bolt actually shocked me back to life. And that wasn't the first time it'd happened. In total, I've been struck six times. It's a miracle I'm even alive."

"Goodness."

"Yeah. It hasn't happened since I became an agent though. I have some measure of control now, but things still explode at least once a month, and when I'm stressed, I shock people all day."

"Don't feel bad. I almost killed a man once. He threatened me with a knife, and the next thing I knew a gust of wind sent him clear across the room. He hit his head and was in a coma for two days. And ... I can't believe I just told a Federal Agent that," I chuckled.

"Well, I am damn good at my job, Annie." Annie. No one had ever called me that. An Annie was sweet, traditional, playful. I liked it. "So, why'd he attack you? Was he a mugger or ..."

"Nope, just an asshole," I said before another sip of Coke. A change of topic was needed before I dug myself into a bigger felonious hole. "So, do you like your job? I imagine it's quite thrilling."

"It can be, I guess. I don't want to do it forever, but ..." He shrugged. "I get homesick a lot. My mom, my stepdad, my sister, my friends back home all think I'm a traveling salesman. I only get to see them a couple times a year."

"Where's home?"

"Garland, Texas. It's this little suburb outside of Dallas. I miss it so damn much some days. The barbecues, cheering on the football team on Friday night, meeting my friends for a beer, having dinner with my family and talking about our days, you know?"

"Not even a little. It sounds wonderful, though."

"What about you? Where's home?"

"Hell if I know," I chuckled wryly. "Used to think I did. Now ..."
I shook my head.

"What about family? Your mom and dad?"

"Dad, and I use that word loosely, died ten years ago and as far as I know Mom's still chasing the Grateful Dead."

"There has to be someone."

"There was—*is*," I corrected with a flinch. "Asher."

"Your boyfriend?"

"That word doesn't exactly cover what he is, but yeah."

"The same one who made you have a nervous breakdown in the hallway?"

"He didn't ... you don't know him," was the only defense I could come up with.

"From where I'm sitting, I ain't missing much, Annie."

"You know, for a Southerner, you are very rude."

"You're one to talk about manners. *I* didn't slam a door in *your* face, if memory serves."

I cringed at the memory. "I'm sorry. You didn't deserve that. And if it makes you feel better, I felt terrible about it all day. But you're still being rude now."

"Well, I've been up for more than twenty-four hours getting the runaround from vampires and their friends, including a hulking Russian werewolf who threatened to do something to me illegal in most states. I would tell you to talk to me tomorrow if you want me to feed you a big plate of bullshit that your life is peachy keen, but my mama taught me never to lie. Sorry. You want that, go try one of your vamp pals. I've found that if their lips are wagging, the words aren't even worth a grain of salt."

"You really have a low opinion of vampires, don't you?"

He shrugged. "I've been around them for two years, and I have yet to meet one who wasn't spoiled, selfish, or just downright evil. I've been to too many crime scenes where companions like you ... well, what I've seen will fuel my nightmares until my dying day. And I don't want that for you. Hell, for anyone."

"First, I'm a consort, not a companion. There is a difference. And second, Asher would never let anything like what you're suggesting happen. He'd turn me if it did."

"And that's what you want? You're what, sixteen?"

"Nineteen."

"What about a career? A family? You just want to follow this asshole, who obviously passes you around to his friends for a midnight snack, around for all eternity?"

"He doesn't pass ... it's this woman. Christine. She's got him all twisted around. We were great before. We ... we were happy. We *were*. If I could just get her away from him ..."

"My grandmamma had a saying: 'No matter how strong the leash, if a dog wants to chase a pig, there is not a damn thing you can do to hold it back, and you'll just break your arm trying to.' I'm sure his wandering eye has precious little to do with you, Annie. It's just who he is. Nothing you can do will change that. *Nothing*. And if that is the case, you just gotta say, 'I love you, but I love me more.'" He shook his head. "All I know is, if anyone, *anyone* puts you in a situation where you feel like you have to forfeit your dignity—hell, your self-worth—then *they* ain't worth a one of your tears, let alone a moment of your precious life. And it *is* precious.'"

The waitress returned with our dinner. Just in time too. The distraction kept me from bursting into tears. Again. I brushed away the strays, and even managed a quick smile for our server. She shot me a sympathetic look back before leaving again. I wasn't hungry anymore. I'd ordered the burger raw but the blood leaking onto the plate turned my stomach. Always with the blood. I just picked at the fries.

Nathan had no such problem. "Don't like it?" he asked with his mouth full.

"I just ..."

"You should eat. You are probably anemic, and you're sure as hell just skin and bones."

I threw my fry down. "You're just a ray of sunshine, you know that?"

"Another thing you could use." He took a huge bite then grinned to get a rise out of me.

It worked. "Okay, wise one, just for the sake of argument, let's say I did decide to up and leave. To give up on my soul mate and walk into the sunrise. I've been with Asher since I was nine years old. I have nothing, no one, save for him. He is the only person who *ever* loved me. He was the only one who ever saw something worthwhile inside me and did what he could to foster it. Not to mention I have no money, and no real useful skills. I tried it alone once, and you know what happened? I became my mother, stealing and shacking up with a *puton* who tried to stab me. And the only reason I was with him was because I was lonely, and I very much doubt you have *any* idea what that depth of loneliness is like. None. It's like you're drowning, but you don't even want to try and save yourself because it's the only way you think you can escape the misery. I can't go through it again. *I can't.* At least now … there's hope he'll come back to me. That things will be like they were."

"Until the next distraction comes along, and you're the walking dead with no going back." Nathan leaned forward, meeting my eyes. "Look, I don't have any easy answers for you. I don't. I wish to God I did, Annie. This might be the hardest decision you'll ever make in your life. And you're right, I don't know you, and I don't know him. But what little I do know, from where I'm sitting, things can't get a hell of a lot worse, can they? I think you know that, but whether you're ready to face it, only you can answer that. But I can tell you that the one good thing about hitting bottom is there's only one way to go, and who knows what's waiting for you up there among the blue skies and sunshine." He sat back in his chair again. "Hell could even be Valhalla," he said with a grin.

"Valhalla?"

"I went through a Norse mythology phase," he said, shrugging. "And a Greek mythology phase. And a *Star Trek* phase. I've had a lot of phases. Right now, it's a chivalrous one."

"Lucky me."

"Damn straight," he said with pride.

I shook my head. "You are a very strange guy, Agent West."

"Coming from you, Miss Asher, and knowing the company you keep, I will take that as a big damn compliment." He nudged my plate toward me. "Now eat. Odin commands it."

"Odin?" I asked with a smirk. "I thought Thor was the one who controlled lightning."

"Just eat," he said, rolling his eyes.

"All hail, Odin," I said, biting into my burger before smiling at my new friend.

He smiled back. "Now, *there's* a gal who can take care of herself." When those words came from his lips, I actually believed it to be true. And I would be damned if I made a liar out of him.

———

Be it the company or loneliness—okay it was really the company—after dessert when Nathan escorted me back to the hotel, I was sad to see him go. Despite his verbal diarrhea habit, he was so bright and sunny. So refreshingly straightforward. And he didn't want a damn thing from me. Not ego boosting, not sex, he just wanted to make me feel better. That was the first time that'd ever happened to me. Riding up the elevator alone, I realized I may never see him again. He gave me his card, but I don't think either of us expected me to use it. Two ships passing in the night enjoying grease and conversation. Still, it would have been nice to have a friend. Someone to have lunch with and just shoot the breeze. To gossip with and go see movies with and chat about life. I hadn't had a real friend in ... ten years.

That realization was like a punch to my already tender gut. It was just so wrong and pathetic. Even at boarding school, I didn't try to make one. Maybe I would have had a better time there had I made the effort. Even when Asher was hundreds of miles away, he consumed all my energy. I worshiped the man, and he repaid my devotion by casting me aside for the first pretty face who crooked her finger. Nathan was right. I couldn't continue on my current course. My body and soul were at their breaking points. They'd been bent so far one little puff of air, and they'd splinter into a million tiny pieces. And a total stranger had seen it before I did.

I almost lost my resolve when I stepped into our suite to find Asher rushing out of our bedroom, relief and anguish washing over his face. Oh, how breathtaking he was in a white shirt, gray vest, and trousers bringing out the red of his hair and blue of his eyes. Even after ten years it thrilled me each time I laid eyes on him.

"There you are! I am sorry, I am so sorry." He scooped me into his arms, and the urge to embrace him back was overpowering. I managed all of a second before I returned the gesture, even inhaling his scent and the glorious sensation of his body against mine. I just couldn't help myself. One step forward, two steps back.

"You have returned. We were growing worried."

I opened my eyes as Christine sauntered from his bedroom, hips swaying, with a satisfied smirk on her pretty face. For once, I was grateful for her presence. Asher's spell broke enough for my resolve to return. I removed myself from his grasp to glare at her. "Oh, I bet you were." My gaze whipped to him. "We need to talk."

"Oh, you are in trouble now, Asher, my love. Those are the deadliest words a woman can ever utter," Christine said.

"*Alone*," I added with a scowl.

"But I love a good brawl," Christine whined.

"Christine, please," Asher said, but really it sounded like an order.

Her nose twitched with displeasure, but she plastered on a grin. "Of course. I shall be in the other bedroom waiting to lick your wounds, my love." She blew us a kiss before crossing the living room, retreating into the bedroom and shutting the door. Not that a door would change a thing. Thanks to vampire superhearing she wouldn't miss a word. Rolling my eyes, I went the opposite direction into the master bedroom.

"I would like to begin," Asher said, shutting our door, "by apologizing. We lost track of time and—"

"I can't do this anymore," I cut in.

"Pardon me?"

"I cannot do this," I said, gesturing around our room, "anymore. I can't live like this anymore. I refuse to."

"*Mo chuisle*, I understand you are upset about tonight, and you have every cause to be, but—"

"It's not just about tonight, Asher. It's about everything. The constant clubbing, the feedings, the … sharing with others. *Her.* She's toxic and evil, but the sad part is, I can't fully blame her for everything. I'm not in a relationship with her. I didn't pledge my undying love to *her*, and she didn't do the same back to me. Unlike you. Two years ago if another man looked at me, you'd gouge his eyes out. Now you shove me toward them so you can watch. How dare you do that? And how dare *I* let you? You know I even tried to get pregnant? I was so desperate to hold on to you, I almost brought a child into *this*. I'm an adult, and our life isn't fit for *me*.

"I love you. I love you more than life itself, but I refuse to share you with anyone, and I refuse to compromise myself anymore. I have given you everything I have: my body, my heart, hell even my soul. I deserve some respect back in return. If you love me even one percent as much as I love you, you will give me at least that. At the *very* least. Or I walk. I will walk out that door, and you will be dead to me. I won't speak to you, I won't go looking for you, you will be nothing but a memory to me. Or we walk out together. You send her away, and we rebuild our life, just the two of us. Please." I stepped toward him, gazed into those piercing blue pools as I had four years before, and whispered, "I need you to do this for me. I need you to love me enough to *want* to do this for me. *Please.*"

Without hesitation, he caressed my cheek as his face fell. "Of course," he whispered desperately. "Of course."

The lodestone around my neck dissolved with those two words. I let out a strangled laugh as the tears spilled. I kissed him once, twice, three times, whispering, "Thank you," until he rammed his lips against mine so hard it hurt. We made love the same way, as if we'd been separated for months and believed we'd never see each other again before or after. All was forgotten, all was forgiven, and nothing and no one else mattered but us. As it always should have been.

Afterward, I lay in my spot, nestled against his shoulder as he stoked my hair. No place, nothing better in this world or the next. "You were truly going to leave me," he said as if it had just dawned on him.

"Yes. I was."

He stopped petting, instead grabbing a chunk of my hair in his fist. "How long have you been contemplating this?"

"Not long. Well, not as a serious option. What does it matter now?"

"I simply had no idea you were so unhappy. You never said anything. You never ... said no."

"I wanted to make you happy. And I'm not blaming you completely, and I'm not saying some of it wasn't fun, but I just let things stretch too far. I broke. Asher, I'm not that person. I'm not made for constant parties and living out of a suitcase. I'm just not. And I'm certainly not a person who wants to share you, especially with *her*. I want our life back. You're enough for me, and I'm enough for you, right? *I* made you happy. Me alone. We were happy. We can be happy again."

"Of course." He kissed my forehead. "Just ... never frighten me again. I am lost without you, *mo chusile*. I do not know what I would do if you left me."

I leaned across and kissed him deeply. "Then don't give me a reason to."

The second time was slower, almost painfully slow as if he wished to punish me. I never begged so much in my life. When he decided I'd had enough, I was literally in tears from pleasure. Oh, how I adored that man.

When we could walk again, and it took some time, he went to shower and I to get a drink from the minibar in the living room. Compared to earlier I was floating on air, even humming like Snow White to her chipper woodland critters. Of course like Snow, the Evil Queen breaks the spell almost immediately. She'd been waiting to pounce. Christine staggered from her bedroom, expression neutral for once. I expected anger. Hate. Recriminations, but maybe I was just projecting. There were a million things I wanted to shout at her, that I'd kept bottled for years, but the glow of victory wouldn't allow me to kick her while she was down. "Hello, Christine. I thought you would have gone out by now."

"And miss your little performance and its X-rated encore? Never."

"Then you know what's happening. We're leaving tomorrow. Without you. I'm sorry it had to be like this, but—"

"Oh, spare me the insincere platitudes, little girl. They are beneath even you." She began slowly stalking toward me. "And they are premature regardless."

"Are they now?"

"Oh, yes. You have talent, I concede that. No girl has ever wrapped Asher around her little finger as efficiently as you. Well, pleasant company excluded," she said with a proud smile. "It took longer to extract him from your clutches than with the others. I almost gave up hope once or twice. But perseverance always wins in the end." Her smile reversed into a scowl just as she stepped one foot from me. "*I* always win in the end."

My eyes narrowed. "If that's what you think, then you haven't kept up on current events. This time tomorrow we'll be on a plane back home, and you'll be all alone. Again."

"For how long? A year? Two if you're lucky? How long until his wanderlust resurfaces? It runs strong within him, little girl. Always has. Some birds are not meant to be caged, no matter how gilded said enclosure is. And if you are the one to lock him in, he will either die inside or break out and peck you to death, as the past months have proved. He will never be *Father Knows Best*. He will never be *The Man in the Gray Flannel Suit*. You will *never* be enough for him. *I* can live with that fact, little girl, can you?"

The knot in my stomach, the same one that coiled when Nathan said the same thing, tightened with each word. "You—you're just running scared. You'll say anything to hurt me. You don't know him, and you certainly don't know anything about real love."

She shook her head. "I cannot fathom how one as bright as you could also be so naive. Folly of youth, I suppose." She shrugged. "Oh, well. The hard road it is. Just know, you brought this upon yourself, lovey."

Still expressionless, Christine grabbed her own hair and yanked. Hard. My mouth dropped open as a huge clump came out in her hand. My jaw thumped to the carpet as a moment later she clawed her own cheek, once again drawing blood. "What—"

"Stop! What the hell are you doing?" Christine shrieked at the top of her lungs. "Leave me alone! Asher! Asher!"

"Have you lost your mind?"

"I'm sorry! Just stop it! Stay away from me! Stop—" The crazy vampire flung herself head first into the glass shelves of the bar so hard she not only shattered them but the mirror behind them. Shards large and small fell around her like snow. "Stop! Anna, stop!" Finally, she threw herself back first into the wood coffee table, cracking it in half. It happened so fast, and I was so shocked, I just stood there as she continued her self-assault. I felt as if I were going mad.

My bedroom door swung open as Asher, dressed only in a towel, hurried out. He glanced from me to the mess that was Christine. "What—"

"Keep her away from me!" Christine shrieked like a wild woman.

"I didn't—"

"She went crazy!"

Asher rushed to help her. "What did you do?" he asked me.

"Nothing! I didn't do this. She—"

"She did not do this to herself, Anna," he snapped, fangs exposed. The knot in my gut all but choked me. The only time I could see the fangs was when he dropped the glamour and wanted me to.

"She did! I swear it!"

As he bent to examine her, I was all but forgotten. Christine looked up, blood and deep gaping scratches marring her perfect face. Even I was taken aback by the horror and gore. Christine clutched onto Asher, all but curled up into his lap for protection. "Keep her away from me! We-we were just having an argument, and she went mad. I-I-I called her a bitch, an-and the next thing I knew she attacked me, then this gust of wind blew me sideways, then—"

"She is lying!" I shouted. Déjà vu whacked me beside the head. I was right back in Paris facing off against Collette, just with the tables turned. The three-fold rule had come back for its due. He believed me then, he'd believe me now. "She—"

"Do not move!" Asher roared. He held Christine tighter as she sobbed against his bare shoulder. "Do not come near her, or so help me ..."

And that was it.

The moment.

The moment when I saw the person Alain warned me about. The monster who would snap my neck and feel not one shred of remorse afterward. Every delusion, every hope I had for us burnt away as if the air were on fire, leaving not smoke but pure crystal-clear clarity. Had I taken another step, disobeyed him, he would have killed me. For her. Because as he bestowed kisses on her face and stroked her hair exactly as he had mine not minutes before, I realized he loved her. A part of him always would. I would never be the sole owner of his heart. His soul. I *would* never be enough. My house of cards toppled.

I didn't say a word, I didn't move a muscle as he gently picked her up like a bride and hummed her a lullaby as he carried her into her bedroom, slamming the door shut with his foot. "Stupid," I whispered to myself. "Stupid little girl."

And before the clouds could return, before he could slink out of that room with false promises and false hope he was no doubt giving her then, I walked to our bedroom, quickly changed, threw my meager possessions into my suitcase, grabbed my purse and coat, and walked out of my old life without a glimpse back.

For my many, many faults, no one could ever say I was not a woman of my word.

———

I just drove. I had fifty dollars in my purse, no credit cards, and no idea where to go. None. I was all alone in the night without a compass to guide me anymore. Even on my Italian misadventure, deep down I knew when the time finally came he would be there. He'd come rescue me. He'd scoop me into his arms and all would be right in the miserable world. I had hope. There is nothing, *nothing* worse in this universe than a lack of hope. Even a glimmer can force one out of bed when there's no tangible reason to. It keeps you company, cheers you on to make those last few steps even while your feet bleed. That was my existence before I met him, living with a selfish bastard who pimped me out because it served his needs. Who only cared what I could do for him. History was repeating itself, and I'd just been too much of a fool to notice it. One little crack, and my life crumbled to dust, snuffing out even that glimmer.

I didn't realize where I was really going until I passed the sign welcoming me to Goodnight. The town even had its own welcoming committee to greet me. I was driving twenty above the speed limit, and the police cruiser waiting behind the sign did not take kindly to that. When the red and white lights began flashing, I almost burst into tears again. It just wasn't my night.

"License and registration, miss," handlebar mustached Deputy Andrews said.

"Yes, sir." The registration was easy, but the license proved a problem in that I didn't have one. I gave him my passport instead. "It-it's all I have."

"This is a rental car? Do you have the rental agreement?"

"The what?"

"Proof you can use this car. It's registered to Peter Cain Holdings. You don't look like a Peter Cain, Miss . . . Asher of . . . Holland? Really. Huh. Never met anyone from Holland before. They don't issue drivers licenses in Holland?"

"I . . . don't have it with me. Sorry."

The deputy jotted something in his notebook. "Okay, well, Miss Asher since you can't prove this is your car, you don't have a license, and I already have you for reckless driving, I'm gonna have to take you in and get this sorted out. Please step out of the car, miss."

It really wasn't my night.

Three hours on my own and I was already in police custody. I was too exhausted in every possible way to protest. The officer escorted me to the back of the squad car, radioed for a tow truck, then drove me in relative silence save for promises we'd sort this out to the Gardenia County Sheriff's Station. Only a half asleep dispatcher greeted us at the station. That angel of mercy brought me a cup of stale coffee. At least Deputy Andrews didn't put me in a cell. I stared into space by his desk as he attempted to get a hold of Peter or someone at the hotel. It was almost dawn, the vampires were settling in for the night and not answering phone calls. I was stranded. "Is there anyone I can call to pick you up?"

Oddly, the first person who sprang to mind was Agent West. His card was still in my purse. I assumed the impulse was due to the law enforcement connection. But it seemed wrong to ask him to take time away from a war to collect me from a backwater town. So though it physically hurt, I gave the only other name I could think of to rescue this damsel in distress. Apparently humiliation was still possible even when an emotional gasket explodes. When Mr. Harmon walked in thirty minutes later, pea coat over his pajamas as if I had pulled the poor man out of his warm bed, I seriously wished I'd just driven off the side of the Blue Ridge Mountains.

"Hey Lucas, thanks for coming down," Deputy Andrews said.

"Of course. So, do I need to sign anything or ..."

"No, she's not under arrest. Just a hefty fine."

"Great. Come on, Anna. Let's go home," Mr. Harmon said, touching my shoulder.

Like a robot, I rose from my chair. The deputy handed me my purse, and Mr. Harmon lifted my suitcase. "We'll call you, Miss Asher, when we have the car sorted out."

"She'll be staying with us. You have the number," Mr. Harmon said. "Thanks, Louis. Say hey to Shirley for Emma and me. Come on, sweetie." The wonderful man ushered me out of the precinct and into his station wagon. "Seat belt."

He didn't ask questions, maybe because he was as exhausted as I was, just drove us back to the house. Mrs. Harmon waited above on the landing in her robe, sporting a sad smile. "The spare room's ready," she said as we walked in. "I put fresh towels on the bed if you want a bath."

"Th-thank you."

"Go on upstairs, sweetie," he said, rubbing my back. "Get some rest."

I took my suitcase from him and nodded. "I ... thank you. You both have been so kind," I said, voice breaking. "I-I don't know how I can ever repay you."

"Don't worry about that now. Just go get some sleep," said Mr. Harmon.

With my head hung, I slowly trudged upstairs, Mrs. Harmon squeezing my shoulder as I passed. I resisted the urge to hug her. The bedroom was simple: just a bed, dresser with lamp, and shag rug, but it looked like Agent West's Valhalla. I shut heaven's door, kicked off my shoes and jacket, climbed under the handmade quilt, and promptly fell asleep. Deep asleep. The kind where you wake fourteen hours later in the same position, every muscle stiff and with a sandwich on the nightstand. A vacuum ran downstairs, almost overshadowed by the music booming on the other side of the wall. Life went on around me. I would have to go on as well.

Fresh towels in hand, I tiptoed to the bathroom to shower. Despite the hell my life had become, I did look better than the day before. The circles under my eyes were more gray than black, the bruises were yellowing, and there were some peaches mixed with the cream of my skin. After the shower, I even felt almost human. Almost. I dressed in brown corduroys and black cashmere sweater, braided my wet hair, threw on pink lipstick and after a tiny pep talk, stepped out to join the world. Tom must have been lying in wait because he popped out of his room at the same time as I left the bathroom.

"Hey!" he said, as chipper as a chipmunk. "Hi!"

"Hello," I replied, eyes to the ground. Who knew what horrors these people thought befell me the night before.

"Did you sleep well? Are you okay? Did you really get arrested?" he rapid fired.

"Um, yes, yes, no."

Tom chuckled. "Well, that's good. I was worried it'd be, 'No, no, yes.' Are you hungry? I made you a sandwich and left it by your bed."

"I saw it. Thank you. I was just about to go eat it."

I started down the hall, and of course he followed me to continue the Spanish Inquisition. "I made it with mustard. Do you like mustard? I can take it or leave it. Did you really sleep well? Was the bed too lumpy? You look a lot better today. I like the pink lipstick better than the red you had on yesterday. Not that you weren't pretty yesterday."

"Um, thank you." I sat on the bed with him joining me as I bit into the sandwich. "This is really good."

"Glad you like it," he said, his chest literally puffing out with pride. "They called about your car. You can pick it up whenever."

"Good."

"Not that you have to right away. No rush. So … how long you planning on staying?"

"I don't know. I'll probably get a hotel room tonight, then—"

"You—you don't have to. I mean, no one ever uses this room, not since Christmas at least. And Mama and Dad said you can stay here until you get back on your feet."

"Back on my feet," I chuckled wryly. "I have no money, no legal means to get any as I have no real ID or employment history, I am now homeless, and the only person I ever loved chose a psychotic whore over me. I don't think I have feet left to stand on."

"Dang. Sorry." He paused. "So, was she an actual prostitute or …"

"Before she was turned, yep. Pretty sure the psychotic thing came later though."

"Huh. Well, your boyfriend sounds like a real jerk. You're way better off without him."

"So people keep telling me."

"Then it's good you listened. My Memaw has a saying, 'If everyone's telling you the sky's falling, you better get your butt inside.'"

Everyone had such wise grandmothers. "She have a saying for what you're supposed to do once you're inside?"

He shrugged. "She'd probably say 'down a bottle of Johnny Walker and enjoy the show.'"

We both chuckled. "Sounds like my kind of woman."

"Well, she comes over every Wednesday for supper, so you *have* to stay at least that long."

"We'll see. No promises." I took another bite of my sandwich. "This is really good. You're a very nice, sweet, talented young man, Tom Harmon. Don't let anyone ever tell you otherwise."

The boy blushed from tip to toes. "Okay."

I finished my sandwich. "Better bring this plate downstairs," I said, rising.

"I can—" he said overeagerly.

"No. I should probably go thank your parents anyway. Goodness knows what they think of me after yesterday. Best not add rude to the list. Excuse me."

A lovesick teenage boy is a lot less intimidating than a put-out homemaker. When I found Mrs. Harmon, she was removing the vacuum bag in the kitchen. Her smile quelled my nerves though. "Well, hello, Sleeping Beauty. You are looking a million times better today. Magic of a good night's sleep, huh?"

"Yes. Thank you." I maneuvered around her toward the sink to wash the plate. "And once again, I am *so* sorry for waking you and Mr. Harmon. I'll get out of your hair as soon as I can, I promise. You have been beyond kind, and … I don't know how I'll ever repay you, but I will. I swear, I will."

She smiled to reassure me once again. "It's okay, hon. And there's no rush for you to go. In fact, I talked to your Aunt Ruth just an hour ago. She's gonna pop by tomorrow. She's dying to meet you. Oh, and Sally McGregor called too. Something about missing potions? You should probably call her back. The store's number is in the rolodex."

Not only did I owe Lord Peter the potions that I smashed, but I still had his car. There was just so much I had to work out, a million tiny logistics required to start over, I didn't know where to begin. The weight of what I'd done almost crushed me in that moment. I couldn't breathe, could barely stand. I'd left him. I had nothing. No one. Everything was gone. My stability, flimsy though it was, my identity, my soul mate, it was all dust in the wind. All I had were the clothes in my suitcase and the kindness of strangers. "I'm, uh … I'm gonna take a walk. I need some fresh air."

"Okay, hon. Supper's at six. Be back by then, okay?"

With a nod and a nervous smile, I walked from the kitchen upstairs to retrieve my coat and book. February wasn't the best time to spend a few hours reading in a park, but the chill didn't deter me. No matter where in the world I found myself, I could locate a park nearby to get lost in a book. Since I was a child it was my one constant. My escape. An anchor. The park in Goodnight, situated in the center of town amid the boutiques and City Hall, was near deserted save for the gawkers passing through. They didn't even attempt to hide their looks and whispers to their companions. In town only a few hours, and I was already infamous. Even without the nosy parkers gawking, no matter how hard I tried I couldn't concentrate on *East of Eden*.

What the hell was I going to do? Go back to pickpocketing? No one would give me a job without a Social Security number and driver's license. Anna Olmstead was most likely declared dead by then. Maybe Lord Peter or another vampire could hire me—*no*. The one silver lining of the mess was I was out of the vampire world. I could die quite happily without laying eyes on another again. No, if I was really doing it, I would do it proper. Honest work, honest friends. I would become a normal person with a normal life. The citizens of Goodnight were witches, and they did it seemingly with ease. I had some jewelry in my suitcase, I could pawn it and at least put down a deposit on an apartment nearby to tide me over until I got a job. If I had to scrub toilets, I would. Goodnight was as good a place to start over as any. My loose ends were easy enough to tie up. I'd drive the potions up in the car during the day, leave them both, then take a bus back. I'd do just that the next morning. I wouldn't have to see Asher or any other vampire ever again. It was doable. And I'd do it.

As always, my time in the park pepped me right up. I had a plan. Resolve. Even a glimmer of hope. I was smart, I was determined, I was a hard worker and most important, I had no choice. Rock bottom had been reached. Onward and upward was the only option left. If only I'd known that rock bottom wasn't the lowest one could go. There was always hell.

———

"Dinner was amazing, Mrs. Harmon. Thank you. I can't remember the last time I had a home-cooked meal."

I'd never had meatloaf before, but it was delicious. I'd have to get the recipe. A lot of her recipes. Asher was the chef, I could barely boil water. That would have to change. If I could whip up a potion, in theory I could whip up a meal. At least that night I proved I was proficient in dishwashing. Tom, who remained glued to my hip since I returned from the magic shop after re-mixing the potions I broke, helped me clear and even stayed to dry. I'm fairly sure Mrs. Harmon did a genuine double take when he offered. Who knew a vampire concubine could be such a good influence? I even promised to help with his Spanish homework. We were deep into conjugating verbs at the kitchen table when the phone rang. Tom picked it up. "Harmon residence," Tom said. "Who may I ask is calling?" He listened, scrunching up his face as if he had a bad taste in his mouth. "It's for you. Special Agent West?"

I actually smiled as I stood to get the phone, which deepened Tom's scowl. "Half an hour response time, Agent West. The F.R.E.A.K.S. will have to work on that."

"My teammate just gave me the message, sorry. We're stretched real thin. Right now I'm neck deep in fiber and autopsy reports."

"Sounds fun. I promise I won't keep you long."

"No, keep me long. Please. I've hit a damn wall, and I am about to hit one literally."

"I'm sorry. Is there anything I can do to help?"

"Actually," Nathan said, perking up, "you know what? Maybe you can. Have you ever heard of a vamp who literally ripped someone's throat out to the point the person was almost decapitated? I mean, even her vertebrae were missing. Because it's been bugging the hell out of me. The working theory was the first victim, Abigail Conlon, was picked up by one or two vamps who knew she was the pack leader's granddaughter and killed her for retribution."

"What makes you say that?"

"The fact she was dumped on the property Conlon outbid Lord Peter on. But it's odd. There are only three reasons for that much damage to the girl. One, it was a frenzied attack, and the vamp went crazy with bloodlust. Two, to send a message about their cruelty, or three to cover up the bite, which doesn't make sense because there was *another* bite on her inner thigh. But according to the autopsy, there were no smears of blood around the thigh wound. It was like they just sunk their fangs in but didn't drink. Nothing adds up, and neither faction will listen to us, and … my roommate snores, and we're understaffed, and I have indigestion, and … sorry. I'm rambling. And frustrated."

"It's okay. And for what it's worth, I've never actually seen any vampire kill before, but from conversations I've overheard about feeding, that kind of brutality isn't consistent with vampires, even when they're starved to the point of death. They're not werewolves. They don't have claws or teeth. They'd have to use a knife for that level of damage. And if she was a werewolf, she'd begin to heal immediately from a vampire bite, right? Unless it was done after her death. And if that's the case, why bite her at all?"

"And why do the exact same thing to the second victim?" Nathan asked.

"Why does anyone do anything? Love, hate, money, insecurity, revenge, jealousy, or just old-fashioned craziness. Pick your poison, Agent West. Frankly, I think the whole situation's ridiculous. I mean, who really *wants* to start a war, especially over a piece of real estate? What does either side get out of it? You're right, nothing about it makes sense, not to me at least. Sorry I can't be more help."

"No, you—you've helped. I think. Thank you."

"Hey, we spent two hours talking about my horrid life last night, I think I owe you one. Or twelve. That's actually one of the reasons I phoned. I just, I wanted to thank you," I said, playing with the spiral phone cord, "for last night. Your delivery left something to be desired, but … you gave me the kick in the bum I needed. Desperately, it turned out."

"What happened?"

"Just, everything you said about him, about me, proved dead on. You pried open my eyes and what I saw …" I shook my head. "I walked out. I left him. For good. "

"Wow. Good for you, Annie. I knew you had it in you."

"That made one of us."

"No, now don't you dare minimize this. What you did took a lot of guts. More than most people got. Hell, more than I do. I don't think I could have. Really. And you know how I am about telling the truth." I smiled, actually smiled at these words.

"Oh, yes."

"So there you go. And are you okay? I mean, do you have money—"

"I'm staying with friends for now, but after that … I'll figure it out as I go along. Valhalla awaits, right?"

"Damn straight. And is there anything I can do to help?"

"No," I said, still playing with the cord. "Really, you've done more than enough. You went above and beyond, practically to the damn sun, for me. I just, I wanted to thank you. It's the least you deserve. The very, very, very least."

"Well, thank *you* kindly, Miss Asher."

"Olmstead. It's really Anna Olmstead, I guess."

"Olmstead. Suits you better."

"Wouldn't go that far, but it's all I have now. I was never officially Anna Asher anyway. Only in my mind, I guess."

He chuckled. "Well, whatever your name is, I do appreciate the call. And the help. You were in many of my thoughts today. And seriously, if you need anything, anything at all, even if it's just to talk, you have my number. Use it, day or night."

"Actually, I plan to be in town the day after tomorrow. Maybe I can take *you* out to dinner. Save you from punching walls and autopsy photos."

"I'd really like that. We're camped out in the meeting room on the third floor of the Sheraton on 7th."

"I will pop by after I tie up some loose ends."

"Can't wait. Bye, Annie. Take care of yourself."

"I'll do my damndest. Bye."

"Dang," Tom said as I hung up the phone. I'd completely forgotten he was still at the table.

"Don't—don't tell your parents you heard all that, okay?"

"Why? I'm not a baby. I know people get murdered and stuff. Especially people who live around vampires."

"Can't argue with you there," I said, sitting next to him again. "But they aren't all bad."

"Including your boyfriend? Mama said something real bad must have happened to you last night. She told me not to ask, but it did, didn't it?"

I grimaced. "Let's just say, you can love someone with all you have, and be so blinded by that love that you fail to see who they really are. What they want. And sometimes the things we can't change end up changing us, and not for the better. You can't change people, not at their core. You either accept them or learn to live without them. I chose the latter. I chose *me*. And that's all you're getting out of me tonight. Now, let's finish your homework. You conjugated third person plural incorrectly. It's *tienes*."

He corrected it on the paper, then glanced at me. "So, the agent on the phone. Are you going on a date or—"

"Homework!"

With my marathon sleep session and general nocturnal habits, I wasn't the least bit tired when everyone else went to bed. Luckily, I had a life to plan. My list of necessities included an apartment or room to rent, of which High Priestess McGregor already provided a lead on. A hundred dollars a month for a fully furnished room was doable, and it'd give me time to save for furniture when I moved out on my own. I'd also need to buy a car, track down my real birth certificate and Social Security card, find a job, get a driver's license, the list took up an entire page. But without a doubt, I could do it. I could survive without him. The gaping hole from Asher's extraction was still bleeding, but I could feel it slowly cauterizing. The scar would be there forever though.

Around midnight, as I walked out of the bathroom back to my sanctuary, I heard sniffling in Bethany's room. Everyone else was asleep, they had work and school in the morning, so I went to check on her. The first thing I noticed, besides her tiny cries, was the reek of urine. "Accident," she whimpered.

"It's okay," I whispered back. "Let's get you cleaned up." I took her tiny hand, collected clothes from her dresser and brought her back to the bathroom. Without protest, she let me clean and re-dress her. "Did you have a bad dream or something, sweetie?"

"A monster came out of my closet and tried to eat me."

"That's awful. I hate monsters." Eyes bulging from her head, she nodded affirmatively. "You know, I get bad dreams a lot too. *Lots* of monsters in my dreams. And I've learned that the best way to banish a monster is just to look him square in the eyes, and shout, 'Go away! This is my dream! You're not welcome here anymore! Go away!' And you turn your back on him, to show him you're not afraid. That you're a brave, strong little girl, and he can't hurt you. And he may scream and howl and maybe even cry, but he has no power over you. Never again." I wiped the tears from her cheeks and smiled. "But you know what the best thing about dreams is? You get to wake up and find out," I gasped and smiled again, "it's not real! It never was. And nothing in it can hurt you. It's over and done with. Isn't that wonderful?"

Bethany nodded and grinned. "Yeah."

I kissed her forehead. "So no more tears. No more monsters. Not for either of us. Mrs. Flossie—"

The cheerful chime of the doorbell not only cut short my words, but also sliced that bleeding hole inside me so wide it swallowed me back into its darkness. His darkness I'd fought so hard to pull myself out of last night. Because he'd found me. I knew it would happen eventually, I just hoped I'd be on sturdier ground when it did, and I certainly didn't want the Harmons in any way involved. How had he tracked me down so fast? No one tied to vampires knew exactly where I was, save for Sally McGregor, and there was no way she'd volunteer the information. The second chime almost knocked the wind from my lungs. He was really there. He had really come for me. My devil was literally knocking on the front door.

"Doorbell," Bethany said.

The creek of the floorboards in the hallway smacked me out of my stupor. When I opened the bathroom door Mr. Harmon, baseball bat in hand, was almost to the stairs with Mrs. Harmon a step behind, muttering, "I cannot believe this. No good deed..."

"Don't," I warned, stepping out.

The bell began ringing incessantly along with a few knocks. Tom came out of his room dressed in his pajamas as well. "What's going on?"

"All of you, go back to Bethany's room and lock the door. Anna, especially, stay out of sight. I'll get rid of him," Mr. Harmon assured me.

"He can't come in unless invited," I instructed. "And don't look in his eyes."

"Good to know," said Mr. Harmon as he and his wife descended the staircase. "Stay with Bethany. Both of you."

I picked up the confused toddler and hurried to her bedroom with Tom right behind me. There was no way I was going to allow the Harmons to face Asher without backup, so I passed Bethany into her brother's arms. "What—"

"Stay here with your sister," I whispered as I rushed out again. "Lock the door."

"But—"

I quietly shut the door and crept across the hall to the corner just before the landing looking onto the foyer began. Out of sight yet ready to help if necessary. I silently prayed to the universe it wouldn't be necessary.

"…Andrews gave me this address," Asher said. I used to love his baritone—that night it sent chills through me.

"And he just *gave* you our address?" Mrs. Harmon asked skeptically.

"It took a wee bit of prodding," said Christine. Of course he brought her. My fear level skyrocketed when she spoke. The situation went from serious to atomic.

"We are most concerned about her," Asher said. "She has been unstable of late. Abusing drugs, harming herself, harming others, stealing cars."

Tom quietly tiptoed from Bethany's room to my side.

"Pathologically lying," Christine added.

"Where's Bethany?" I mouthed.

"Hiding in her closet," Tom whispered into my ear. "What's happening?"

"We were going to check her into a treatment center last night," Christine continued, "but then she ran away when she discovered the plan. I don't know what she has told you, but it should be taken with a grain of salt."

What she lacked in a soul, she made up for it in the acting department. Were they believing this? Hell, I would have. Just enough truth behind the lies. Tom shook his head.

"If she is here," Oliver said—they brought him too? "It would be in your best interests to let us speak with her. We do not wish her harm. Truly. We only wish to speak to her. It would be the best thing for all parties concerned. Please."

I was about to step into sight, but Tom grabbed my arm to stop me at the same time. Mr. Harmon said, "Look, I don't know what to tell y'all. She was here last night in a right state, but when she woke up, I threw her butt into a taxi. Haven't seen her since and don't want to. We have no idea where she went. Really. Sorry. Best of luck finding her, though. Y'all have a nice night."

I let out the breath I held as I heard the door creak closed. Thank the—

"She left without her coat?" Asher asked.

Merde.

"Excuse me?" Mr. Harmon asked.

"That is a thousand-dollar coat I had tailor made for her in Moscow. She would not leave it behind, especially in the midst of winter."

"She must have forgotten it," said Mrs. Harmon. "Or maybe she left it on purpose. Bad memories and all."

The two seconds of silence was deafening. I was almost relieved when Asher called, "Anna..."

He wasn't buying it. I was about to step out of my hiding spot but noble, sweet Tom beat me to it. "You need to leave now," he said with as much authority as a sixteen-year-old could muster.

"Tom, go back to bed," Mrs. Harmon hissed.

My self-appointed savior continued down the stairs. "I've called the police already. They're on their way."

"That is not necessary," Oliver said. "We are—"

"Anna," Asher shouted with disapproval, "*mo chuisle*, please. I wish to talk, nothing more. You owe me that at least."

"She doesn't owe you anything," Tom spewed out, "you-you child molester!"

Christine chuckled cruelly. "What have you been telling them, Anna? You may as well come out, little girl. Sir Galahad blew your ruse."

"Please just g—" Mr. Harmon said.

I stepped onto the landing, suddenly wishing I wore more than a white slip. Asher preferred me in negligees or nothing, so my sleepwear choices were limited. I'd expected to just run to the bathroom and back. The five minutes between then and the present seemed like an eternity ago. I gazed down at them all: the elder Harmons huddled together blocking the door, bat still in hand; Tom at the foot of the steps, hands balled into fists, ready to channel his inner Batman; and my old family on the other side of the threshold all staring up at me. Malice in her brown eyes, apprehension in the gray, and relief in the piercing blue. My own moved upwards. I couldn't look at him. I had to remain strong. "I have nothing left to say to you. I said it all last night. I told you what would happen. You taught me to keep my promises. To keep my word. I only wish you'd learned that lesson as well. So please leave. Now. Don't make this any harder than it already is."

"Oh, boo fucking hoo," Christine said, rolling her eyes.

"You heard her," Tom said. "She doesn't want to talk to you anymore."

"Please leave," Mr. Harmon said forcefully as he began to close the door.

"Oh, fuck this," Christine said. She pounded on the side of the house hard enough to jolt us, while saying, "Mommy Homemaker!" Mrs. Harmon must have glanced into Christine's eyes, and even with a millisecond of contact, Christine wormed inside her mind. "Invite us inside."

"Come in," Mrs. Harmon said robotically.

Christine literally pushed past Mrs. Harmon with the men following behind. This was not good. At all. The moment they walked in I could practically taste the threat of violence in the air, as if the room were already thick with blood. The knot strangled my stomach, and I grew nauseous. Oliver glanced up at me, eyes pleading for me to do something. Anything. All other thoughts ceased except, "*Get them out of this house*," which was screamed through a bullhorn inside my brain.

"Get out," Mr. Harmon said. "I dis-invite you from this house."

"How adorable, you have viewed a vampire film," Christine cooed. "It does not work that way, Daddy."

"Anna, it is time to come home," Asher said forcefully.

"Yes, Anna, go get your suitcase *now*," Oliver insisted through gritted teeth.

I nodded like a flicked bobblehead and started toward my room. Had I been thinking clearly I would have just walked directly downstairs and out the door, but I was on autopilot. I was told to get my suitcase, so I did. I hadn't unpacked so I just zipped it up, grabbed my purse, and hurried back out. "I-I'm ready."

I made it three steps down before Tom said, "No! She doesn't have to go anywhere with you!"

"Boy, shut your mouth," Oliver snapped.

"It's okay, Tom," I said, still walking.

"No, it's not okay, Anna! He doesn't own you!" Tom turned to Asher. "You don't own her. She doesn't want to be with you anymore, don't you get that? She doesn't love you anymore. Bullying her isn't going to change that, you-you monster. If you really loved her—"

I blinked and Asher was an inch from Tom, lifting the boy by the jaw and snarling. "How dare you question me, boy?"

"Asher—" Oliver warned.

"Hey, get your goddamn hands off my kid," Mr. Harmon said, raising the bat and advancing toward them.

"Lucas—" Mrs. Harmon pleaded, reaching for her husband.

Too late. All too late. It was too late the moment they crossed that threshold.

Christine pounced on Mr. Harmon before he could reach his son. There wasn't a moment for me to react. She was five feet away, then upon him, fangs impaling his jugular like a rabid dog. His howl of pain, Mrs. Harmon's shriek of terror, and Tom's gurgling cry as he fought against Asher's grasp still haunt my nightmares to this day. As Mr. Harmon crumpled to the floor, blood pouring everywhere, the hysterical Mrs. Harmon darted toward her dying husband.

I didn't know where to look next: at the horrified Oliver as he backed away from the blood, at Asher slowly crushing the gagging Tom's windpipe as the teen clawed and kicked to no avail, or at the advancing Christine as she went for Mrs. Harmon. My overloaded mind finally decided. I raised my finger and shouted, "*Lapsus!*"

Christine flew into the living room out of sight, allowing Mrs. Harmon to reach her husband, collapsing to his side and pressing the wound to quell the blood. But I chose poorly. The moment Christine rocketed out of sight, a sickening crack overshadowed all the carnage as Tom's windpipe collapsed. Crushed like glass. Asher released him, another for the ground.

"No!" I cried.

I sprinted down the steps, finger raised again, but in a foot race between a vampire and witch, the vampire will always win. Two steps and Asher was there, slamming me against the wall with his body and covering my mouth with his hand. "Please do not make matters worse, *mo chuisle*," he whispered.

Cue worse.

"Mama!" Both mine and Asher's gazes whipped down the hall as Bethany began running toward us. "Ma—"

"Bethany! Run! *Run!*" Mrs. Harmon shouted. The girl listened, spinning on her bare foot, taking off the way she came. Like a wild woman, Mrs. Harmon leapt up and dashed toward the staircase, shrieking the whole short trek. In another blink, Christine reappeared behind the mother. With one swift movement, the monster snapped her neck, silencing the mother forever. I screamed and squirmed under Asher, even biting his hand, but he caught my eyes. Everything locked shut. My limbs, my mouth, even my mind was no longer my own. Out of reach. I could hear, I could see, but nothing more. No feelings, no thoughts were available to me. Forced catatonia. He literally took all of me. He removed my soul. "There is my girl," Asher whispered as he released my shell.

"Speaking of girls," Christine said, nodding up toward Bethany's room. "The brat saw us."

"We can wipe her memory," Asher said.

"It can be retrieved with magic. We should burn the house anyway. We do not want a repeat of Warsaw, do we?"

Asher's face contorted with distaste. "No, we do not."

"So, should I…" she nodded again.

"I will."

The two vampires glanced at Oliver, who until that moment had just watched in shock as the events of the past minute unfolded. The bastard actually smirked. "Why should you two get to have all the fun?"

"Good lad," said Asher. "Christine, please go start the car."

She obeyed, not giving her victims a second glance as she left. One minute. Less. Less than one minute to snuff out the lives of an entire family. Madness. Utter madness. And just the beginning. Asher picked up my suitcase, took my hand as if we were about to stroll down the Danube, and led me down the stairs. We stopped right beside Tom's corpse, bloodshot eyes staring up at me, pleading for salvation even in death. It's the only time I was glad to feel nothing. "Oliver, finish here quickly, then drive Anna's car back to Washington. We shall begin making arrangements to leave this country as soon as possible."

"Yes, sir." Oliver hurried up the stairs and down to Bethany's room. Monster.

Asher and I stepped over the still bleeding Mr. Harmon to reach the front door. Asher grabbed my coat from the peg and gently slipped it on me. With a tender, sad smile he buttoned it. "I am so sorry, *mo chusile*," he whispered. "I did not intend for any of this to happen anymore than you did. I still love you though. I shall make this up to you, I promise." He kissed my frozen lips, then picked me up like a bride, retrieved my suitcase too, and hustled me away from the house of horrors into the waiting car, even buckling my seatbelt. How considerate of him. "Drive."

"Well," Christine said as she shifted the car into gear, "who knew the suburbs could be such fun."

And we monsters drove off into the darkness from whence we came.

———

I often wondered if the numbness I experienced that night, that lack of a single emotion, was how vampires went through their existence. No fear, no pain, no thoughts for others. It must be. How else could they do all I witnessed? That night my forced apathy was a gift. Losing your soul, your essence, could be a blessing at times. Had I not been rendered soulless, I probably would have thrown myself from the speeding car, happy for death as my body hit the asphalt going seventy miles per hour. Or I would have lost all grip on reality as Asher and Christine made plans for our departure. The duo spoke as if I wasn't there, which for all intents and purposes I wasn't. For the two and a half hours it took to return to DC not a single thought crossed my mind. I stared straight ahead at the road with Asher's arm wrapped over my shoulder. He even pulled me into my spot so I rested in the crook of his neck. I could smell the blood on him. He missed a smear near his ear when he and Christine stopped to wash up. I just stared at that spot and continued my inexistence.

Christine dropped us off at the hotel to make arrangements for our departure, and Asher hustled us up to the suite to pack. The evidence of the previous night's histrionics had been cleared away as if it never happened. They even replaced the coffee table and mirror behind the bar. Better to pretend it never happened that way. Asher dragged me to our bedroom and placed me on the bed like the good wind-up doll he probably always wanted me to be. "You needn't worry, *mo chuisle*," he said, moving into the bathroom for his toiletries. "After tonight, I shall never allow her near you again. Never. Once Oliver returns our quartet shall take the first plane out of this wretched country, then go our separate ways." He came back out and stuffed his toiletry bag into the suitcase on the stand. "You were correct on all fronts, my love. She has grown far too unstable of late. Tonight proves as much. There was no need for such violence. None." He glanced at me and frowned. I just stared at the suitcase. My lover kneeled before me, meeting my eyes with his pained ones. "You do believe me, yes? I meant no harm to those people or to you. Especially you. I swear it on our love." He paused. "Please tell me you believe me, *mo chuisle. Please.*"

With a mere thought, he opened my jail cell, and all at once every emotion banging to be let out rammed through the door. Fear, sadness, shame, horror, guilt, twelve tons of guilt coursed through my veins and my soul. Too much. Far too much. I began trembling, seething as the volcano within me, dormant yet accumulating for years, began to rumble. My jaw clenched shut, and my

177

breath escaped in ragged spurts through my teeth. Asher knelt there, trepidation locking all the muscles in his face. When I couldn't hold it in anymore, I slapped him hard enough to bruise us both. Twice. He took them both. "I deserved that," he said calmly.

The volcano erupted. "You … fucking … monster!" I shrieked. I bashed him with my fists on the face, the shoulders, I just kept pounding and shrieking and pounding even more. "I hate you! I fucking hate you, you bastard! You monster! I fucking hate you!" He let me continue my assault for five seconds before he grabbed my flailing limbs, spun me around, and held me with my arms crossed in front of me like a straightjacket. "I hate you," I sobbed as I crumpled against him.

He lowered us to the floor with me on his lap. "I am sorry," he whispered between the kisses to my hair. "I am so sorry, my love. I am so sorry. Please forgive me. I shall do anything you ask. I am your willing slave. I love you. Just please forgive me. *Please.*"

I knew where this was going. Part of me wanted to. My body was just conditioned to respond to his caresses, at the narcotic feel of his lips and words against my flesh. I couldn't lose control, not then. The he'd win, and I'd be lost again. I took deep breaths to calm my sobs. "Let me go, Asher," I warned.

"I am so sorry, my Anna," he whispered with another kiss, this time to my neck.

"I said let me go!" I shouted, wriggling from his grasp. I think he was so shocked by my resistance, something that had never happened before, he released me. I sprang up and backed away, literally shivering the sickening sensation of him off my body. "You don't get to touch me *ever again,*" I said through gritted teeth. "You ... *disgust* me. I want to rip off my fucking skin to cleanse myself of you, you ... devil."

"You do not mean that, *mo chuisle,*" he said, rising. "You are upset and—"

"I'm upset? *Upset?* I-I-I just watched as you *butchered* an entire family whose only crime was being kind to me when I had no one else."

"I told you, it was never my intention for that to occur. Christine—"

"Christine is a sadistic, crazy, unpredictable psychopath. None of which you were unaware of. Hell, I think you like that about her! *You* brought her there. *You* choked a sixteen-year-old boy to death and are acting as if you'd merely swatted a fly. *You* ordered Oliver to murder a two-year-old. *You* made me watch it all. You took away my free will because it didn't suit you. At least Christine isn't in denial about what she is, Asher." I shook my head in disbelief. "Alain was right. He was a hundred percent spot on about you. He warned me this day was coming, and I was too blinded by love and hope and stupidity to listen. He said you were cruel and vindictive, and if I ever wised up and deigned to leave you, if I wounded your pride, you'd make me rue the day I ever set eyes on you. But I thought I was special. That my love would somehow transform you into the man I wanted you to be. A man who loved and respected me back. I was so fucking naive," I said to myself.

"You are not, *mo chuisle.* I do love and respect you," he insisted breathlessly.

"No. You may think you do, but ... you love what I do for you. How *I* make *you* feel. I'm just a possession to you. I used to think you stole me away for my sake, to save me from that cesspit, because you saw something special in me. But I could have been anyone. Any needy soul willing to feed your ego and make you believe you're a good person. That you're worthy of love. *You're not,*" I hissed.

"Love, *real* love requires sacrifice on both ends. It's a partnership. It's give and take, and I can't keep giving. You have taken almost everything from me, Asher, even my self-worth. Even my identity. You made me feel as if I don't exist without you. That I'm nothing if I'm not loved by you. That is unforgivable. *Unforgivable.* And I refuse to give you that power over me anymore. I refuse. And if you love me, truly love me like you claim to, you will let me go. You will let me walk out of this *nightmare* that we have created, so I can stand on my own two feet. Have the life that, no matter how much I may want it, *you* cannot provide me. I need more than you. I love you, I probably always will, but I love me more. *Let me go.*"

Asher shook his head through my whole plea. "No. *No.*" He advanced toward me, and I did my best not to shrink away, but tension locked my whole body in place. "Look at me. *Look at me!*" He attempted to catch my eyes, but I moved my head away. "I love you. I love you with everything I have. My life, my heart, my soul are yours and yours alone. We can repair this. I shall do whatever you ask," he said desperately, even grabbing my hands. "We will return to Holland, just the two of us. We will never leave again, if that is what you desire. I-I-we will have a child. A dozen."

"It won't work," I said, voice breaking.

"It will," he whispered, now on the verge of tears.

"It won't!" I shouted. "A year, two, and you'll get restless, and we'll be right back here."

"That will not happen. I promise, *mo chuisle*, I promise."

"It will. You know it will," I cried back. "I can't do this anymore. Please, *please* let me go, Asher. Please."

Still sobbing, I ripped my hands from his and stumbled toward the door. My entire body felt as if it weighed a million pounds. I only made it three steps before he cried, "No. No." He moved in front of me to block my slow trek. "I love you." He grabbed my arms again, but I yanked them from his grasp. "Do you hear me? I love you." He tried to kiss me, but I moved my lips from his. "I love you."

"Stop it," I whispered.

His lips pressed to mine but only succeeded for a second before I twisted away. "I love you," he cried back. "Do not leave me. You cannot leave me. Never. I need you so much. I love you." He clutched my wrists and pulled me against him.

I struggled, but he just gripped tighter. "Let me go," I said forcefully. "Please."

He forced his lips to mine again and squeezed tighter, hard enough to leave bruises. No matter where I turned my head his lips assaulted mine. I hadn't even noticed he was backing me against the bed until my legs hit the edge. "I love you so much. Do not leave me. I am lost without you. Please."

We collapsed onto the bed with him on top of me. Panic overwhelmed me. "Asher, get off me! Get off!" I flailed my arms, but he would not let go, pinning me to the mattress. Bile rose into my throat. "Wait! Stop! No! Please!" I choked out.

"You will not leave me. I love you so much," he said to himself.

Any vestige of the man I loved was gone. The man I loved never would have ignored my pleas, my sobs, my struggles against him.

I thought he had taken everything from me already. How wrong I was. One violent motion ceased all my protests, and I floated out of my violated body. I left it for him to do as he pleased as his bloody tears rained down on my cheeks. I was aware of them but couldn't feel them. Thank the universe I couldn't feel a damn thing. I just stared into space and waited for it to be over. "I love you, my Anna. All mine. *I love you.*"

When he was spent, when he got what he wanted from my body, he gazed down at my blank expression, my own tears streaming from the corners of my eyes, and he gasped. Shock and revulsion swept over his face like a tempest. "Oh no," he whispered. "No, no, no, no, no, no," he said as he removed himself from me. His shaking hand covered his wide-open mouth. "What have I done? I am sorry. I am so sorry. What have I done?" Asher backed away, climbing off the bed, but his unsteady legs buckled a second later. "I am sorry. I am so sorry," he said through the hard, wracking sobs. "What have I done? Oh, what have I done?"

His cries brought me crashing back to earth. He was so pathetic. So broken. He meant it. Watching his torment, I didn't doubt his remorse. I still don't. He would take it all back if he could, every last heinous act. And as I stared at him, curling into a ball on the floor, filled with such utter self-loathing, I knew what I had to do. I rose from the bed, rearranged my coat and slip to regain some dignity, and bent beside him. "Asher..." I whispered. Tentatively, I reached down to stroke his wild, downy hair.

His bloody eyes looked up at me, and he let out a wail I hadn't heard since our first night in that cemetery. I put up no resistance as he collected me into his arms once again, sobbing against me. I embraced him back as tight as I could until he released me. I wiped those tears away without a hint of fear or hesitation. "I am so sorry," he whispered. "I am so sorry, my love. I love you. I love you more than I have ever loved another living soul. Please never doubt that. Please do not leave me. I need you. I am lost without you, my Anna. Please do not send me back to hell. *Please.*"

I kissed his uncertainty away. And mine. No matter how hard I fought, no matter where I tried to run, one universal truth could never be changed. He was mine and I was his. 'Til the close of the dream.

'Til death.

———

The song "Don't Fear the Reaper" woke me at ten when the alarm went off. With the panels down, the bedroom was close to pitch black but even still I could make out the soft features of his handsome face at rest. It really was the face of an angel. I touched his cheek, his lips, his closed eyelids and long lashes before extracting myself from his cold arms. The valets were due at noon to collect the coffins and take us to the private plane Christine arranged. London, then we'd find a home in the countryside, just the two of us. We'd start fresh. It was all settled. I sat up in our bed, stretching like a cat, then sighing. Time to go.

My clothes, white slacks and pink cashmere sweater, were already laid out and I even put on make-up and a matching pink headband. Asher taught me to always look my best, especially when you feel your worst. I stepped out of the bathroom and surveyed the room, stopping at my slumbering Asher. He seemed so serene, so beautiful with a tendril of his auburn hair falling against his white forehead. Vampires weren't dead during the day, more in a light coma that is filled with vivid dreams much like us humans. He must have been having a splendid one judging from the faint smile across his lips. Was it about me? About the night before? I did hope for his sake it was the best dream of his entire existence. I turned away, put on my bloodstained coat, picked up my purse and still packed suitcase, opened the bedroom door, and, before I stepped out, I pressed the button to open the shutters. As I walked out, the light of day slowly filtered into the room behind me.

His tortured, agonizing screams began as I shut the suite door. Nothing. I felt nothing. I hadn't felt a damned thing since he pinned me to our bed. Perhaps it was a mercy. Without the disconnect, the numbness, I probably wouldn't have had the strength to do what needed to be done. With all emotion gone, my only course of action became crystal clear. He would never let me go. *Never*. He would scorch the earth until there was nowhere for me to go but into his arms. Him or me. For once, I made the right decision.

I engaged the fire alarm as I calmly walked down the hall. All the human companions and staff panicked around me in the stairwell, some even sobbing in fear. No one paid me a second glance, not even on the DC streets as I trekked the seven blocks to the Sheraton. I didn't bother to knock on the meeting room door. There was only one man, a vaguely familiar thirty-something redhead in jeans and flannel shirt inside reviewing a tackboard with maps and pictures on it. "Uh, may I help you, miss?" the man asked.

"Are you the F.R.E.A.K.S.?" I asked in a monotone.

"I'm, uh, working with them," the man said, stepping toward me. "Are you ... okay?"

"I'm here to report multiple murders. Last night my boyfriend John Asher and two other vampires, Christine Caple and Oliver Smythe, killed four people in Goodnight, Virginia. The Harmon family. And I just burnt my boyfriend alive at the Elysium Hotel. I'm here to turn myself in."

The redhead stared at me, his long jaw falling open. "Um, let-let me just … have a seat, doll. I'll be right back." The man quickly walked out, leaving me alone once more. I did what the man said, I sat and stared at the crime scene photos. Normally, I'd throw up a little in my mouth at the sight of ravaged dead bodies but not then. What are pictures when you've actually had an innocent person's blood on your flesh? The girl couldn't have been more than eighteen when some bastard literally ripped out her throat. The wound on her thigh was even a little intriguing.

At least I wasn't alone with the pictures for long. About a minute later, the red-haired man returned with an emaciated fifty-something gentleman with a full head of gray hair. "Hello, miss," the elder said as he entered.

"That's not a vampire bite."

"I'm sorry?" the man asked.

I pointed to the picture. "There's no puckering from when the fangs extracted, and the punctures are too close together. That's not a vampire bite."

"Um, thank you for telling us," said the man as he approached. He slowly lowered himself into the chair beside me as if any swift movement would result in his injury. "Mr. Dahl, would you please get our guest something to drink? A Coke from vending perhaps?"

"Yeah, sure," said the redhead. "I'll be right back."

"Is Agent West here? I want to see Agent West," I said as he departed.

"I'm afraid he's in the field right now, but I'd like to help you, if you can." The gentleman smiled at me. "My name is Dr. George Black of the F.R.E.A.K.S. What's your name, dear?"

The question singed like acid, cracking my thin veneer of apathy. My mouth twitched, but I couldn't answer. The man with the kind eyes took my hand. Another crack. "Who are you, dear?"

Kaboom.

"I-I-I-I don't know," I whispered before I burst into tears. Dr. Black squeezed my other hand and let me sob. "I'm no one. He's gone, and I killed him, and I'm no one now. What have I done? Oh … what have I done?"

———

It was a busy day for the F.R.E.A.K.S.; even I added to the drama. They were hot on the trail of Lord Peter's bodyguard Ivan, or Monster, as he was called around the vampire scene. Everyone knew to avoid him even without being told. Even amid vampires he was intimidating. Six-four, pale blue eyes, built like a tank and never without a scowl, even when he was leering at my breasts. It didn't surprise me at all to hear he was a serial murderer.

The F.R.E.A.K.S. were stretched so thin, no one gave leaving a confessed murderer alone a second thought. Not that I was a flight risk. Where did I have to go? Dr. Black escorted me into a hotel room, and only came to check on me if he had more questions. About two hours of lying in a stranger's bed with only the Harmons' and Asher's howls of agony to keep me company, I broke quarantine and returned to the conference room. Unfortunately, High Priestess McGregor had arrived by then. I interrupted Dr. Black comforting her, just a simple hug between colleagues, but when the witch set eyes on me, her disgust and hate radiating from her hard brown eyes, I retreated back to my isolation. I'd already caused so much pain, I couldn't bear to cause a second more.

About seven hours after my escape, while I stared at the television watching Joan Collins battle Linda Evans on *Dynasty*, there was another knock on the door. "Annie?" Nathan asked as he stepped in with a bag of fast food. "Hey. Brought you something to eat."

"Thank you," I whispered as I sat up, "but I'm not hungry."

He joined me on the edge of the bed and passed me the bag regardless. "You need to eat." I didn't move. "Hey, you promised me dinner. It ain't Morton's, but it'll have to do." I hadn't eaten in almost twenty-four hours, but I didn't realize how starved I was until I saw and smelled the fries he laid out. I ate one. Two. Then I couldn't stop. "Knew you were a woman of your word."

"My one saving grace," I said with my mouth full.

"I wouldn't say that."

"The guests at the Elysium Hotel might beg to differ." I paused. "Did the hotel burn down?" I asked with a knot in my gut.

"How'd you know that's where I was?"

"You smell like smoke."

He sniffed his rumpled suit jacket. "Oh. No. The fire was contained to ... your suite."

"Christine?"

"It's a madhouse there. They're still processing the scene." He paused. "Your room was a mess, and vampires can burn to nothing, especially when daylight's involved. We did find a body in a nearby room drained of blood, but there may be no connection. Just to be safe we locked the place down. No one went in or out until we did a full sweep of every room and garage. We didn't find her."

"So she either died or got away before lockdown. And there was no body in my room? None? So he could ..."

Nathan touched my hand to calm me. "The bedroom was cinders. No one could have survived. Not even a vampire. You're safe now. He can't hurt you anymore, okay?"

I couldn't stand the feel of Nathan's hand on mine, not because it didn't feel good but because it did. I yanked mine away, balling it into a fist. "So, um, am I under arrest?"

"I, uh, I have no idea. Sorry. Like I said, everything's nuts. Was before you even got here. Might be cold comfort right now, but *you* helped us to avoid a war." My weary eyes narrowed in confusion. "Last night. The information about the bite, the ripped throat, teeth and claws, the motive. Talking to you, I realized the whole thing screamed setup. The first two murders were staged. This Ivan made it appear a vampire was the UNCRET. Tensions were so high both factions weren't asking questions, just jumping to conclusions. We were so focused on the macro, we forgot to review the micro. We had the first victim's diary, but no one bothered to read it until last night. It turns out Abigail Conlon was seeing someone, an older werewolf she met at Club Vertigo. Just called him 'I.' Ivan Illovitch fit her description. We put the pieces together about an hour before you arrived. The werewolves are chasing him down right now. *You* did that, Annie. Who knows how many others would have died without you." He moved up the bed and gazed into my eyes. "What happened to those people last night wasn't your fault. I'm sure you did everything you could to protect them."

"I should have known," I whispered. "I should have known what he'd do. I never should have involved them, but I didn't have any place else to go. They were helping me. They were good, nice people, and …and …" Just when I thought there were no more tears. Wishful thinking, I guess.

This time I didn't shy away from Nathan's embrace. I had no fight left in me for anything. "Hey, hey," he said, giving me a hug. I squeezed back. "It's all okay now. Everything will be okay."

"I couldn't do anything. I tried but … oh, that little girl. That poor baby. She was so frightened, and Oliver …" The image of Bethany's sweet face brought fresh sobs. "She was two years old, Nathan. Two, and he …"

"No one told you?" Nathan asked as he pulled away. "Annie, Bethany Harmon's alive."

"What?"

"She walked into the sheriff's station late last night with no memory of how she got there. They're working on retrieving her memory right now. The police did find three other bodies in the burnt-out house, but the girl's alive. Not a scratch on her."

I covered my mouth as I gasped. At least a thousand pounds lifted off my shoulders. "Really?"

"I don't lie, remember? She's alive, Annie. I swear it. And we're working on finding this Oliver. We think he's run to Lord Peter, who has been less than cooperative. There's a big meeting set for after sundown to hash this mess out. You'll probably have to be there." He touched my hand again. "But I'll be there too. I'll do whatever I can to help you. I promise."

"Why are you being so nice to me?" I whispered.

"Because …" he said, squeezing my hand, "if anyone ever needed a friend in this world, Annie Olmstead, that person is you. I'm more than happy to oblige."

"I've never had a real friend before. Not really."

"That … is the saddest thing I have ever heard in my life," he chuckled. "Really." He shook his head. "Well, then I am glad to remedy the situation. And as your new friend, I insist you eat every bit of this fine greasy feast before I do, then I'll take your formal statement and get us ready for the meeting." His smile wavered to nothing. "I am gonna need to know every detail though. *Everything*," he said as if I already wore a scarlet "R" on my chest.

When it came to that part of my horror story, I did lie. It was the only time, and I did it not because I didn't trust him, but because I wasn't ready to admit it to myself, let alone say it aloud. The "official" story was he locked me in the bathroom, I broke out and decided he needed to die or he'd hound me until the grave. At the time, Nathan seemed to believe me. He asked a lot of questions, but the Olmstead genes kicked in, and the lies flowed.

"I was right," Nathan said, closing his notepad after over two hours of hell.

"What about?"

"You did everything you possibly could have done for those people. For yourself. You got grit, Annie Olmstead."

"Is that a good thing?"

"Oh, Annie, it's everything," he said with a grin. I managed a tiny smile back. Even in the most grave of circumstances, he could always bring a smile to my face.

The ringing telephone disturbed our first nice moment in hours. Nathan reached across to answer it. "Yes?" He listened. "Yes, sir. We're on our way down." He hung up and treated me to another smile, this time sympathetic. "They're ready for us. You okay to do this now?"

"I don't know. Do I have a choice?"

He squeezed my hand again. "You got this, Annie. Come on. I'm right beside ya."

And he was. The entire march downstairs, even while I waited outside in the hallway for half an hour. He would have stayed longer, keeping my mind occupied with small talk and questions about magic, except he was summoned inside. My stomach knotted a dozen times when he disappeared out of sight. I hadn't realized how calming his presence was until it was gone.

As I waited, I willed myself numb again. There were three potential outcomes to this meeting, one worse than the last, but I knew that when I turned myself in. I could be imprisoned for years, which was the best case scenario. Guaranteed three meals a day, a roof over my head. It was more than I had sitting in that hallway. The second option was that Lord Peter could request my execution. Under vampiric law, as a consort, if I murdered a vampire for any reason other than self-defense, the punishment was immediate death. As I sat in that hallway, that fate didn't seem terribly dreadful either. The third, where they let me go into the big bad world, was a hell of a lot more frightening. Despite what Nathan believed, whatever resolve from twenty-four hours ago I ever possessed burnt away with my lover. No hope. Asher had taken that glimmer I'd fought so hard for from me in the end too. The greatest of his sins against me.

Nathan stepped out twenty minutes later. "They're ready for you now."

I held my head up high as I walked inside to face my fate.

My tribunal was gathered around the table, some of whom I'd already met: Dr. Black at the head, High Priestess McGregor to his left, the debonair Lord Peter to his right with Oliver beside his only ally, and the redheaded Mr. Dahl sitting behind a huge bald man in his fifties with blue eyes. Every heavy hitter in the North American supernatural community. If I weren't so terrified, I would have been honored. The moment I entered, the tension in the room was already palpable, especially between Lord Peter and the bald man, who were too busy sneering at one another to give me the slightest notice. Mrs. McGregor merely glanced at me before hanging her head. Oliver stared straight ahead, hands folded on the table. Only Dr. Black and Mr. Dahl gave me anything resembling a friendly greeting, if sad, pitying smiles qualify. Nathan pulled out my chair across from Dr. Black, then he sat beside me.

"Hello, Anna," Dr. Black said. "We've heard from Mr. Smythe and Special Agent West about the events of last night and this morning. Now, if you could, in your own words, tell us—"

"This is fucking ridiculous," the bald man cut in. "We heard what happened already. Rehashing it would be just wasting more time when we should be out looking for the cocksucker who murdered my granddaughter!"

"Alpha Conlon, please," Dr. Black chided.

"What? She left her boyfriend, he got pissed, killed some people, and she took care of the bastard for you. Seems pretty fucking cut and dried to me."

"You insensitive bastard," the High Priestess spewed.

"What? Look, Sally, I am damn sorry about your witches, I really am. I can more than relate, but the only reason I'm at this table is because that fucker," he said, pointing at Lord Peter, "knows where Ivan is and is holding out to save his little butt buddy here. For all we know, he put Ivan up to all this to start a war!"

"I did no such thing, and I have resented the implication this is my doing from the start," Peter spewed back. "I had absolutely no knowledge of Ivan's misdeeds and would have turned him in posthaste had I. And let us not forget the four of my people *your* wolves slaughtered."

"And I already told you, they've been dealt with."

"And I am supposed to take your word for it?" Peter asked.

"My word is my bond, bloodsucker. How dare you question it? I—"

"Alright, everybody please calm down!" Dr. Black snapped. "You all agreed to cooperate with one another. Every single person at this table has the same goal: justice for your respective clans."

"Then let's get on with it," the werewolf said. "What does he want for Ivan?"

"Leniency for my subject. Per his statement, Mr. Smythe believed he was simply going to retrieve Miss Asher—"

"Kidnap her," Nathan cut in

"Retrieve her," Peter continued, "and Mr. Smythe took no part in the tragic killings last night. He even went out of his way to ensure there were no further deaths. Need I remind you there is a little girl alive because of his quick thinking. All Oliver is guilty of is a poor choice of friends and destroying evidence."

"Is this true, Miss Asher?" Dr. Black asked.

I glanced at Oliver, who stared down at his hands. "If Bethany is alive, then yes. He didn't lay his hands on anyone."

"He also did nothing to stop the situation," McGregor said.

"There was nothing I *could* do," Oliver said.

"Bullshit," said the Priestess. She turned to Dr. Black. "George, you can't let him get away with this."

"If it gets me Ivan, oh yes he can," Alpha Conlon chimed in. "Your guy's been taken care of already by the girl here, mine's still out there. He's a rabid dog, Sally. You saw the pictures of my Abigail. Hell, look what he did to his own kid. We need to find him, and find him *now*. If it means pretty boy over there gets a slap on the wrist, so be it."

Dr. Black pondered this for a few seconds. "What do you propose, Peter?"

"You mentioned being short staffed, and that your last vampire agent met her final death several months ago. We have spoken, and Oliver is amenable to joining your organization for a decade instead of serving his time in your internment facility. Not only will he bring a vast network of connections in the vampire world to the table, but as last night proved, he is quick on his feet, good in a crisis, and dare I say it, even heroic on occasion. I cannot recommend him highly enough for the post. And should he flee, or simply not live up to your expectations, I shall kill him myself. This I vow."

Dr. Black looked at High Priestess McGregor. "Not good enough," she said.

"Thirty years," Dr. Black countered. "Nonnegotiable."

Lord Peter whispered to Oliver, who nodded, then said, "I agree to the terms."

"Great. Settled. Now, where the fuck is Ivan?" the Alpha asked.

Lord Peter removed a piece of paper from his pocket and passed it across. "I own a cabin in Warrenton. He is there. The directions are in the envelope."

The Alpha leapt up. "Guess we're done here."

"Not yet," Mr. Dahl said. "The boy. Ivan's son. What happens to him?"

"Who the fuck cares, Frank? George can square him away."

"He's a traumatized boy," the Priestess said. "A *werewolf* boy. He should be with others of his kind."

"I don't want that mongrel," the Alpha said. "He's psychotic like his father. He damn near gutted one of my men!"

"Because we literally broke into his house and terrorized him," Mr. Dahl pointed out. "I would have done the same."

"Me too," chimed in the witch.

"He ain't pack, and he ain't our problem."

"I'll take him," Mr. Dahl said quietly.

"The boy cannot be placed in regular foster care," said Mc-Gregor. "If I'm not mistaken, the law states any known werewolf under the age of eighteen is under the guardianship of the reigning pack regardless of his or her formal affiliation with said pack. He—"

"I said I'll take him," Dahl proclaimed louder that time.

Conlon rolled his eyes. "Yeah, Jenny'll love that."

"She'll learn to," Dahl said. "And we are bound by law to oversee his care until he's of age. She is correct about that right, Dr. Black?"

"Yes."

"Then I volunteer to oversee his care," Dahl said.

"Fine. Whatever. The little monster's yours. Can we leave now? Is this kangaroo court adjourned yet?" Conlon asked.

"There is one more item on the agenda," Lord Peter said before turning his cold glare my direction. "Miss Asher."

I sat up straight in my chair and willed the knot in my gut to uncoil.

"What about her?" Conlon asked. "Your guy kidnapped her, she fought back and won. Good on her."

"It is not that cut and dried. Per her statement to Agent West, when she committed the act, she was not in immediate danger therefore she did not act in self-defense. Miss Asher maliciously murdered her consort, in cold blood, and endangered many other lives in the process. By vampiric law, she is culpable for multiple atrocities and must be turned over to me for the appropriate punishments."

"Now, wait a minute," Nathan said. "She might not have been in danger at the moment, but she did try to leave your vampire once and look what happened. She was terrorized, kidnapped, made to watch as an entire family was massacred, physically assaulted, and held hostage. Where was your vampiric law then? Isn't it also meant to protect *her*? You," he said, gesturing to Oliver, "you knew this Asher. If she ran again, would he have gone after her again like last night?"

"Without a doubt," Oliver said.

"Then even without her being in immediate danger, that still sounds like self-defense to me. He left her no other choice," Nathan said.

"Her crimes are not under the F.R.E.A.K.S. purview," Lord Peter countered. "The case against Asher and Christine, yes, as their victims were a different caste. But this was consort on vampire crime, therefore only vampiric law applies, and you have no jurisdiction."

"She's a witch," Nathan pointed out.

"She is a consort first."

"So he," Nathan said, nodding to Oliver, "the one who stood by and did nothing while three people were butchered, gets off scot free, but Annie faces a possible death sentence? Does that seem right to anyone?"

"It is—" Lord Peter began.

"Agent West is right," High Priestess McGregor proclaimed. "Everyone at this table is making concessions for the greater good, Peter. What good would it possibly serve to punish this young girl? We all heard her account. She has suffered enough already. This Asher got nothing less than what he deserved as will this Christine when you locate her," she added with a hard edge.

"Yeah, let the girl get on with her life for God's"—the vampires hissed—"sake," Conlon said. "If what Texas said here is true, she helped crack my Abby's case. And she tried to stop the killings last night, unlike others. *She's* the heroic one here. Hell, George, maybe you should take her onboard too. Two for the price of one. She is one of you super-witches—right, Sally? Knows vampires, knows witches, has no problem killing? Sounds like an ideal F.R.E.A.K. to me."

"She'd be an excellent addition, Dr. Black," Nathan chimed in as well. "And having a witch would be useful, especially a High Priestess."

"The girl needs to be punish—"

"*I* insist, your lordship," Conlon said with a hard edge. I knew he was only taking my side to aggravate the vampire, but I was grateful none the less. "All in the spirit of cooperation, right, Sally? George? Like you both said, it's why we're all here."

"If the deal's good enough for him," Nathan said, nodding to Oliver too, "why not her?"

Dr. Black looked at the perturbed Lord of Washington. "Peter?"

"Ten years," he said.

"Six months," McGregor countered.

"Two years," Dr. Black said with finality. "Is that agreeable to you, Miss Asher?"

"I-I-I suppose," I said, still in a haze.

Conlon rose again. "Then we've covered everything. Guess the summit's over. Hallelujah. Let's do it again sometime. Come on, Frank. Time to skin that fucker." With his friend in tow, the werewolves stalked out of the conference room.

Peter stood next. "Well. Then. This was relatively painless. Miss Asher, Oliver, I leave you in Dr. Black's capable hands. Good luck. You shall both need it." He nodded to Mrs. McGregor. "Always a pleasure, Sally."

"And if you find that woman—" she began.

"I shall hold her in custody and notify you both immediately. Good evening all."

I breathed a literal sigh of relief when he departed. My head still gyrated with all the current events; I couldn't focus on just one. Then it was Mrs. McGregor's turn to rise. "Well, that went better than I anticipated. No blood drawn. I'm shocked. Perhaps now we can convince them to make it a yearly event."

"I was thinking precisely the same thing," Dr. Black said.

The witch turned her gaze to Oliver and all kindness dropped as did Oliver's eyes. Coward. "You got off easy, *sir*," she said through gritted teeth. "You should die for what you've done. Instead, you've been given a chance for redemption. To make up for all your, I'm sure, considerable crimes. Don't squander that. Make their deaths *mean* something." She stared at me. "Both of you. Live a good life, live it to the fullest. Live it for *them*."

"Yes, ma'am," I said softly.

The most powerful witch in the country, my kin, now probably lost to me forever, nodded at me, at George, then left to resume her life as well. Nobody was left in the room but us F.R.E.A.K.S.

"Well, this is a surprising turn of events," Dr. Black said, "but hopefully one that will prove to be beneficial to us all." He rose from the table too. "Mr. Smythe, Miss Asher, let me be the first to welcome you to the F.R.E.A.K.S. Now, if you'll excuse me, I have many unexpected arrangements to make. Nathan, stay with them until I return, please?"

"Yes, sir."

"Then I leave you in good hands. You two rest. Training will begin tomorrow." With a nod for each of us, the last of the power players departed.

Oliver fell back in his chair, and his entire body relaxed. "Well... this should be interesting."

I just sat in my chair staring into space until Nathan asked, "Are you okay?"

"I have no idea."

Twenty-four hours. Twenty-four hours before I had sat at a table with the nicest people alive, my heart full of hope and happiness for my new, wide-open future. Now they were dead because of me, and

I was in a position to make sure no one ever met a similar fate. It meant something. It all *had* to mean something. And if it didn't, then I'd *make* it mean something. Their deaths would not be in vain. Nor would Anna Asher's. She died reclaiming her soul from the darkness. She died fighting for the future, and she won. *I* won. I would never let that darkness return. I wouldn't squander the opportunities the universe provided. I swore to the universe, to the dead, to all who listened, I'd make the most of every single one. My future husband, the father of my children, and even then my best friend, squeezed my hand again. I squeezed back. Every. Single. One.

And Anna Olmstead Asher West always keeps her promises.

PART II

RAY OF LIGHT

AGE 29
STOKER, KS

"Oh, my God, this place is so rad! Is that a naked lady?"

I'd forgotten how child-inappropriate this mansion is. Priceless paintings and bric-a-brac laying about, antique furniture worth tens of thousands, and an entire room in one of the basements filled with enough weapons to invade Wyoming. Not to mention the inhabitants now include a vampire, a Pusher, a blind medium, a werewolf, and another witch. Save for Dr. Black, and unfortunately Oliver, the old gang from Nathan's and my F.R.E.A.K.S. tenure have since retired. My family's life is in the hands of veritable strangers. But we're blessed to have them.

Nathan and the boys recovered from the shock far quicker than I did. My husband's first act was to call Dr. Black for advice, which consisted of packing a bag and hopping the first flight to Wichita to hole up at the F.R.E.A.K.S. manor until the team traced Asher. Running and hiding worked for me. Nathan required persuading on this course of action. His inner Alpha male now unleashed, he insisted on remaining in Garland to help the agents with the investigation. If not for the boys I'd want the same, but after a heated argument where I had to remind my pig-headed husband *he* was the one marked for execution by a sociopath with unlimited resources and a grudge, Max ran into the room in tears, close to hyperventilating. His terror shocked us both out of our fear and rage. Nathan gave in to our baby boy's pleas and agreed to accompany us to Stoker. So the Wests fled into the night with a dead Swiss National rotting in our living room and half-assed excuses for our family about our impromptu vacation. Another birthday to remember.

"Joseph Thomas West, get away from the painting and get into bed! Don't make me tell you again!"

With a pout, my son obeys. He's handling this whole situation far better than I anticipated. Hell, better than I am. He inherited his father's quick resilience and sunny disposition, without question. To him we're just on one big adventure. A bad man broke in, Mommy chased him away—they weren't allowed in the living room—and now he gets to miss school, visit Mommy and Daddy's old workplace, spend time with real FBI agents who carry guns, and watch TV all day. Little boy heaven.

Max unfortunately takes after me. He knows, no he *feels* the danger and fear radiating around the air, then he internalizes it. My baby's had so many stomachaches in his life he had to see a specialist, and that was before all this madness. He's been glued to me and Nathan since this all began. As Joe explores his new surroundings with awe, Max sucks his thumb as he rests his towhead on my husband's shoulder, just staring into space, deep in his own mind. I wish I could start him in therapy *right now*.

"Come on," Nathan says from the bed. "Family pile."

I shut the bathroom door and, like Joe, walk over to the king-size bed to join Nathan and Max in one big family pile. Nathan lifts his free arm to allow us both into his embrace. Maybe Joe's just hiding his fear better because of late he hates family pile—calls it "Gross." Tonight he crawls between Nathan and I, and even pulls my hand up to his racing heart. I snake my arm under my husband's neck so I can pet Max's downy hair. One second like this, all of us together, touching and I'm infinitely better. Max too as he stops sucking his thumb. "It'll all be okay, guys. Mom and me and everyone here won't let anyone hurt you, okay? We're safe now."

"How long are we gonna stay here?" Joe asks. "My soccer game's on Saturday."

"Sorry, champ. You'll probably have to miss it."

"But that's so unfair," he whines. "Why'd the bad man have to come now?"

The children know precious little about my past except that my parents are dead, I moved around a lot, and Daddy and I met when we were working for the FBI as analysts. That's all *anyone* knows about me, even Nathan's parents and sister. I'm already dreading the day the boys are old enough to ask the right questions because I will tell them the truth. They deserve to know it. They wouldn't be alive without it. But today is not that day.

"I don't know, sweetie," I say honestly, "but we'll make sure he goes away and never comes back, okay?" I say with a kiss to his head. "Until then, you have our permission to watch as much TV and eat as much ice cream as you want."

"Really?" Max asks, finally perking up.

"Yep," Nathan says. "But you have to be brave and strong and listen to all the grown-ups here, okay? Remember, we're guests, so you must be on your best behavior."

"Okay, Daddy," Max whispers.

There's a gentle knock on our door. "Come in!"

Oliver steps in. I haven't set eyes on that man in almost eight years, and he's still as gorgeous as ever. I wouldn't say we became friends during my two years of F.R.E.A.K.S. duty, just begrudging acquaintances and colleagues. The first month we barely spoke, barely looked at one another unless absolutely necessary. If I did, I just saw the Harmons or recalled our depressing nights together. And I know a large part of him blamed me for his indentured servitude, though he never came out and said it. He avoided me, I avoided him, and he didn't even attend our wedding, in the library downstairs, it being daylight, or wish me well when Nathan and I left. No, we'll never be friends, but the vampire takes one look at us Wests all cuddled together, and a brief smile crosses his lips. For a vampire he's a decent sort. "I apologize for interrupting. Your presence is required in the conference room."

"Hi," Joe says.

"Hello, little one." His gray eyes move to Max, who once again sucks his thumb. "Other little one."

"Okay, boys," says Nathan, extracting himself to try to sit up. No such luck. Max clings to Nathan's arm, holding tight with all his might. "Come on, Max, it's okay."

"No!" he whines.

"Stop being a baby," Joe chides.

"Sweetie, we're just going to be downstairs," I say, petting his hair. "We'll be back soon, I promise." I pull him into a kiss. "No one is going to hurt you, okay? I mean it. No one. I promise."

"Me too, buddy," Nathan says.

"I promise it too," Joe says.

After searching all our faces with his soulful brown eyes for artifice and finding none, Max loosens his stranglehold. "Okay."

Nathan turns to Joe with a proud grin. It's almost as wide as mine. "If you need us, just press 97. It's the conference room." He kisses Joe's hair. "Take care of your brother."

"Okay."

I hug both my sons, and caress my baby boy's chubby cheek. "I love you both so much. *So* much."

"We love you, Mommy," Max whispers.

"Try to get some sleep, okay? We'll be back soon," says Nathan.

Nathan and I climb out of bed, tuck in the boys, and follow Oliver out. Both Nathan and I sigh in unison after the door shuts. "They appear to be handling the situation quite well," Oliver says as we begin walking.

"I hope so," I say.

"They are beautiful boys," Oliver adds. "You should be proud."

"We are," Nathan responds curtly. He never did take a shine to Oliver. Wonder why.

"Thank you," I say. Oliver nods. "So, any news yet?"

"George sent two agents and our new medium to your house. They are still processing the scene while Andrew attempts to question the assassin, but—"

"That bastard's ghost is still in our home?" Nathan asks.

"That's a good thing," I point out. "He may be able to tell us Asher's whereabouts."

"Yes, it is just a shame Mr. Fournier is not alive," Oliver says. "We could have used other forms of persuasion as well."

"I'm sure my wife will keep that in mind next time she's literally fighting for her life," Nathan snaps. "Making your job easier for you. Sorry for the inconvenience."

"I meant no disrespect, West. To either of you. I am sure Anna did not intentionally . . . inconvenience us."

As we stroll down the hallway to the stairs, it hits me. I killed a man. I have really taken another living, breathing, human being's life. All my years with Asher, all my years as a F.R.E.A.K., even with Dario, I had never crossed that final threshold. It may have been an accident, and it may have been self-defense, but regardless. It is another blotch of darkness on my soul, courtesy of Asher.

"Annie, sweetie, you okay? You've gone real pale," says my husband.

"I-I'm fine. Just . . . a long, horrible day. I'm tired."

Nathan slips his hand in mine, giving it a squeeze before kissing the top. "It'll all be okay. You beat back this bastard before, we'll just make sure we wallop him so hard this time he never gets up again."

"So say we all," Oliver says.

Somehow I manage to push the day's gruesome memories aside and allow the beautiful ones to flood back, inspired by walking the halls of this mansion. My home for two years. Where I fell in love with the man by my side. When I came to this palatial five-story manor after my month of training, those first few hours I was afraid to leave my room. Everyone knew my past. What I'd done. I had no idea how the others would treat me. Would it be like boarding school? Like those girls, the agents also knew each other for years, had formed tight bonds forged from misery, and I was an interloper. My fears proved groundless. Nathan plucked me out of my bedroom and introduced me to everyone as the girl who averted a war. His vouching for me, his taking me under his wing, was all it took for the others to accept me. My saving their lives once or twice in the field might have had something to do with it too. But most of the credit goes to my ray of sunshine. I slip my hand in my husband's, who smiles and squeezes tight.

The rest of the new team waits in the conference room around that familiar table with Dr. Black at the head per usual, as his underlings review the file. We'd met them all when we arrived: the FBI agent Lau, the curvy werewolf Tara, the twenty-something Pusher Leif, and witch Martina. Lot of turnaround in the F.R.E.A.K.S. I still keep in touch with some of our old teammates, who have all moved on to greener pastures, some together like Nathan and I. Agent Brewster and Jade got married a few months after we did, but I was too pregnant with Joe to attend the wedding. The F.R.E.A.K.S. definitely lose more agents to intermarriage than death, present company included.

"Did the boys settle in alright?" asks Dr. Black.

"Yes, thank you," I say as I sit.

"I cannot recall the last time there were children under this roof. This might be the first time ever," says Dr. Black.

"And we appreciate you opening your doors to us all," Nathan adds as he takes his old spot by my side, "more than you know."

"So, please walk us though what transpired today in as much detail as possible, Anna," Dr. Black says.

As I comply, the others take notes. Halfway through my tale, Nathan takes my hand again. I don't even mind the electrical shock that accompanies the act. I know it's driving him mad he wasn't there to protect us. I personally thank the universe he wasn't. They'd have two bodies to process had he been. "Thoughts?" Dr. Black asks when I'm done.

"Without a shadow of a doubt, this was Asher's design," Oliver begins. "Quite frankly, I am just surprised it took him this long to strike."

"Me too," I say under my breath. Nathan shoots me a sideways glance.

"First question to answer is how he found her," Agent Lau says.

"No, the first question is how y'all didn't know he was still alive?" Nathan spews.

"There have been a handful of sightings and rumors through the years," Dr. Black says, "but none that could be substantiated. As you are aware, the vamp community can be very ... tightlipped, especially with outsiders and law enforcement."

"Well, you know the secret handshake," Nathan says to Oliver.

"And believe me, West, I have not been idle since last we met. I have a network of associates who have, on occasion, fed me information on said rumors of our mutual friends. Unfortunately those associates are few and far between. Quite frankly, their loyalty to Asher far outweighs their loyalty to me. They have obviously closed ranks around him and Christine."

"That bastard has to have some enemies," Nathan says.

"Byron maybe," I say. "Alain ... he'd help for sure."

"Not out of nobility though," Oliver adds snidely. Still on bad terms with his sire it seems.

"And we care about his reasons because ..." Nathan snaps, garnering a glare from Oliver.

"Well, do we know where to find either of them?" Tara, the werewolf, asks.

"Byron stays mostly in London, and if not, then his island in Greece," Oliver says. "Alain ... your guess is as good as mine. I do not know nor do I care. And regardless, as I said before, they will not speak to law enforcement."

"It can't hurt to try," Lau says.

"I concur," says Dr. Black. "I'll reach out to the Rogue's Gallery in London to locate this Byron."

"Start with Lord Richard," I suggest. "If Asher went to anyone for help, it'd be to him. He may know where both are."

"We should contact all the European bureaus," Oliver says, "and have them brush up on the case and recheck all the locations Anna provided ten years ago. All the flats, all the nightspots ... He has obviously grown careless through the years, otherwise we would not all be gathered at this table now."

"Excellent idea," says Dr. Black. "We'll also see if the bureaus have anything on this assassin."

"Didier worked for Lord Augustus of Vienna," I say. "Augustus and Asher weren't close, but a lot can change in ten years."

"You are proof of that, Mrs. West," Oliver says with a grin.

"Could this Asher be in Dallas?" Leif, the Pusher, asks.

"I have spoken to a contact close to Lord Fredrick," Oliver says. "He does not believe Asher is within the territory, no."

"Plus a preliminary search of Fournier's hotel room and rental van indicate a private plane was on stand-by at Love Field," Dr. Black adds. "The flight plan filed included three coffins as cargo set for New York City, then on to London."

"So he's probably in London right now," Nathan says.

"No, by now he knows Didier has failed and probably fled," I say.

"London is as good a place to begin as any though," Oliver says.

"I'll call the Gallery the moment we're done here," Dr. Black says.

"And on the plane here I wrote down everything I could remember. Other friends, addresses, habits, his favorite brands," I say, removing the paper. "It's all mostly in Europe, so you should pass it on to those bureaus as well."

"Thank you," says Dr. Black. "Anything else, team?"

"What else *is* there to do?" Leif asks. "This guy's a ghost. Literally until today. Unless we use her and the kids as bait—"

"Absolutely not," Nathan says.

"I'm just saying, you can't stay here forever," Leif clarifies. "It's been ten years, every agency in the world has been trying to track this guy. We know what he wants, and what he's willing to do for it. That's half the battle."

"We're not there yet," Dr. Black says. "We have a spate of new leads now: London, the money trail, the papers for transporting the coffins, we will run them all down. Lau, you coordinate with the FBI on the financials. Leif, you stay in contact with Garland and run point on any leads they garner. Oliver and I will tackle our foreign friends, and everyone else, get some rest to take over when the first shift needs a break."

"What about us? What can we do?" I ask.

"Sleep. Be with your children. You've provided more than enough to begin with. We *will* find him," Dr. Black assures us as he rises along with the rest of the team.

Nathan and I do the same. "Thank you," my husband says. I grab one of the files before we all disperse.

The boys are watching *Captain Planet* when we return. Ten minutes after Nathan and I crawl into bed with them, the boys sandwiched between us, all my men are asleep. After twenty minutes of attempting to join them in slumberland, I give up. It was futile to even try. I have some reading to do.

After slipping on my clothes again and retrieving my pilfered file, I sneak downstairs to the two-story library. Oh, I adore this room. I practically lived in here during my F.R.E.A.K.S. tenure, reading every book on two walls when I wasn't on a case or out with Nathan. Hell, I was married in this very room, by the fireplace almost eight years ago. Being forced to become a F.R.E.A.K. was the best thing that ever happened to me. Well, the second best.

We fell in love gradually, so gradually I didn't even realize it was happening. Neither did Nathan, or so he claims. We were just friends. Buddies. I couldn't handle any more than that, not at first. Maybe he sensed that. So we stayed friends. Friends who went out to karaoke clubs with our fellow F.R.E.A.K.S. Who watched movies together late into the night. Who listened and gave advice as he talked about the girls he was dating, though it always left a knot in my stomach. I mean, why would he want *me*? I was damaged goods, and he was the kindest, sweetest, most generous man ever to walk the earth. So whenever the thought of taking it a step further crossed my mind, I quickly quashed it. Friends would have to be enough. It was more than I deserved.

After a month of slowly wearing me down, I agreed to travel to Texas for Christmas with the West family. That bunch immediately quelled my nerves. The moment I stepped into their home, they acted as if I'd been a West forever. I learned to make Nathan's favorite chicken-fried steak from Mrs. West. His sister, Donna, took me shopping. His friends even cheered me on as I rode a mechanical bull in a honkey tonk. It was so normal. So warm. Everything I'd always dreamed of when I was with Asher.

After Christmas dinner, stuffed to the gills with ham, Nathan and I plopped down on his parents' sofa to watch *It's A Wonderful Life* and fell asleep. As Jimmy Stewart ran through his hometown, filled with the joy of being alive, I woke and found myself curled against my best friend's chest, his arms draped around me. He was so warm, so handsome, and smelled of cinnamon and pine. I gazed up at his gentle face as he slept, this wonderful, challenging man who never let me get away with anything. Who believed in me. Who held my hand when I finally admitted all of Asher's crimes against me. Who found me a rape survivor's support group in Stoker and stayed by my side that first meeting. Who thought me worthy of meeting his family. Who was proud to call me his best friend.

Be it the wine at dinner, the glittering Christmas lights on the tree, or … okay, I'd wanted to do it for over a year. I almost had more times than I could count, but that night my resolve burnt to ashes. I lowered my lips to his. One sweet stolen kiss as he slumbered. When I pulled away, his eyes were wide open, perhaps he'd been awake the entire time. Before I could apologize he grabbed me and kissed me back. *Really* kissed me. Not with the fervor of claiming me, of trying to devour me like Asher always had, but with the perfect mix of passion and tenderness.

At first I was too afraid to kiss him back, then I fought against myself not to. He could do far better than me. What if this failed? I'd lose my best friend. I couldn't survive losing another man I loved. I couldn't. But it felt so damn good. *I* felt good. Alive. Right. So I lost the fight.

Desire soon swept away any hesitation, any fear, any illusion that I didn't want this man. That I wasn't in love with him. And though it wasn't that intense, all-consuming madness I had with Asher, it was pure and true and hard earned, nurtured through friendship and mutual respect. I wouldn't have made it that far without him. He was my champion, my best friend, the one who helped me discover what real love is. Sacrifice. Putting another before yourself. Struggling through the hard times. Partnership. I wanted that. I wanted that real love. Nothing else mattered in this life. Nathan West taught me that. So when he proposed to me on my twenty-first birthday in this very room, without hesitation, I accepted. Two weeks later, on the official day of my release from the F.R.E.A.K.S., we were married in this room as well. And one week after that while we honeymooned in Hawaii, as that white picket fence was being installed at our new home, I realized Nathan had provided me another gift on my birthday, our son Joe. And the days of wine and roses began in earnest, sweeter and more beautiful than I had ever dreamed possible. Until the darkness crept into our paradise. And no matter the cost, no matter if I have to drag that bastard into the fires of hell myself, there will not be a next time.

I just have to find him first.

I crawl into the lounge chair by the bay windows and open the file. My stomach knots involuntarily when I set eyes on the photo inside. I'd forgotten how blue his eyes are. How dark his red hair was, almost the color of wine. And he wasn't nearly as handsome as my memory led me to believe. He barely has lips, and his cheeks are so hollow. I suppose the rose-colored goggles that love provides wipe away the imperfections, at least the minor ones. In my dreams, he was still perfect. That beautiful angel I laid eyes on twenty years ago. I barely have the dreams now, twice a year if that, but in them we're making love or just strolling arm in arm in the sunshine through a garden filled with roses and lavender. And there are still moments when I'm practicing ballet or watching a movie we saw together, I do wish he was beside me. Yes, just as I'd feared, a part of me still loved him. Even now. And that same twisted, abysmal part of me is joyous he doesn't hate me for my betrayal. That he still thinks about me. That he still might love me. He could want to kill me. Hell, he *should* want to kill me. But I don't believe that was his motive.

Ten years. Ten years he was out there. He was *alive*. Searching for me. Waiting for me. He took great risk trying to reach me. Capture. Death. Maybe it was a trap. That was a real possibility. Maybe this gesture *did* come from hate, not love. Perhaps both. My heart held equal parts of both for him. I gave that heart to him twenty years before and, try as I might, he still held a part of it, miniscule though it may be. I feared until my dying day he always would. What would

I do when I finally saw him again? Would I have the strength to banish him once more?

Only one way to find out.

———

Nothing. Almost thirty-six hours, and nothing. The whole of the supernatural community searching and not even a whisper. Not a lead. Lord Richard stonewalled the Rogue's Gallery, all of Asher's properties are deserted, and even the bank account that wired the money to Didier was untraceable. They've closed ranks around him. Again. I knew this would happen. It was always going to come down to me.

As I take one last look at my boys and husband playing *Castlevania II* in the living room on the Sega, whipping those electronic vampires into submission, dread washes through me. I meant what I vowed. There is not a single, solitary thing I would not do to keep them safe. Nothing. I would lay down my life for them in a heartbeat. I'd even … there is *nothing* I will not do. And now is the time. This ends, once and for all. If Asher wants me, he can have me. Time to teach that bastard to be careful what he wishes for.

Nathan senses me staring and glances over. I muster a smile, and even blow him a kiss, before pivoting around and leaving them to their vampire slaying to begin my own. I've been waiting for them to be distracted before I packed. I've already made the plane reservation. Wichita to London via Boston. I should reach London by midnight, and I've already pilfered Dr. Black's registry of supernatural agencies' addresses and phone numbers, should I need them. I'll call to inform Dr. Black of my plan during the layover.

Sometimes it's better to ask forgiveness than permission. I only hope Nathan and the boys will agree with this philosophy.

Since I didn't unpack much—for this very contingency—all that is required is to retrieve my toiletries, remove Nathan's clothes from our communal suitcase, and write a note explaining the logic of my endeavor. I just hope my husband doesn't find it for a few hours to give me a head start. He'll understand. He *has* to understand. I—

As I zip up the suitcase, I hear the bedroom door shut. *Merde.* When I spin around, my husband is staring at the suitcase as if it were a gremlin then up to me with the same displeasure. Nathan *really* loathes gremlins. "Going somewhere?"

"N…" But I've never lied to him but that once, about the rape, and I promised I'd never lie to him again. Never. And I keep my word. "There is no other option. This is how it has to be."

"Leaving me? Your children? Sneaking off? *That* is how it has to be? We're not even gonna have a discussion about this? You just decide to shut me out?"

"There is nothing to discuss. It has to be done."

"Alone? You don't trust me to have your back? Is that it?"

"You know that's not true, and I resent you for even saying it," I snap back. "Someone needs to stay with the boys."

"They are perfectly safe here, and you know it."

"And so are you," I counter. "It's not *me* he wants to kill, Nathan."

"No, it's just *you* that murderous rapist wants to kidnap and do God knows what else with for all eternity. And you're running right into his arms."

"Only so I can get close enough to stick a blade through his black, dead heart."

Nathan strides toward me. "Then I am gonna be right by your side holding your other hand while you do it."

"Nathan … he'll kill you. He. Will. Kill. You," I say, drawing out every desperate word. "And I couldn't live with that. I couldn't. I won't."

My husband grabs my upper arms to force me to meet his determined gaze. "Now, you listen to me, Anna West, and you damn well listen good. We've got two little boys who need their parents, both their parents, so we've got no choice but to come back to them. Nothing is gonna happen to either one of us because you are gonna watch my back like I'm gonna watch yours. Just like old times. Like always. Then we're gonna go home. We're gonna watch our sons grow up, we're gonna play with our grandchildren, and we're gonna die in our bed holding each other when we're ninety, with smiles on our faces. I promise. We just gotta to do this first. *Both* of us. This is *our* life, the one *we* built. Together. You don't gotta carry this one all by yourself. Not this time. I love you. I made you a promise years ago I wouldn't leave your side when you needed me, no one's gonna make me break that vow now. Not even you, Annie." Nathan releases me and takes a step backward. "So, Mrs. West, where are we headed first?"

I leap into my husband's arms, hugging him as tight as my arms can manage. Oh, I love this man. He always knows just what I need. No matter how much I feared for his safety, I didn't want to face this alone. "I love you so much. *So* much."

"I love you too. And if we got that, that bastard can't touch us. No greater power in the universe, right?" Nathan pulls away to kiss me. "Let's beat the devil with it."

LONDON, ENGLAND

With the almost fifteen hours of flight time, and six-hour time difference, by the time we land on English soil we're exhausted. After checking into our hotel in Piccadilly and phoning Kansas, we fall asleep the moment our heads hit the pillow. Five far too short hours later, I force myself awake and Nathan along with me. We order room service—tea, lots of strong tea—then deal with the multiple messages that racked up while we slept. In the end, Nathan convinced me to let Dr. Black in on our plan. Since we're civilians now, he couldn't exactly order us to stay, but did lay out his reservations, none of which hadn't crossed my mind a dozen times already. Despite his hesitation, common sense won in the end. He agreed that if we could live with the potential consequences, and if we share any concrete leads we uncovered, he'd feed us any new information as it came in. He even informed the Rogue's Gallery we were in town in case we need their immediate assistance. I really, *really* hope we don't.

The boys were a tougher sell. Joe was all ready to fly out and fight the vampires with us, but Max had to be literally pried from my body as I held back my own tears. I almost cancelled the whole trip then. When your baby's in real pain and begging you not to abandon him, it's as if you're experiencing his agony times twelve. I physically hurt as his tears soaked through my slacks. The struggle ahead of us is the equivalent of a pillow fight compared to the strength it took to get me to walk away from my babies. Nathan held my quaking hand the entire drive to the airport. Damn Asher for causing my children one second of pain. He deserves to die for that sin alone.

The first message is from the lead inspector of the Rogue's Gallery, Felix Frye, welcoming us to London and requesting we phone him. Nathan and I decided it was best if we involved the authorities as little as possible. We're on Asher's patch of land now. Leaks are possible. Plus we may have to engage in less that legal means and acts of persuasion in the coming days. It's just better for all parties involved that we remain dark right now.

The next message is from the boys, who have recovered from their abandonment trauma though the power of a night out roller skating with Oliver and Tara, followed by eating their weight in sweets and an all-night movie marathon. Who knew Oliver could channel Mary Poppins so efficiently.

The third message is from Dr. Black with the latest updates, the most promising of which was a rumor that Christine was spotted on the Orient Express days before, destination unknown. So nothing useful. At all. *Merde.*

"What now?" Nathan asks beside me on our bed.

"We continue with our plan. I invite myself to tea with an old friend."

The Gallery interviewed him yesterday and got nowhere. I *will* do better. When I ring the bell at his Chelsea townhouse, I pull my coat tight around me. Damn is it cold. I forgot how frigid England can be. It never gets below forty in Texas. Nathan absolutely got the better job, waiting in the coffee shop across the street. I decided this task is best done alone, but my husband insisted he remain close in case I needed backup. When my old friend opens his door it is immediately evident this precaution was unwarranted. The past fifteen years have not been kind to him. He's gained at least thirty more pounds, and the excess has weighed down his shoulders so he's hunched over and even requires a cane. "Hello, Clifton."

The old man's brown eyes expand to double their natural size as his mouth drops open. I was probably one of the last people he ever expected to see again. I never did get to say good-bye to him. By the time Asher came for me in Rome, he'd already dismissed Clifton, and at fifteen I didn't really need a babysitter anymore. The last time we saw each other was when he brought me back to boarding school. I refused to say a single word to him the whole trip. I did write him a letter after Rome, but he didn't respond. For all I know, Asher never posted it as he said he would. Another way to keep me all to himself. "Anna," Clifton says as if he'd seen a ghost.

Without preamble, I step forward and embrace him. I wasn't sure how I'd feel when I saw him again. Anger? Shame? Sadness? But there's nothing but relief. Joy. On his side as well. It takes him a second, but he squeezes back. "Hi." I release him. "Long time no see."

"Yes," he says, still in shock.

"I-I wrote you. Did you …"

"No. No, I never received a letter."

"Why am I not surprised?" I start rubbing my freezing arms. "May I come in? I'm about to become an icicle."

"Of-of course." He steps aside to allow me in. No surprise his tiny townhouse is immaculate with nary a dust bunny in sight. It took him a whole year of chidings, punishments, and plain old guilt trips before my cleaning skills reached his standards. My home would be a pigsty if not for his tutelage. "Um, would you like some tea?"

"No, thank you," I smile. "You're looking well."

"You used to be a far better liar, Anna," Clifton says with a quick grin back. "This weather is doing nothing for my arthritis. Let's sit down." He gestures to the right and I follow him into the modestly decorated living room. He takes the maroon sofa and I take the matching lounge chair.

"I'm sorry for coming over uninvited but—"

"You didn't want to take the chance I'd refuse to meet you."

"Exactly." I pause. "Still. *You* taught me better than that." Another pause. "How have you been? Really?"

"I am getting old, Anna. I do not recommend it," he says with a gracious smile. "You grew up to be as beautiful as I always knew you would be. And you married, I see."

I glance at my modest diamond solitaire and gold band. "Eight years. Nathan. I have two boys as well. Here," I say, digging into my purse. I remove my wallet as I join Clifton on the sofa and show him one of the pictures of our trip to Niagara Falls last summer. "The older one's Joe. He's all his father. Direct, charming, sociable, a realist. Mr. Happy-Go-Lucky. My big ball of sunshine.

And that's Max. He looks like his father, but … poor baby got my moodiness. Sometimes he's just one raw nerve taking everything in, good and bad. He's my sweetheart though. And that handsome devil's Nathan. My husband. That man helped save my life. Without question."

"Let's make a trade," Clifton says before nodding toward the bookcase. "Second shelf, last album."

After I retrieve the album I rejoin him on the sofa. He opens it to a photo of ten-year-old me at the *barre* in our old Paris flat in my pink leotard, and below it another photo of Asher and I practicing our fencing. I haven't seen a photo of myself before age nineteen in over a decade. I was so … tiny. So young. I'd never thought of myself as ever being a little girl, I surely never felt like one, but here was the proof I was, at least in body. It wasn't until I had children that I realized how truly precious having a real childhood is. Until this week the only concern my boys had was failing a spelling test. I had to grow up so fast. Children shouldn't have to worry about where their next meal is coming from or have to fight back some molester. I was cheated out of mine, I'll be damned if my boys are.

Clifton flips the album's page. The next photo is of Clifton and I in front of the Arc de Triomphe as the sun hangs above it. Oh, I remember that day. I wanted to play normal tourist, so we hit all the hotspots as normal people did. A German tourist took this photo. And below that one, Asher and I in the kitchen as he cooked for me. He got really, really good toward the end. I can't help but smile at that photo. He *was* good to me in those early years. For the first time in my life I felt safe. Loved unconditionally as a child should be. I should have been content with that. Things would have been so different if I hadn't been so insecure. So greedy. It was true what

I said the night we first made love. *I* seduced him. I knew exactly what I was doing. What man can resist a nubile, naked nymphet literally begging for him? No matter what anyone says, not Nathan, not my therapist, I am at fault for that progression. I wanted all of him. All his attention, all his love. Guess it was something we had in common.

"Take whichever one you wish," Clifton says as I continue to flip through.

I stop at one of me reading a book on the couch. "Oh, goodness, the Galway cottage! Oh, how I adored that place."

"Some of the happiest times in my life," Clifton says.

"Mine too." I remove the shot of Asher, Clifton, and I at the dining room table as I blow out my twelve birthday candles. "This one. Definitely this one."

"He did the best he could. We both did."

My smile drops as I look up to my sad friend. "I know."

"We are what we are, Anna. And trying to change that core is like attempting to spin straw into gold. It only happens in stories." We let that fact hang in the air, souring it. He takes my hand. "I am aware of what he's done to you. What he's still trying to do. If I knew where he was, I would tell you. I would. But I've been out of that world for almost two years, and I have had no contact with Asher in fifteen. I believed him dead, and I have seen no evidence to the contrary until now."

"Did he have any close friends or enemies in London? I mean, he must have brought some people over to the flat after he sent me away."

"Oh, yes. Lord Richard and that trollop of his were frequent guests."

"What about enemies? He has to have a few. Alain, for instance?"

"Him, I don't know, but during a party, Asher did come to blows with one gentleman, George Byron. He's the lover of my last employer, Master Tobias, so I spoke to him frequently. The ire toward Asher was still present at least two years ago when his name was mentioned."

"Do you know where I can find Byron?"

"He and Master Tobias often went to one of Lord Richard's clubs, Blue Heaven. It's in Whitechapel on Strype Street, I believe. I would begin there. And if I can be of further assistance—"

"Actually, I was hoping you'd say that. If you could call around, find out anything you can from your old employers, I would really appreciate it." I retrieve pen and paper from my purse to jot down the F.R.E.A.K.S. main number. "Here."

"Aren't you concerned Asher will hear about your search? That you're in Europe?"

"I'm counting on it." I smile again. "Thank you. You were always good to me, even when I didn't deserve it."

"Thank you for the picture. I'm glad you're doing so well," says Clifton.

"It's due in large part to you, you know." I stare at this hurting old man. The same one who picked me up from dance class, who nursed me through illness, who taught me how to keep house. I lean in and kiss his cheek. "Really. *Thank you*. When this is over, you should really come visit us. Meet the boys. I mean it. You're the closest thing to a mother I ever really had," I chuckle sadly. "You're family."

"Oh, you sweet girl," Clifton says, twisted hand caressing my cheek. "How dreadful for you."

I manage a sad smile. "Anyway," I say, rising. "It *really* was good seeing you. Truly. I'll see myself out."

"Anna…" he says just as I reach the living room threshold. I spin around. "He did love you, you know."

I shrug. "Just not enough." I grin again. "See you at Christmas. I won't take no for an answer." I blow him a kiss. "*Ciao.*"

When I step outside, Nathan's pacing nervously on the other side of the street. His shoulders slump with relief when he sets eyes on me. Without looking either way he charges toward me. "How'd it go? Are you okay?" he asks eagerly. "Do you—"

I peck my husband's fears away, then grin. "I'm great." I kiss him again. "Just great."

"He helped?"

I pull out the picture, presenting it to Nathan. "Even more than I'd hoped."

Nathan studies the photo with a smile. "My God. I never realized how much Joe looks like you." He gazes up, and says, amazed, "You were so young."

"I'm as shocked as you are, Mr. West," I say playfully. I lock arms with my husband and lead him down the street. "That's not all Clifton gave me."

"What else?"

"He gave me an excuse to show you Harrod's. *We* need new clothes."

"Why?"

"Because we have a club to infiltrate, husband of mine, and vampires don't wear khaki."

Being a suburban housewife with two small children doesn't afford me many opportunities to relive my wild youth. Getting dressed up in revealing clothes, staying out all night, drinking until I'd convinced myself I was having fun. Yeah, I have not missed it one iota. Give me lullabies, watching sitcoms with Nathan, and asleep by ten any day of the week. This girl's seen Paris and definitely prefers the farm, yet tonight, *bonjour Pairee*.

It's been a while since I had to dress up for anything but a potluck dinner, and I know tongues would wag if I showed up at Audrey's Tupperware parties wearing this ensemble. Compared to some of the outfits I used to don, this one is practically nunnish: a sequined deep blue dress with a plunging back but draped front, and mid-thigh skirt that clings to every contour. Ballet has kept me trim, but the years have collected their due. My stomach isn't as flat as it used to be and my breasts, especially without a bra, have lost their perk. Breastfeeding two babies tends to have that effect. As I appraise myself, I hold them up, then let them drop. Yeah, Mother Nature can be a real cow sometimes. With a frown, I step out of the bathroom.

"Holy…" Nathan's mouth plops open. "You are so keeping that dress."

"You don't look so bad yourself, Mr. West."

My husband cleans up quite nicely as well. He's dressed in black slacks, leather jacket, and V-neck gray sweater we bought to complete the ensemble. I'm surprised he agreed to a V-neck. The closer one gets, the more starkly his scars comes into focus. He was always self-conscious about them, and I never knew why.

Each of the seven lightning strikes he's endured through life left their marks. Their exquisite marks. It was as if God himself painted a tree on his flesh with bare fir-like branches on his back, his chest, his leg, and his arm. When I first caught sight of them a year after we met, purely by accident as Nathan went out of his way never to remove his shirt, I felt no revulsion. Instead, I had the strongest urge to trace the taut, beautiful, ravaged flesh. I do just that every chance I get now.

"Mrs. West," he says with a seductive smirk, walking toward me, "compared to you, I'm a troll in a cave." He wraps his arms around my waist, pulling me against him. "You are the foxiest bitch I have ever laid eyes on."

I drape my arms over his shoulders. "And you are quite the smooth talker there, Shaft."

"Worked for me earlier. Can't blame a guy for trying for round two." He kisses me deeply. "You do grow more beautiful with every passing day, you know."

"Really? You prefer me *now* more than when I was nineteen?"

"Annie, when you were nineteen, I didn't want to sleep with you, I wanted to feed you a damn sandwich." My eyes narrow. "Okay, maybe I wanted to sleep with you a *little*."

"And when I'm ninety and all wrinkles and sag?"

"I will be chasing you around our couch with my walker."

That sentiment earns him another kiss. "You really are the best thing that ever happened to me, you know that, right? I love you. I love you so much. So damn much. And thank you. Thank you for our children. Thank you for our life. And I am *so* sorry this is happening to you because of me."

He strokes my hair. "This isn't your fault, Annie. It's his and his alone. And we will find him, and we will make sure he never, *ever* comes near us again."

With another smile, and another peck, I extract myself from my husband's loving arms. "Well, he isn't in this room, and it took me almost an hour to do my hair and make-up, so the sooner we get this over with, the sooner we can come back here and you can ruin it."

"I love it when you take charge like this." He even growls.

Oh, I adore my goofball husband.

After a few touchups for us both—how do his glasses get so smudged?—we're out the door. Most days we're asleep by ten thirty, but a vampire party doesn't start until at least eleven. Thank goodness for the six-hour time difference. The entrance of Blue Heaven is tucked away down a narrow alley in Whitechapel, not one of the nicest neighborhoods in London. Prostitutes and drug dealers inhabit half the ancient streets. We almost walk right by the alley even though the cab drops us at the exact address. If not for the couple laughing and stumbling down said alley, I wouldn't think to venture down there. When we do we find a staircase down to a door. It isn't until I reach the bottom step I see the club's name painted on the brick wall. *Merde.* This place must cater more to vampires than humans. There are no innocent eyes keeping the monsters in check. Nathan and I exchange a worried glance before, with a sigh, I open the door.

The club is more of a lounge with low music playing through the medium-sized space, about the size of a boutique, filled with couches, a small bar and dance floor with blue lights providing the only illumination. The copper reek of blood instantly assails my nostrils. Oh, that takes me back, and not in a good way. We're barely through the door and I already want to leave. This is one step down Memory Lane I wish we could avoid. No such luck. As we hang our coats, I notice the vampires on the nearby couch are getting quite the naked workout. I suppress a shudder. I will not be sitting on anything in here without a Hazmat suit that is for certain. The bouncer, a bull of a man with muscles atop muscles and head shaved bald, stands in front of a velvet rope blocking the rest of the entrance.

"I'm sorry," he says with a Cockney accent, "this is a private club. Members only."

"Anna Asher. Official consort of elder vampire John Asher, and guest." The bouncer's eyes widen in shock. I cock an eyebrow. "Heard of me, have you? I'm honored."

"He isn't here."

"Good. I'm not here to meet him. Now, may we pass or do I need to remind you of the laws of consortship? My one guest, a former United States F.R.E.A.K.S. Special Agent and I have every right to enter any and all public spaces where vampiric activity occurs."

The bouncer's face contorts as if he's smelled dung, but he removes the rope. "Welcome to Blue Heaven, Consort Asher. Enjoy yourself."

"I will. Thank you," I say with a cheeky grin. Taking Nathan's hand, I walk straight to the bar. Thank goodness that worked. Plan B was to wait outside in the cold and flirt with vampires until one agreed to sponsor our entry.

"Welcome to Blue Heaven," says the buxom bartender. Even in the dim light, I can see the bruises on her neck and wrists from vampire bites. Guess she's on the drink menu too. "What can I get you?"

"Two ginger ales please," Nathan says.

"Oh, I love your accent," she says as she pours. "I adore Americans. Your first time in London?"

"I used to live here," I say. "We're actually supposed to meet an old friend of mine. George Byron. Is he here yet? We're a bit early."

"Oh, no, he's here," she says, nodding toward the far corner where one man straddles another, kissing and fondling with abandon. Compared to the couple one couch down, this is positively PG-13.

I look to Nathan. "What do you think? Tampa or Wyoming?"

Nathan considers it. He was in the F.R.E.A.K.S. longer than me. I defer to his strategic experience. "Wyoming. He is a poet, not some crazed werewolf. No need for the big guns."

"Then see you in a sec." After a wink to my partner, I saunter over to our distracted quarry. Oh, I am *very* much going to enjoy this. "Room for one more?"

The men call their tonsil hockey game to gaze up at my smirking face. Byron returns the gesture, but not his partner, who is fourteen if he's a day. Not a fan of competition, I guess. I meet Byron's eyes for a moment while licking my lips. Byron's grin grows when I nibble the lower one. "The more the merrier, I always say."

The boy climbs off the vampire, shooting me the glare of death, as I take his place on Byron's lap. It's probably as hygienic as the couch. The bastard's smile grows as I snake my arm around his neck. "Hi," I say huskily.

"Hello," he replies, sliding his hand up my thigh. "An American, are you?"

"Yes." I cross my legs. "And I came all the way here for *you*, your lordship."

"You're a Lord?" the boy asks.

"Don't you know you're in the presence of greatness, young one?" I ask the boy.

"Well, he shall learn that soon enough, pet," Byron says, placing his other hand on the boy's crotch. "You have me at a loss, though. Have we met before?"

"Now you've hurt my feelings, George," I say with a pout. "Going to have to make you pay for that. I'll give you a hint, though." I lean in and whisper, "You ruined David Bowie for me, asshole."

As I sit up, the vampire's eyes narrow on my steely face until it comes to him. "You."

"Me. All grown up. Surprise."

Nathan, who's been listening from a nearby table, takes his cue to pounce. "Mind if I join the party?" he asks, plopping beside the boy on the sofa.

"Lord Byron, my husband Nathan. Nathan, this is Lord Byron. You remember, I told you about him? The man who tried to fuck me when I was thirteen and drunk out of my mind? Sweetie, you used to be a Special Agent, isn't that considered attempted rape, even under vampiric law?"

"Alright, you have made your point," Byron says.

Nathan turns to the boy. "And how old are you, son? How much have you had to drink tonight?"

"Stop it," Byron orders. "Let him alone. Kevin, please go wait for me at the bar. I shall join you in a moment."

The boy eagerly obeys. Nathan scoots closer to Byron as I climb off his lap to flank the vampire as well. "Still like 'em fetal, I see," I say.

"What exactly do you want, Miss Asher and ... friend? Come to seek your revenge? I hear you are a vengeful little bitch when crossed. Is it my turn to be burned alive?"

"Tempting, but actually, I'm here to ask for your help."

The vampire harrumphs. "You are joking. Or mad. Why on earth would I help you?"

"Because we're two kindred, vengeful souls? I heard what Asher did to you. Beating you. Humiliating you. Blacklisting you from society. In a way, you're lucky. He butchered people for less than what you did to me."

"He could just be biding his time," Nathan adds.

"And goodness knows what he'll do if, when he and I do come face-to-face, I tell him about that time you tracked me down at boarding school. Oh, it was horrific how you all but forced yourself on poor, depressed, desperate, vulnerable me in retaliation for the two beatings he gave you."

"I can't imagine he'll take that news well," says Nathan.

"He would never believe that," Byron counters.

"'Oh, Asher,' I begin, voice cracking, "'I didn't tell you before because I didn't want you to think any less of me. I just missed you so, and he wouldn't take no for an answer. It ... it hurt so much.'" My expression becomes neutral. "And that's just off the top of my head. He hates your guts already, it wouldn't take much to push him over the edge. And if I've lost everything that matters in my life already, why the hell would I give a damn about yours?" I lean back. "Or you can help me find him before he finds us, and your name never escapes my lips again."

"Or perhaps I can provide further incentive," Nathan says. He holds up his hands and bursts of electricity crackle between them, lighting up the darkness. My husband, the human Tesla coil.

"Alright, stop. Both of you," Byron says. "Your threats grow tedious. Asher is no friend of mine. I shall tell you what I know, which is precious little. Though I personally did not lay eyes on him, I heard he was in London a few days past, but has since fled to destinations unknown. He and his shenanigans are the talk of Europe, though. Rumors swirl like snow in a cold winter's night. He's in Africa, Vienna, Berlin, Paris, all of the above. Pick a location. You know the bastard better than I."

"Well, who would know? Besides Richard, who were his friends? Who would he trust?" I ask. "Tobias?"

"Tobias is in Stockholm, and they were mere acquaintances," Byron says. "If anyone aided Asher, it would be Richard. They were mercenaries together through two wars. Brothers in arms until the bitter end. But though he would help your lover, I very much doubt he would help *you*."

"What about Alain?" Nathan asks. "Any idea where we can find him?"

"As a matter of fact, yes. He owns a theater and several boutiques in Monte Carlo. Has for decades."

"What's the name of the theater?" Nathan asks.

"*Le Theatre de Rosa*. He is even known to act in several productions. He is quite good."

"And he's in Monte Carlo now?" I ask.

"I assume so. I am not his keeper."

"And there's nothing, no one, anything else you can tell us?"

"Well, I did hear you are not the only comely female in search of Mr. Asher. Dear, psychotic Christine was asking similar questions a few months past, but I, like everyone else, assumed him dead. Still he must be quite the lover to have two such beautiful creatures chasing after him."

Nathan's jaw tightens. "Any idea where *she* is?"

"Most likely a pace behind Asher now. From what I have heard, she has always trailed after him like a lost puppy. Pathetic. But last I heard, she was in Vienna. Of course the majority of our lot are. The Vienna Opera Ball is in a few days. Even I am attending. Now, I have told you all I can. Please leave me be."

I glance at Nathan, who nods. We're done here. It isn't as much as I'd hoped, but it'll have to do. Nathan and I stand. "Good to see you again, Lord Byron."

"Yes, may it never happen again," he says with a smile.

I blow the bastard a kiss before following Nathan toward the door. "Well, that was easier—" The sight of the familiar tall man waiting with the bouncer by the exit cuts my premature statement short. "*Merde*."

"What?" Nathan asks.

Lord Richard never takes his eyes off me as he glides toward us, handsome face a mask of polite neutrality. It can't fool me. Oh, I really hoped to avoid him, at least until we had proof he aided and abetted Asher to use as leverage to get him to talk. We could be in real trouble here. Nathan senses it too as he moves shoulder-to-shoulder against me and cups his hand in case action is required.

"Consort Asher," Lord Richard says, holding out his hand.

Courtesy dictates I kiss his ring or curtsey to show my respect. Supplication is more accurate. Still, I perform my duty, with a smile even. "Your lordship."

"I had to see it with mine own eyes," Richard says. "Little Anna Asher, all grown. And still as beautiful as ever."

"You are too kind, sir. And may I present my husband, former Special Agent with the F.R.E.A.K.S. of America, Nathan West."

"Howdy," Nathan says with a scowl.

Richard barely gives him a glimpse. "Yes, I had heard you took a husband," he says with a fake smile.

"I'm sure you have," I say, matching his expression.

Both our pleasant masks drop in unison until only scowls remain. "You are either mad or idiotic for setting foot in my city, let alone my club, madam."

"No, just desperate."

"Quite a bit of that in the air," Richard says. "Shall we continue this little reunion in my office?" He glances at Nathan. "Alone."

"No way," says my husband.

"It's fine, Nathan," I say. We're really not in a position to negotiate. Since we're not here in an official law enforcement capacity, and I am forever bound by vampiric law, any act of aggression against a lord gives him the right to kill us here and now. "We're old friends, right?"

"Among other labels. Shall we?" he asks, gesturing toward the back.

"I'll be fine," I whisper as I squeeze Nathan's arm. I hope. Richard leads me past more copulating couples to his office. "Nice place you got here," I say with a grimace.

"Asher never took you to a club such as this?"

"No, he did," I say with displeasure. "I just choose to repress those memories, thank you very much."

Richard opens the office door to let me pass. "Ashamed?"

"More than words can express."

The office is a simple affair, just chairs, desk and window into one of the private rooms where a naked woman is pressed against the glass while a man rests on his knees, pleasuring her. Another reason Asher and Richard got along so well, they're both voyeurs. I learned this firsthand when we were invited on Richard's yacht during those last months. I was quite the showgirl that week.

Reading the distaste on my face, Richard shuts the blinds. "The years have made you prudish, Miss Asher."

"The years have made me learn the value of self-worth, Lord Richard," I say as I sit.

He lowers himself into the chair behind the desk. "He never forced you."

"No. Not until that last time. Or did your best friend neglect to tell you about *that*?"

"Is that why you burnt him alive?"

"He's lucky I didn't castrate him too."

"But you did," he counters, "in all but body. And now you have come to finish the job?"

"I didn't start this, Richard. *He* sent an assassin into my house. *He* tried to kill my husband. *He* attempted to harm my children. *My children*."

"And now the goddess Nemesis has come to claim her vengeance," he says with a sneer.

"This isn't vengeance. It never was. I just want him to leave me alone. Nothing more, nothing less. What I did ten years ago was an act of self-preservation. He wouldn't listen to reason then, maybe he will now. I promise I will at least try to reach that reasonable part of him again, unlike the others searching for him. I owe him that. But as his friend, you should know he has been marked for execution. He attacked two former Federal agents and their family, not to mention nobody has forgotten the events in Goodnight. There is not a single law enforcement officer in this world who does not know his face or what he is capable of. *I* might be the only person searching for him who *would* hesitate to cut off his head. And anything you tell me will not leave these four walls. My husband and I are here alone. No official law enforcement affiliation. Your name will never leave my lips, I swear on my children. And if I reneg, well, I have no doubt you can kill my whole family with one phone call. But it won't come to that. So I'm asking, no … I'm *begging*. I just … need to find him. Please."

Richard leans back in his chair, studying me with his cold brown eyes. "Still as determined as you are beautiful." He shakes his head. "I did warn you both about this, if you recall. He, especially, should have known better, taking a lover so young. There are so few happy endings in our world, why compound the odds by being with one who has not settled into their own skin yet? But he always was a fool for love." He pauses. "Of course I am the bigger fool for enabling him for so long. It has caused me naught but misery. I warned that man to leave well enough alone. To stay dead. That the world would forget about him and move on but …"

He shakes his head again. "He came to me still raw and frail from your assault, seeking asylum. A quiet place to recover, to heal, to hide. Against my better judgment, I granted the request on the condition he retire from society until I deemed it safe. I even gave him use of my manor house on the isle of Jersey. A few trusted friends could visit whilst I did, but regardless it was exile. And as we both know, Asher does not manage peace and solitude well. You left a hole in him, Anna," says Richard with a hard edge. "He came to me a shell and as the years wore on, what grew in that vacuum, no storybook monster was ever so frightening. Anger, depression, moodiness, nothing else remained inside him. He starved himself, refused to leave his coffin for a fortnight, even began having whole conversations with himself. Finally, a few months past, he began talking of seeking out the sun. Ending his life.

"He told me about the same urge twenty years past, and that *you* saved him. How it was driving him mad not knowing your fate. Your not knowing how much he still loved you. How simply hearing your voice and the happiness within it could alleviate some of his torment. I took my friend at his word." Richard pauses. "So I gave him your telephone number."

"How did you know where I was?" I ask, my pulse quickening.

"You are not the only one with powerful friends in this world, Mrs. Anna West of Garland, Texas, former agent of the F.R.E.A.K.S," he says with an edge. "I kept informed for this very contingency. But I only gave him the telephone number and warned him it could go no further. He could hear your voice and nothing more. He must remain dead. I thought that would be enough for him. I assumed it was because the next time I saw him, he was up and about, even inquiring if he could renovate the manor. Brighten it up. Modernize it. He was more alive than I had seen him in a decade. I had no inkling of what he was planning, that he would have so little respect for me and all I have done for him that he would stir up the maelstrom I now find myself pulled into. Ungrateful bastard."

"What happened?"

"Four nights ago he arrived at this very club, no warning given, once again in need of my assistance. He revealed the entire debacle: hiring Fourtnier to assassinate your husband, to abduct you and the children so you could reside with him in *my* Jersey home, but that the plane had never left Texas. That something had gone wrong."

"So what did you do?"

"The only thing I could: I told him to run far and run fast from my territory. That he was no longer welcome, and that I would aid him no further. He failed in the one thing I had asked, to not draw attention to himself. He could clean up his own bloody mess."

"So, where did he go?"

"There I cannot help you. Plausible deniability, Mrs. West. I remained ignorant, so I could answer with all honesty I have no inkling where he has gone to ground. Nor do I care to know."

"Could he be back in Jersey?" I ask.

"No. He was not even allowed to return for his clothing. I made it clear, under no uncertain terms, if he failed to comply with my edict, I would take his head myself. And that, Mrs. West, is the extent of what I know of our mutual acquaintance. If I had to venture a guess, he is still in Europe, or he will return to the continent as soon as word reaches him *you* are here."

"Well, I'm not waiting around for that to happen. As they say in football, the best defense is a good offense."

"How quaint."

"Well, if you don't know where he went, do you know anyone who might? Others who may be in a charitable mood?"

"No. With INTERPOL and every supernatural police squad on high alert, no one would be so foolish to involve themselves in this quagmire. He is well and truly on his own now."

Merde.

I rise from the chair. "Well, please contact the Rogue's Gallery if you hear of anything else. You may earn some Brownie points with them. Can't hurt, right? I'll back you with whatever you tell them, on that you have my word." I nod. "Thanks for all your help."

"I did not do it for you." Richard pauses to scowl at me. "You destroyed him, you know. You took a strong, powerful, fierce warrior and ground him into dust."

"I didn't destroy him, Richard. I meant what I said when I signed that contract. I trusted him. I wanted nothing more than to be by his side until the sun burnt out. I loved him with everything I had. It just wasn't enough for him. *I* wasn't enough. So I didn't destroy him, I simply refused to let him destroy *me*. If that makes me selfish then … we both know who I learned that from, huh?" I manage a smile. "We'll be gone by tomorrow and you will never see me again. That I promise as well. Goodnight, your Lordship." I turn and walk away. "As always, it was an education."

Nathan waits right beside the door. We both let out long sighs as I shut the door. When I stepped in there, I really did put my chances at leaving without bloodshed at 70/30. Nathan did as well, as his bony shoulders finally relaxed in time to our sighs.

"Are you okay?" he asks.

"I'll be better when we get out of here."

"Amen to that." My husband takes my hand and leads me down the hall. The scowling bouncer removes the rope to let us pass, and Nathan helps me with my coat. I blow a kiss to the glaring Byron before stepping out into the cold night. It is still far chillier in there than out here.

"So, does he know where Asher is?"

"I don't think so. He seemed … done. Everyone has their limit, and Asher sure does know how to push people to theirs."

"Then what's our next move? Monte Carlo?"

"Yep. By way of Jersey."

"Jersey?"

"It's a little island between here and France. It's where Asher's been living. If living is the right word."

"You think he's there now?"

"Richard says no, but Asher left in a hurry. It's worth a look."

"Then Jersey it is. I do love the beach. You want to leave tonight?" Nathan asks.

I wrap my arm around my husband's waist as he drapes his over my shoulders. "What I want is to call our boys to wish them a good night, then have my sexy husband ruin my hair and makeup. At least twice."

"You read my mind, Mrs. West." He pecks my lips and we continue to stroll the streets of London. Out of nowhere, Nathan bursts into giggles.

"What?"

"N-nothing," he laughs. "It-It-It's just … I just met Lord Fucking Byron." He shakes his head. "Oh, Annie. Boring you ain't."

THE ISLE OF JERSEY

IT DOESN'T TAKE MUCH investigating to locate Richard's manor. Everyone on the isle and their mother apparently knows about the strange, agoraphobic tenant at the cliff side Lionheart Manor. Some have even claimed to have seen the thin, pale man creeping about town or strolling the beaches. At night, but no one has the memory of actually meeting or saying a single word to him. And that's just what we learn from a resident on the ferry ride to the island. The lovely woman even invites us to tea with her and her husband. Close communities, gotta love them.

The same invitation is extended by the couple at the pub where we enjoy lunch. They were full of gossip about the so-called Phantom of Lionheart. He was a former solider wracked with PTSD, he was a burn victim who didn't want others to see his scars, he was an exiled prince with a price on his head. Strangely, all fairly accurate. Per the bartender not even the cleaning staff who went into the manor once a week had met the phantom. They received their orders from the caretaker Philip and his wife Ellen, even during the massive renovation. It was still the talk of the town, the fact the mysterious recluse finally allowed strangers into his house to prepare it for his long-lost wife and children to join him, or that was the most widely spread rumor. How Nathan and I managed to maintain our smiles through that story is beyond me.

We need to catch the five p.m. ferry to reach our train in Normandy, which should then reach Monte Carlo by midnight, so there's no time for sightseeing on the picturesque island. Though it's in the high forties and chilly, the sun has deigned to make a rare appearance today. The blue/green water twinkles in the light as it crashes against the clean, sandy beach. After renting a car for the day, and getting directions from the clerk, we drive along the narrow streets lined with interconnected brick shops and over hilly green glens as we venture across the small isle. As far as places to be exiled goes, Jersey would be top of my list.

Our drive ends at the twenty-foot tall wrought-iron fence, chained and padlocked, with only the top of the dark brick manor visible from this far away. "What you think?" Nathan asks from the passenger seat.

"Well, we're not exactly invited guests. Pop the lock and sneak in?"

"Breaking and entering. Mama would be so proud. Let's do it, Bonnie."

I reverse the car back up the driveway to park on the street. "You got it, Clyde."

Car concealed from anyone inside the compound, we sprint back to the fence and I use a spell on the lock. Easy as pie. Nathan and I hustle along the iron until we can use the tree line for cover to reach the manor. It's much smaller than I envisioned, only about half the size of the F.R.E.A.K.S. mansion, yet far more imposing. Dark gray brick with ivy snaking up the mortar, and even strangling some of the gargoyles on the corners of the flat roof. The few windows are blacked out either from heavy drapes or shutters. I'd hate to see what this place looked like before he began renovating. Norman Bates wouldn't even feel at home here. But what really damn near knocks the air from my lungs is the literally shiny, glittery new playset next to the stone veranda. Two swings, monkey bars, see-saw, even a fake castle with a slide. I very much doubt Richard installed that.

"Jesus Christ," Nathan says as he stares at this happy monstrosity.

"Come on," I say, taking his hand.

We enter the house of horrors through the magically unlocked glass veranda doors. Just stepping inside brings chills, as if he's imprinted on the walls, watching us. Or that could be the mirrors along the wall with a *barre* lining the same wall. It takes my overwrought mind a moment but a horrible realization finally breaks through. The bastard recreated my dance studio from our house in Holland. The same grand piano with green padded bench, a stereo with a CD stand filled with classical music, and a gray wingback chair in the corner. He'd sit in that exact chair and watch me, sometimes for hours, or would accompany me on the piano as I glided around the room, always completing my performance with a deep kiss to my audience of one. How could something that made me so joyous then turn my stomach now?

"Wow," says Nathan.

I don't linger. If I do I'll give in to my intense desire to throw the boom box against the mirrors, and I probably won't stop until I've earned a thousand years of bad luck. We're here to search for a Rolodex or any paperwork that may generate a lead: deeds, bills, treasure map, anything to track him down. The living room is far less disturbing, save for an entire wall of VHS movies and the copy of *Moby Dick* left open on the ottoman. It's as if he's just popped out to run errands. There's nothing here of interest except for the dozen or so pictures of me in frames scattered around. Me at nine working on a puzzle in our flat in Cairo. In Paris at the *barre*. In Galway as I helped him make dinner. A snapshot of us kissing I took myself when I was sixteen. At least he kept the naked ones hidden.

The library proves more fruitful. There isn't a treasure map in his desk, but I do locate a spate of invoices for the renovation and checkbook with the name Jay Asher printed on the checks. He has at least one credit card in that name as well. The phone bill only has numbers for England but I stuff it in my bag with the rest. We're going to have to call Dr. Black to have them chase the financials and alias.

We go room-to-room on the first floor, finding nothing else of interest but antiques and a ridiculous amount of photos of me, before venturing up the dark, creaky stairs. The first few bedrooms haven't been touched in decades. Most of the furniture is covered in white sheets to protect from the dust. Nothing, nothing and more nothing. What we have is good, useful, but there has to be…

I open the fourth door and gasp.

Oh, Asher.

It's as if a toy store exploded. Trucks, train set, a Matchbox car track, football paraphernalia, video games galore, everything two little boys could dream of to pass the time in their prison cell. I'm stunned into silence, Nathan too, because we check the two closed doors attached to the sitting room without a word: just a bathroom with Mickey Mouse towels and a bedroom filled to the brim with more toys and twin beds, one with "Max" and the other with "Joe" written above them. My stomach is so knotted that stranglehold is the only reason I'm not vomiting all over this abomination. I rush back to the hallway with Nathan a step behind.

Two more rooms. Just two more. It can't get much worse, right?

Nothing behind door number five. But number six … the four poster bed with blush colored canopy, my favorite color, is fit for a king. And if I didn't want to sleep there, then there was always the matching pink coffin with space for another judging from the empty stand beside that pink monstrosity. "What the hell?" asks Nathan.

"He was going to smuggle us here in caskets, remember? Mine would just be more a permanent sleeping arrangement."

After a pause, Nathan whispers with disbelief, "He was going to turn you."

"Probably. What better way to keep me close?"

"That sadistic fucking …"

"It doesn't matter now. Come on, let's get this over with. Go check the bathroom, I'll take the closet."

It seems the photos and furniture weren't the only remnants of our nights in Holland he smuggled in during exile. My clothes from over a decade ago take up half the closet with his right beside. The scent of his aftershave and cologne knocks me back a dozen years. One whiff and I'm back in our living room curled up in his lap with my head on his shoulder listening to Puccini and inhaling his aroma like a coke addict. Heaven. Then. Stomach churning now. I shut the wardrobe.

"Nothing in the bathroom," says Nathan as he steps out, "except some fancy shampoo and a bidet."

"Nor here. I'll check the dressers, you get the nightstand."

Waste of time on my part. Nothing in the dresser save for a few pieces of lingerie with the tags still attached. Ugh.

"Hey, Annie. Check this out." Nathan holds up a leather-bound notebook and envelope from the nightstand as he crosses the room toward me. "Found this. The return address is from Garland. Vinnie Spano P.I. Agency."

Inside the envelope are surveillance photos. Over a hundred shots, most taken with a telephoto lens, within the space of the week judging from the variety of clothes. Me picking up the boys from the bus stop. Nathan and I out to dinner. Another dozen of me and the boys around town. Me with my friend Audrey chatting on the sidewalk. Nathan at his desk at work. The boys, my mother-in-law, and Nathan when he collected them from her house two weeks ago. Me at the dance studio teaching. Along with the photos is a log of all our activity that week. School pickups, duration of shopping trips with what I purchased, Nathan's appointments with locations, addresses of the boys' friends. A damn roadmap of our lives.

"Jesus wept," Nathan mutters. "How did we not know?" I put everything back into the envelope, shoving it into my purse. "How did I ... how—"

I touch his cheek. "Hey. If this isn't my fault, it sure as hell isn't yours."

"I am the man, Annie. I am supposed to protect my family, and I let this … psycho fuck sneak back into our lives, our *home*. He's been stalking us for almost two months. I was a goddamn Federal Agent for four years. I should have sensed this. I should have … I should have …" He shakes his head.

"There is nothing you could have done, Nathan. There was no way to prepare for this. To foresee it. And you're here now. *We're* here now. We will find him, and we will make sure he *never* comes near us again."

"You're damn straight he ain't gonna bother us again, because I'm gonna kill him," spews my husband through gritted teeth. "I swear to God or whoever or whatever is listening, I am going to rip out his black, rotten, corroded heart and make the bastard choke on it."

"Hey. Hey," I say, pulling the man I love into my arms. He hugs me tight. "*I'm* supposed to be the dark dour one. You're Mr. Sunshine, remember? Don't you *dare* let him take that away from you, okay? Not for a second. We'll find him." I kiss his neck. "I prom—"

The creak of wood in the hallway cuts my sentiment short. Nathan drops his arms and steps away, hands at the ready to fry any oncoming monster. I pull out the silver nitrate Mace, though with the shutters open I doubt there's a vampire coming toward us. Stuff still stings though. There's another creak. "Who's there?" a man shouts from down the hall. "I have a gun!"

Merde. Nathan glances at me, and I shrug. "Woodbury?" I whisper.

"Lodi."

I nod. "Please don't shoot," I call as I slip the Mace back into my coat. "We're friends of Richard's! We're not armed!"

The barrel of the rifle rounds the corner first and we hold up our hands, palms out in Nathan's case. Saved our bacon in Lodi with that witch, though probably not needed today. An elderly man with wild gray hair in a brown wool jumper and equally old, short woman literally cowering behind him step into view. "Who are you?"

"A-Anna. Asher. I'm Anna Asher. You must be Philip and Ellen. Pleased to finally meet you both."

Both sets of eyes narrow on my face before growing wide once more. "It is you," the man says, lowering the shotgun.

"Who's he?" Ellen asks.

"My valet."

"Are the children here too?" the woman asks.

My jaw tightens, as does Nathan's, but I somehow shut my anger away. We need them on our side. "No. Just us. For now. May we please lower our arms?" The man nods, and we all relax as best we can. "We're sorry for startling you. Richard didn't phone to tell you that we were coming?"

"No," says the woman. "And surely he told you Asher is no longer in residence."

"No, he did, but Richard said we could come have a look around anyway," I lie.

"He did?" Ellen asks.

"How else would we find this place if his lordship hadn't told Miss Asher about it?" Nathan counters.

"It's very important we locate Asher before anyone else does," I say. "There is a literal bounty on his head, and he has many,

many enemies. We don't want him harmed. If there's anything you can tell us, anything at all. You were the two closest to him all these years."

"We weren't close," Philip says with a huff. "We got his blood, he told us what to do about the house, and we did it. Nothing more. He weren't exactly Mr. Friendly."

"Until a few months ago he moped about, just reading or watching the telly when he got up at all," Ellen adds. "At least until a month ago when he told us you and the boys were coming to live here."

"You mean when he kidnapped them all," Nathan snaps.

"What? We don't know nothing about no kidnapping," Philip says. "All he told us was you and the two boys were going to live here, that we needed to fix this place up for you, and to start searching for a governess for the children. Mr. Asher left five days ago saying you and the children were coming back with him, but the night after that Lord Richard phoned and told us to close up the house. That Mr. Asher weren't allowed on the property no more, and if he did show up, we were to phone his lordship immediately. He hasn't come back though."

"He hasn't called or sent for his clothes?" I ask.

"No," says Ellen.

"What about his friends? Does he have an address book?" Nathan asks impatiently. "There has to be *someone* through the years who came to visit or someone he mentioned who he could turn to." The couple shake their heads no. Nathan steps toward them, his scowl deepening. "Come on! Think!"

Philip begins to raise the shotgun again, but I grab Nathan, receiving another electrical shock but still holding on. "Stop it," I warn. He ceases moving but still fumes, breathing heavily in and out through his nose like a bull. In ten years of knowing him, through over fifty cases with the F.R.E.A.K.S. exposed to the worst humanity has to offer, I've never seen him this enraged. "I'm so sorry for my friend. This has been most upsetting for us all."

"We can't tell you nothing else," Philip grumbles, "because we don't know nothing else. The only people who came here came with his lordship, and Mr. Asher barely spoke to them."

"Except for that one girl," Ellen reminds her husband.

"A girl? Brown hair and eyes? About sixteen? Pillowy lips?" I prompt.

"That's her," says Ellen. "She just showed up at the gate about six months ago. Mr. Asher had us turn her away. She came back every night for over a fortnight, but he refused to see her. That last night she got so upset, she glamoured Philip to invite her in, then smashed all of the photo frames in the house. She was about to burn the photos in the fireplace when Mr. Asher finally rose from his coffin and literally tossed her out on her bum without a word said."

Definitely Christine. "Has she come back since? Did she mention where she's been living?" I ask.

"We didn't exactly have a conversation," Philip says.

"She must have mentioned—" Nathan says, taking another looming step.

"You calling me a liar, sir? I said she didn't," Philip snaps, moving his finger to the trigger. "And that's all we know. Now, get out before I shoot you. You're trespassing."

Merde. Somehow I manage a gracious grin. "Well, thank you for your assistance. If Asher does return, or you think of anything else to help us find him, please call us." I pull out a piece of paper to scribble down the F.R.E.A.K.S. main number. Philip reluctantly snatches it from me.

"Thank you. We don't want to trouble you further. We'll see ourselves out. Come on, Nathan." I take his hand and lead him from the room, down the hall, and out the front door into the bright, blue day.

"They know more than they're letting on," Nathan says as we continue up the gravel driveway.

"Most likely."

Nathan stops dead. "Then what the fuck are we doing? We should march back in there and—"

"And what? Torture the elderly couple? Make an enemy of one of the most powerful vampires on Earth who happens to know our home address?"

"He helped Asher! He hid that … murdering, rapist bastard for years! He led that psycho right to our doorstep! And those people," Nathan shouts, pointing at the house, "were gonna stand by while he kidnapped my children and turned my wife into a walking corpse! I don't just wanna torture them, Annie, I want to fucking kill them! I—"

I grab my husband by the coat, receiving a few hundred tingling volts through me, but still yank him against me into a firm hug. His heart thumps wildly, so fast I worry he's about to have a heart attack. At first he stands as rigid as granite, but I hold on. After a few seconds, hesitantly he raises his arms, lowers them again then gives in to me, embracing me as desperately as I do him. This man is my strength, my light, and if he loses that, his beautiful sparking essence, we'll both be adrift forever. "That house…" he says, voice quaking.

"I know."

"He's insane."

"I know."

"I'm gonna kill him, Annie. He has to die."

I squeeze the love of my life tighter. "I know."

We stand in the middle of the driveway, in the monster's beautiful prison, clutching one another until all his rage, all his hate dissipates, and my Nathan returns to me. Damn you, Asher. Damn you for pushing this wonderful man into your darkness for even a moment. And damn me for the same sin. Never again.

"I love you," I whisper. "I love you *so* much."

"Not half as much as I love you," Nathan whispers back. "I won't let him touch you again. Never again. I promise."

Took the words right out of my mouth.

MONTE CARLO, MONACO

JERSEY WAS ALMOST WORTH all the emotional *Sturm und Drang*. Almost. While waiting for the ferry, we phoned Kansas with the leads from the financials. Dr. Black promised they'd interview the private investigator Asher hired along with tracing the bank account and credit card number we uncovered. The boys were gone, but when we reached our hotel in Monte Carlo several hours later, they deigned to give us five minutes before Agent Lau and Tara took them roller skating again. Max even perked up when he told me about the Big Bird skates he always selects, though he may choose Scrooge McDuck today.

As I listened to their chipper voices chat about watching *Doctor Who* episodes with Oliver and playing magic with Martina, my body physically ached for them as if I were going through drug withdrawal. I would have sold my soul in that moment to be able to scoop them into my arms and inhale their scent, that strange mix of shampoo and strawberry fruit rollups they adore. Before this we've never spent but one night apart. If they're missing us or upset in any way, it does not come through over the telephone. Really, thank the universe for that fact and the F.R.E.A.K.S., even Oliver.

After we hang up, I need to take a few minutes alone in the bathroom. I can barely shut the door before my hands begin to tremble. By the time I flop on the toilet, I can barely draw breath. One conversation with my children and what little vigor I still possess leaves me. I can't let Nathan see me like this. I can't. I've been using all my willpower to retain my strong veneer for him. In our decade together I have never seen him this grim. Not at crime scenes, not when his development company faced a lawsuit, not even when his stepfather was diagnosed with melanoma. He's barely spoken, barely released my hand since we left that house of horrors. He even wanted to follow me into the ladies' toilet at the train station "just in case." My husband, who apologizes when someone bumps into *him,* snapped at the porter when Nathan accidently made him drop a suitcase. I've been so focused on him I haven't allowed myself permission to process my own emotions. They've been skating on the fringes of consciousness, but I walled all the fear and horror away until this moment.

With the faucet running and holding a towel up to my face to mask the sound, I burst into tears, even folding in on myself, hugging my knees. This is madness, absolute utter madness. Asher, oh Asher, what have you become? Was Richard right? Did I do this to you? How could you do this to *me?* He was going to kill me. Turn me into his undead bride. Use my children to keep me in line. Imprison us all in that mausoleum. Wipe Nathan from our memories after killing his flesh as well. Evil. And sad. *So* sad.

Yes, fool that I am, a tiny part of me sobs for him as well. I cannot help it. Locked away from the world he so loved, haunting that house, that *prison,* with no human contact. His own personal hell with no escape in sight. Perhaps he really did go mad. I always believed I'd be the one who couldn't live without him, that if we separated I'd wither and die. Lose my mind. I almost did in Rome. If he's experienced half the misery I did in those two years, I wouldn't wish that on any soul, even his.

What am I going to do when I come face-to-face with him? *If* I do. Alain's the end of the line. Asher's smart enough to cease using the Jay Asher alias and bank account tied to his crimes. We didn't talk much about his finances, but I got the sense he had multiple accounts under multiple names for this very contingency. When I joined the F.R.E.A.K.S. I told them a few I recalled which, at least during my tenure there, never had any activity. So Alain is our last, best hope. Our Hail Mary Pass as Nathan would call it. We're out of moves. Out of options. Out of hope. I just want to go home. To hug my children, sleep in my own bed, chat with Audrey over coffee, laugh at Urkel with Nathan, teach my ballet classes. Get my damn life back. I worked so hard for it. How dare he try to take it from me?

Nathan knocks on the door, drawing me from my misery. "Annie?"

"Be right out." I rise from the toilet. "*Keep it together, West,*" I whisper to myself.

Oh. I wipe the tears, splash cold water on my face, and smile in the mirror for practice. Be strong, Anna. You are descended from Vikings, men and women who conquered the world. Bloody well act like it. When I step out of the bathroom, Nathan anxiously waits only a foot from the door. "Are you okay?"

"I'm fine. Did you find the theater?"

"It's only about a kilometer away. Not only did the concierge give me directions, but he actually knows Alain. He goes by the last name DePlass."

"Good work, husband of mine."

"Thank you, wife. So, how do we play *this* one?"

"I should go alone. He—"

"Hell no."

"He—"

"*No*," Nathan snaps as all the lights in the room flicker. I can practically see the electricity crackling around his aura. "Together or nothing."

"What? Don't I look like a girl who can take care of herself?" I ask with a seductive grin. He doesn't take the bait, if anything the scowl deepens. "Your caveman is showing, husband."

"Together or nothing."

I sigh. I'm too exhausted to fight. Plus I don't think we have enough money left after this endeavor to replace all the electronics in the hotel if he loses control. "Fine. But remember: we need him. No anger, no frustration, no snapping, no electrocuting. Treat him as you would a client."

"His ass will be thoroughly kissed by the end of the night."

"That's the Nathan West I know and love." I peck his lips. "Come on. It's a beautiful night to take in the theater."

The door to *Le Theatre de Rosa* is locked when we arrive but a quick spell sorts that out. Alain has done well for himself. The theater easily seats five hundred with red velvet cushioned seats, matching red carpet, arching ceilings with fading murals, and a grand crystal chandelier hanging above. As actors rehearse on the immense stage, my old friend observes in the back, I assume jotting down notes of critique. He's so immersed in the drama onstage he fails to notice our approach.

"Looks like a hit to me," I say in French. We've only ever spoken in that language, I don't know if he even knows English. "*A Streetcar Named Desire* by Tennessee Williams if memory serves."

Alain spins around in his seat. If he's shocked by my presence, it fails to register on his pretty face. Nothing does. His expression is deceptively neutral as I slide into the seat beside him. Nathan remains standing. "I certainly hope so. We could use a hit. No one desires to experience live theater anymore, it is all film and television now. Such a shame. It is enough for one to become a Luddite." He pauses to gaze behind me. "Is this the husband? Not at all what I imagined. He seems quite plebian."

"Is he talking about me?" Nathan asks.

"Yes, I am," says Alain in English.

"Nathan West, Alain. Alain, my husband Nathan West."

"*Enchanté*," Alain says.

"What were you saying about me?" Nathan asks again.

"Simply that you are quite … tall," he replies with a gracious grin. "Please sit, Mr. West. Those long limbs of yours must be weary after your long journey from Londontown." Alain pauses to return his attention my way. "I was wondering if you would grace me with an appearance during your quest across Europe."

"You heard about us?" Nathan asks, taking the seat beside me.

"Of course. It is all anyone is gossiping about. Last night alone I received three calls, one from the Lord of London himself, regarding the reappearance of the infamous Anna Asher."

"What are they saying?" I ask.

"Simply that Asher wished to reclaim his consort, and when the bid failed, he once again had to go to ground because said consort and her electrifying husband wished to claim his head."

"Yeah, because this is all her fault," Nathan spits out.

I touch my husband's hand to calm him. "He hired Didier to kill Nathan and kidnap me and my children," I clarify.

"Yes, I heard that version as well," says Alain.

"Suppose all *that* was her fault too," Nathan says.

"Nathan …" I warn.

"It is fine, Mrs. West," Alain says. "I take no offense. A husband should defend his wife's honor against malicious gossip. You do have precious few friends left in our world. To us you are merely the strumpet who attempted to burn her lover alive, then skipped off into the sunset without a glimpse back. Not to mention your turncoat antics against my poor youngling Oliver. I have heard he still remains a slave to your government to this very day. You betrayed two beloved members of our community, and we all have mighty long memories, Mrs. West."

"They deserved everything they got," Nathan says.

"Most would disagree with you," Alain counters.

"Then they're soulless, fucking morons," Nathan says with a smug smile.

So much for ass kissing. Though his apathetic expression doesn't sour, I can sense Alain is losing his patience with my better half, mostly because *I* am losing my patience with him. "Nathan, can you please give us a minute alone?"

"No, I—"

"Go sit in the back and watch the rehearsal. *Now.*" The combination of my scowl and hard tone works on males of all ages it seems. Nathan glares at us both but obeys, retreating to the back row where he can keep an eye on me. "He's not usually like this. All the traveling, all the stress..." I shake my head. "We went to Asher's house. It was... he was..." I roll my eyes and scoff. "I think Asher's lost his mind. Truly. He really believes he can make everything right. Just as it was. He'd lock me away, and I'd magically fall in love with him again. That all he's done to me, that I've done to him could just be washed away, and I'd rush into his open arms forever and all eternity."

"He always was a hopeless romantic," Alain says.

"There is a difference between hopeless romanticism and a plain old lost cause," I point out. "I abandoned him. Hell, I tried to kill him. I married someone else. And he wants to play happy families? He should hate me."

"Do you hate him?" Alain counters with a raised eyebrow. "If the rumors are true, it would be justified."

I consider the question, the same one I've been asking myself for a decade. "If you asked me that a week ago, it would have been an unequivocal 'No.' I made my peace with him, with my past, years ago. But I hate him for what he's done to my family."

"That is not the same thing, and you know it," Alain counters. "The line between love and hate can be wafer thin more often than we care to admit, especially when dealing with that man. I speak from experience. You wish never to lay eyes on him again, while at the same time find yourself inexplicably drawn to him. His love is a drug that never leaves your system. You desire it more than blood, yet loathe yourself and him for that weakness."

I sit staring at the actors playing at tormented love onstage for a few seconds. "I have an *amazing* life. I'm married to my best friend, a man who supports me in every way fathomable. I have two beautiful, healthy, smart, sweet boys. I'm active and respected in my community. Even my in-laws love me, and I love them. I have everything I have always wanted. I'm *happy*. Really.

"But sometimes...I think about the years with him, and there's a flash, just a moment, when I would sell my soul to be back there. And in those moments I missed him like a suffocating person misses air. I *craved* him."

"I am aware of the feeling."

"What we had—massively fucked up though it was—it was real. At least on my end. When it was good, there was nothing better in this whole universe to me. There were times when I was afraid I'd burst into tears because I couldn't contain my joy. Where I would have been content to die because the moment was so perfect, I thought nothing could ever top it. But he always found a way, another perfect moment better than the last. He was my *everything*. Nothing else compared to one of his caresses. Nothing else mattered. Not even myself. And I miss that a little. I do. Life was simple. And despite everything, I missed him. I missed our conversations. I missed holding his hand in the movie theater. I missed watching him cook. I missed the feel of him against me. No matter what, I think I always will. And I forgive him. I do. He did me a lot of wrong but ... he made me who I am today. He loved me as much as anyone could.

"He still must or he wouldn't have gone to all this trouble," I chuckle sadly. "Maybe he believes he's saving me. That I've settled, I don't know. All I do know is when that moment is up, when Nathan cracks a joke or Max smiles at me, it is just as real. More so because it's equal. Consistent. There's no grand all-consuming passion, no pendulum swinging between love and hate, no compromise of morals or my sense of self. I am Anna West, wife of Nathan, and mother of Joe and Max, which is *more* than enough for me. Anna Asher's dead. I buried her a decade ago, and no matter how hard he may try, he cannot resurrect her. If Asher's unable to understand that, accept *me*, then ... he's a threat. And I'll do what needs to be done. Just as I did ten years ago. There's no vengeance, no retribution in this, just pure survival."

"And you require my assistance."

"I have no right to ask, I am aware of that. You've done so much for me already. You looked out for me when no one else really was. And I didn't appreciate it then, not really, but ... I do now. More than you can ever know. If there is any good to come out of this situation, any at all, it is that I can correct the fact I never really thanked you. I always regretted that. So truly, from the bottom of my heart, thank you," I say, voice quivering. "You were right. Everything you told me was right, I was just too young, too self-involved, too in love to recognize it. It took me some time, but I finally did, in large part to you. You helped save my life, Alain. You did. So again, thank you. *Thank you.*"

He stares ahead too, deafeningly, oppressively silent but after a few seconds says, "I wish I could tell you my actions were solely charitable or even partially." He shakes his head. "I do not know how much you are aware of my tumultuous history with our

Asher. More downs than ups, but in our way I suppose we did love one another. Perhaps even respected each other. We have committed many atrocities against one another but always found a way to move past. Until, like you, he went a step too far. He turned my Oliver against me. One night a century of petty resentments built up, exploding out with my sire not only fanning the flames but siding with Oliver at every turn, simply because I refused to stay in the Americas with them. Because I chose to leave him, my sire, youngling and I all but killed one another. I have not seen nor spoken to my youngling, my blood since. To this very day he loathes me. So when I saw an opportunity to sow the seeds of discord with the person my sire adored, to draw even a sliver of blood in that bastard, I leapt at the chance. I did not care one whit what it would mean for you. Nor did your well-being factor into my decision to inform Christine that Asher would be in attendance at the opera ball."

"*You* brought her there?"

"It *was* inevitable she would resurface, I simply hastened the reunion. I did wish to give you a fighting chance though, hence my warning. But I am sorry. Truly."

The knot in my gut twisted with this revelation. I suppress the urge to slap his face, instead balling my hand into a fist. *Calm down, Anna. We still need him.* "Then make it up to me now. Rectify some of the turmoil you've caused. Help me. You know him better than almost anyone. You have the same circle of friends. You can ask around, put out feelers. You said it yourself, there have been rumors. You feed them to us; we chase them down."

"And why would I do that? What would I receive out of this interaction besides the label of turncoat?"

"The knowledge of a good deed done?"

Alain scoffs.

"Okay, how about a pound of flesh? You and I both know I am the only one who'll be able to get close enough to extract it? Hell, you want one? I promise you three. Plus I'll even put in a good word with Oliver for you. When this is all over, on my children's lives, I will sing your praises to him. Tell him you only agreed to help me so you could avenge Asher's crimes against him. Maybe that will help begin healing your relationship, I don't know, but it's a chance you should take. What's more important than our family, Alain? So if not for me, and not for yourself, do it for your youngling. Show him you're willing to risk your reputation to garner him some damn justice and in the process get your own. But I need to find him first, and I cannot do it without you. So for yourself, for your child, *help me*."

Alain studies me, eyes slowly narrowing in time to the corners of his mouth rising into a grin. "I see Asher taught you the art of manipulation."

"No, he doesn't get credit for that. If anything *I* taught *him* a thing or two."

"I do not doubt it, Mrs. West." His smile falters as slowly as it rose. "Rumors have placed him from Paris to Cape Town to Minsk, none credible."

"Who else would help him like Richard did?"

"With the amount of pressure and scrutiny law enforcement is placing on our community? Only Christine. She has been searching for him for a decade. He might just now be desperate enough to run straight into her arms."

"So where is *she*?"

265

"Most likely where everyone else is: Vienna. The ball is in three days."

"No, she's crazy but not that crazy. She's still a wanted fugitive for Goodnight."

"That has not stopped her from attending these three years past. The Goodnight Coven is respected, but their reach does not extend to the European vampire community. There is no, what do you call it, co-op among our communities here. As long as she refrains from causing ripples to the world at large, she is free to rejoin our society. It helps that she is so … generous with her favors to all members of our clique."

"Meaning she pays for protection in the bedroom." I pause. "But just because she's there, doesn't mean he'll attend."

"He will if given the proper incentive."

"Like …"

Alain's lips purse in disapproval. "You, silly girl. *You.* He has been searching for you far longer than you have him. Whatever desperation, whatever hunger you are experiencing, Mrs. West, multiply it by ten years. With a few phone calls, the whole of Europe could know you and your inconvenient husband shall be attending the ball to locate willing friends to aid in your endeavor. He will know the exact spot, the exact time of where you will be. If the tables were turned, would you pass up that chance?" he asks, right eyebrow raised.

I recognize his plan for what it was: an act of desperation. A trap with me as bait. In truth, we don't have the financial resources or just plain time to trace Asher beyond the end of the week. We have lives. The boys have already missed so much school, and Nathan too much work. They've given enough of their lives to my previous dysfunction. And money. Our savings is all but dried up. This was it. The best, worst plan.

He would be there. As soon as Alain said the words, I knew this was the course of action required. The *only* course of action. I'd be the sacrificial lamb tied to the gilded stake in hopes the predator would strike. And he would.

He had to.

"Okay. I'm in."

"Then the curtain rises." Alain smirks. "I do love a good drama. Especially the tragedies."

I feel like crying already.

VIENNA, AUSTRIA

I NEVER THOUGHT I'D see this place again. I never *wanted* to see this place again. At least I don't resemble a walking corpse this time. However, the night *is* young.

The Vienna Opera House is far grander than I remembered. The whole of Vienna is beautiful, with its baroque castles and gardens amid the low stone and brick buildings older than the whole of America, ensconced along the tranquil blue Danube River. We had time, since arriving this morning, to explore the City of Music. The immense Hofburg Palace, the golden monument of Johann Strauss, the cathedrals with their cherubs and gargoyles keeping watch—they are far lovelier in the daylight. Strolling along the Danube's banks hand in hand with my husband was a brief oasis in our otherwise hectic trip. For those three hours we just walked and explored, all our troubles could not touch us. There was no strategizing, no worry, nothing but Mr. and Mrs. West and the majesty of Vienna.

Right now that stroll seems like a lifetime ago, not hours. No room for tranquility now. The moment we stepped into this House, we entered a snake pit. There are precious few who don't desire to sink their fangs into us. Literally. Job well done, Alain.

He was correct in his assessment. A few well-placed phone calls, and by the next night not only did we have tickets to the hottest party in Europe, but according to our patron there wasn't a vampire on two continents who didn't know the Wests would be at the ball in an attempt to gain an audience with Lord Augustus. He even arranged a discount on Nathan's tux. If I ever have another son, I know what we're naming him.

As my dapper husband and I stroll through the opulent foyer with the murals of angels watching over us on the walls and ceilings, I notice more than a few incredibly pale people staring, then whispering to their companions. We are quite a fetching pair. As always, Nathan stands a head above everyone, and with his brown hair slicked to the side and contacts in he hasn't looked this handsome since our wedding. I'm no slouch myself tonight. I'd remembered a gown in *Vogue* from a few months ago, and somehow Alain tracked it down. A lovely surprise when we checked into the hotel this morning. Fits like a glove. A bright red satin sleeveless ball gown with a rose embroidered in black crystals on the full skirt. I'm even sporting the same lipstick shade Asher always insisted I wear. The boys no longer have college funds so this had better damn well work.

Come and get me, you bastard.

He is here. I can sense it, sense him, like ripples on the air that only certain animals register. Whatever our connection, faint as it may be now, it still exists, and it's tingling now. I scan the foyer, locking on every male Asher's height and weight, but no luck yet. Nathan performs the same task. There are so many people here, five thousand to be exact, it's hard to examine them all and who knows how much his appearance has changed. He is in hiding after all.

Perhaps we should have brought in the authorities, or even let Dr. Black know where we were as Nathan insisted. My husband found himself outvoted. It was two against one as Alain and I dismissed the idea. Lord Augustus is well connected, word of their law enforcement involvement would more than likely reach him. That was absolutely not a chance we could take, full stop. If this plan should fail, the only other option left to us is witness protection. Changing our names, leaving our home, never seeing friends or family and praying Asher never finds us again. *No.* My husband and children will not have to endure that. Plus with all the bodyguards of foreign dignitaries around, one speck of trouble and an army of men with large guns would descend on the source. We're trained agents with supernatural talents and weapons taped to our bodies. Nobody better mess with the Wests.

We make it through the foyer gauntlet to the overflowing ballroom. The orchestra plays a jaunty polka as the upper crust bounce around the dance floor or chat with their contemporaries off to the side. There are too many people both on the main floor and five tiers above to clock all potential threats.

"Holy shit, is that Steven Spielberg?" Nathan asks, pointing at the auteur.

"Yeah, and you know who the blond is? Princess Diana. Your sister's gonna die when she hears you were in the same room as Princess Di."

"She's even prettier in person."

I squeeze his arm with mine. "Head in the game, husband."

"Right. Right," he whispers, shaking his head. "Sorry. It's just… holy shit, is that Tom Cruise?"

"Probably. They're just people, Nathan."

"Well, forgive me if I'm not as jaded as you."

He's nervous. He could barely fasten his cufflinks at the hotel, his fingers trembled so hard. If I allowed it, I'd be the same mess. Not tonight. Every emotion I possess is locked away until I have the luxury of opening the box again for a much needed break-down. But tonight, I must remain focused, sharp like the blade of the silver knife taped to my back. It's the only way I'll get through this night.

"We need to locate Augustus and Alain," I say. "Let's do a sweep down here and then move to the boxes."

"Do you think Augustus will actually see us?"

"Doesn't matter. Come on."

We travel the oval room, checking every available face for our prey. I recognize a few monsters from boarding school, a vampire or two from the old nights, and not a friendly face in sight when they spot me as well. My debutante "date" Gerhardt is one of the familiar faces, though his hasn't aged a day in over a decade. Guess his lover Heinrich made good on his promise to turn the teen. Forever seventeen, a fate worse than death. I smile at the boy, who promptly excuses himself from the group to rush off. My smile grows. "We have about five minutes before we're summoned," I whisper to Nathan.

At the five-minute mark, as we're halfway up the side staircase to the second level, Gerhardt swans down straight toward us. "Gerhardt! Lovely to see you again. How have you been?"

Once more, he refuses to return my smile. "Lord Augustus requires your audience in his box."

"Just the man we came to see," Nathan says.

"Not him," says the vampire, nodding at Nathan.

"And who's gonna stop me. You?" Nathan asks menacingly as he takes a step up. "Try and I'll send ten thousand volts straight into your head, frying your brain and boiling your stolen blood."

"I—"

"Don't test me, kid. I am in no mood." Nathan's lip twitches. "Lead the way, rent boy."

Having no real option, save for causing an unwanted scene, the vampire escorts us to a fourth-level box filled with the glowering undead. I was never popular with my old circle of "friends," but at least they hid their derision before. I'm surprised they aren't spitting on me now. Byron appears about to, actually hissing as I pass him. But Asher instilled in me a sense of pride and calm while facing adversity, so I keep my head up and Mona Lisa smile plastered on.

At least there's one friendly face here. That face isn't that friendly at present, but I know it's an act. Part of the scene to come. "I told you she would be here," Alain says, sipping his bloody goblet beside the Lord. He stares into my eyes, and the faint smile drops. "Despite my express insistence a few nights ago."

"When have I ever heeded your advice?" I ask with a cocky grin.

"And look where that mistake has led you, little Anna Asher," Alain counters.

"Mrs. West," I correct. "My name is Anna West now."

"If you say so, dear," Alain says, words dripping with derision.

I roll my eyes then divert them toward Augustus. "Your lordship," I say with a curtsey. "I am not sure if you remember me. I'm—"

"I know who you are," Augustus snaps. "The whole of Europe knows who you are and whom you seek. I have personally been accosted *twice* by the law this past week. I assume that is your doing."

"Any known friend of Asher was interviewed. They didn't target you specifically," Nathan clarifies.

"And this must be the lightning bug husband," Augustus sneers, sizing him up from top to toes. "Definitely a downgrade, Miss Asher."

"Mrs. West," Nathan corrects.

"A rose by any other name," Alain says with a smirk. "Though you have taken her bloom, Mr. West."

"No. Your psychotic, evil friend Asher did *that*. Or tried to, at least," Nathan counters.

"Nathan," I warn as I touch his arm. No shock. He's calm. Good. "Lord Augustus," I say, taking a step forward, "I apologize for any trouble we've caused you, I truly do, but I cannot stop the harassment. Nothing can except Asher's capture."

"It all goes away if you help us catch him," Nathan clarifies behind me. "We know Didier Fournier worked for you once upon a time."

"He worked for *many* people," Alain chimes in.

"We don't care if you facilitated the recent contract," I say. "The past is the past. We just want to find Asher."

"However, INTERPOL *is* digging into your financials and phone records as part of their ongoing investigation, which will continue until Asher is apprehended," Nathan cuts in. "We now know Asher's phone and bank routing numbers. One link and you lose your little fiefdom and possibly your life for facilitating the death of a former federal agent. Is he worth that?"

The lord's thin lips purse in disapproval. "How dare you come here, making negative assertions about my character and threatening me?"

"It's not a threat, sir. Merely a reality check," Nathan says.

"Whatever it is, *sir,* you are ruining my night," Augustus spits. "I do not know where your wayward lover is, Miss Asher, I have neither seen or heard from the man in over a decade, nor do I care to. Now, I suggest you both leave my city before I lose my temper, and INTERPOL has a true reason to investigate me. With the hornet's nest you both have kicked, it would be impossible to narrow down the exact person that stung you both to death. *Leave.*"

"I warned you this would be a waste of time," Alain says smugly.

I glower at Alain before returning to my husband's side. "Come on. I need a drink."

I attempt to take Nathan's hand, but he jerks his away as if my touch would slice his hand in half. "Don't." Nathan spins around and steps toward the door. Two men stand in front of it and don't move until Augustus clears his throat. Still glowering, they step aside and Nathan stalks out with me at his impatient heels. Mission accomplished. Alibi established. I can breathe again.

On to Act Two. Tampa redux.

"Nathan, please wait!" I shout as I rush to his side.

"Have I ever mentioned how much I really, *really* hate fucking vampires?" Nathan asks, shaking his head. "I need a drink. Or twelve."

We locate the bar on the main level, and Nathan orders a Whiskey Sour. I stick to Ginger Ale. Nathan knocks his back with one gulp. "Take it easy," I say.

"Your old friends are uniformly assholes, you know that?" he states loudly before turning back to the bartender. "Another."

"No, one's enough," I insist. I grab his hand again. "Come on. I want to dance. Let's dance. Come—"

He violently yanks his hand from my grasp again. "I don't want to fucking dance with you. And stop trying to manage me like I'm a fucking child, Anna."

"I'm not."

"The hell you aren't! I'm pissed, alright? And I have every fucking right to be pissed. We've spent all our savings, I haven't seen my kids in a damn week, and oh, your ex-boyfriend is trying to kill me, and it's all your fucking fault! So no, I don't want to dance with you. I want to go home."

"Is everything alright here?" the man beside Nathan asks in a Swedish accent.

"Oh, fuck off," Nathan snaps at the gentleman.

"Nathan!"

"You know what, Anna? You can fuck off too. I'm tired of chasing your damn ex-boyfriend around Europe. I'm tired of living under his fucking shadow, being constantly compared to him, your 'great love,'" he snaps, using air quotes, "and coming up short. Well, I'm sorry I'm not some ancient jet-setting asshole who treats you like shit and gnaws on you like a chicken bone every night. I'm sorry I don't take you to balls, and introduce you to dead poets who want to get into your pants. And I'm sorry I knocked you up, and you had to settle for me, okay? But I'm done. *Done.* You want each other? You can fucking have each other."

At first I just stare at my husband, my mouth dropped open and trembling as he glares at me. Not good enough. I toss my drink into his furious face. "Go to hell, Nathan. Go. To. Hell." I glance at the Swedish Samaritan. "You. You want to dance?"

"I—"

I take the stranger's hand and drag him past our captivated audience comprised of more than a few vampires. Excellent. That piece of theater would be pointless without people to spread it around. The sacrificial lamb is now caked in blood. If my need of rescuing from my brute of a husband doesn't entice Asher, nothing will. It worked with a werewolf in Tampa, why not a vampire in Vienna?

As the Swede sashays me around the dance floor, being smart enough not to speak while doing so, I catch sight of my scowling husband sitting at a table shooting me daggers when he's not pretending to sip his whiskey. Eyes on each other at all times, rule number one. At the end of the dance, the Swede passes me off to the Russian for the schottische; who is replaced by the Scottish Laird for the Viennese waltz. I don't even swat that one's hand away when it rests on my rump. I'm so "beaten" and "miserable," just staring into space as we twirl, I don't see the point. Really, I have the strongest urge to knee the bastard in his kilted bollocks. Half an hour around the dance floor and still no sign of Asher.

I'm beginning to think he doesn't care about my manhandling. Or he's turned on by it. He could go either way depending on which way the wind blew.

My molester insists on another dance. Then another. Come on, you bastard. Bite. Just as the fourth is about to begin, Alain taps the Laird on the shoulder to cut in. "May I have the honor, Miss Asher?" My scowl deepens on the outside, but inside I want to hug him. I put up no resistance as he wraps his arm around my waist, takes my hand, and begins twirling me around the room.

"Always rescuing me," I whisper.

"Word finally reached me of your marital tiff. Excellent work. You are the talk of the ball."

"Anything on our friends? Was Augustus telling the truth?"

"Yes. He has no knowledge of Asher, and Christine has not been seen in society for almost a week. And no one has set eyes on either tonight."

"He's here," I say with utter certainty. "I can all but smell him."

"How … disturbing." Alain pauses. "Well, at least you can re-claim your belle of the ball title tonight if nothing else."

"No, someone else can have that honor, thank you very much. I never wanted it in the first place."

"Oh, come on, Mrs. West. Part of you must miss the glamour and intrigue of your previous life whilst you fold underwear and wipe snotty noses in the life you now find yourself shackled to."

"Shackled to? You make it sound as if Nathan keeps me locked in the house to act as his maid."

"Then why him, out of your undoubtedly many suitors? Though we have only been acquainted a short time, I am under the impression that despite his considerably impressive supernatural talent, he is rather … milquetoast. Was it simply because of the child?"

"What? No, that was a lie. I found out I was pregnant *after* we were married. And he is anything but milquetoast. I once watched him beat the hell out of a ghoul with its own arm. I married him because I fell in love with him. Because I wanted to build a life with him. He is the kindest, sweetest, funniest man I've ever met. He's my best friend. My lover. My cheerleader. A loving, amazing father. He gave me the strength to beat back the darkness. He is my Valhalla. The best thing that ever happened to me. My gift from the universe." I spot the man himself circling the room, still frowning at me, but for a moment, just a moment when I catch his eyes, the ire vanishes. A flash of a smile crosses both our lips in unison. I look away first before my hard-fought brick wall topples and my emotions spill out, knocking me out of this fight. "I have a favor to ask you."

"Another? They are piling up, Mrs. West," he chides.

"I know, just … look after Nathan. Please."

"I beg pardon?"

"No matter what happens to me, however this ends, I want you to make sure Nathan returns home. He's not to leave your sight tonight, not even for a moment. I don't matter. Just … if it comes down to me or him … *him*. Always him. Please." Alain stares down at me and after a second, a smile grows across his face. Confused, my eyes narrow. "What?"

"Nothing, just … the last time we spoke, your husband made me promise the same about you. You before him."

I can't help but chuckle. Great minds think alike. "Well ... you were my friend first, therefore I win. Besides, Asher wants *me* alive. At least in the beginning." I pause. "And if it comes to *that,* it would be better if everyone thinks I was dead. I know him. I know them both. Nathan won't stop searching for me, and if he becomes a nuisance, Asher will not hesitate to eradicate him. He's proved that once already."

Alain stares at me again, though instead of amusement, his pretty face betrays his concern. I knew deep down he cared. "You intend to go with him."

"If I have to," I say without hesitation. "It's simple math, really. If he gets what he wants, my family factors out of the equation."

"But what of you? Are you really willing to spend centuries with that man? You know what he is capable of."

"There is *nothing* I wouldn't do to keep my family safe," I say with a hard edge. "Including never seeing them again. They shouldn't pay for my sins. It may be the only way. So, if it comes to that, I'm trusting you to make sure my sacrifice isn't in vain."

"You trust me?" he asks, barely hiding his shock and pride.

"Yes. You are family after all."

"Well, the Borgia's have nothing on us, do they?" he asks with a grin.

The song ends, and Alain and I stroll over to my irate husband and his empty whiskey glass, but he rolls his eyes and takes off in the other direction toward the bar. I glance at Alain, who follows after him without a word. You can always count on family, right? I take this opportunity to sit down and rest my feet. I don't care if it is uncouth, I kick off my shoes and rub my toes. Sure enough the woman across the table shakes her head. I narrow my eyes at the judgmental bitch. That's enough to scare her away. I sigh. What—

Her.

Across the dance floor. Long wavy brown hair, right height and weight, back of her purple dress plunging so far I can see her bum crack. When she glances to the side even her profile's the same. I quickly slip on my shoes and leap up. The bitch's mine. Finger at the ready, and the paralyzing hex on my lips, I stride through the dancing masses. She's vanished when I reach the spot. *Merde!* I...there!

She's halfway to a side door. I push and shove my way through the crowd this time. I'm not losing her again. The door opens onto a small, dimly lit hallway. My heart beats so fast and hard I feel the drumming in my ears. Christine still in sight, I quicken my pace. I've been dreaming of this moment for over a decade. *Just don't kill her, Anna.* Not yet anyway. She's about the step into the powder room when I shove my finger against her bare back. I've got you, you bitch. "*Placi*—"

The woman twists around, blue eyes wide in shock. Damn it! It's not her. The resemblance isn't as pronounced up close. This woman's nose is thinner, and her eyes are set closer together. The doppelganger begins chastising me in Finnish, and I back away. "Sorry, sorry." She scoffs before retreating into the bathroom away from the crazy woman. Damn it. Damn it! I take a few deep breaths to calm myself as my confused audience watches. I almost hexed an innocent woman. Paralyzed her without a second thought. Who—

"Excuse me?" I spin around to find a waiter, sans tray, standing behind me. "Mrs. West? Lord Augustus requests your immediate presence in his box."

Great. "Thank you. Tell him I'll be there in a mom—"

"*Immediately*, madam. He was most insistent on that point."

Merde. We really can't afford to anger him further. "Could you please do me a favor? In the salon at the bar, there is a very tall and thin American man. Will you please tell him I'm going?"

"Of course, madam."

I nod at the waiter before continuing down the hall to a staircase. This cannot be good. I don't think I'm in physical danger. Augustus won't assault me without provocation and certainly not in public, at least I don't think he will. At worst he could officially order us to leave, and since I'm here as a consort, I'd have to obey. In that case I'll beg, get down on my hands and knees if necessary, pride be damned. I'm not leaving. *I'm not.* Not without seeing Asher, speaking to him. I am not leaving.

The Lord's loyal subjects have thinned, off enjoying the night, when I return to box. Only a handful remain, including Augustus who is too busy feeding on a nubile redhead to notice my approach. I clear my throat, yet it takes another several seconds for him to realize I'm in the room. His hand remains up her skirt, but the vampire removes his mouth from her bleeding neck to scowl at my intrusion. "What?" he snaps.

"You wished to see me?"

"*You*? Why would I want to see you?"

"You didn't …" That damn knot twists inside me so tight it takes effort not to double over. *Merde.* I make it three steps back

281

the way I came before I notice Alain striding toward the box. Alone. I quickly bridge the gap between us.

"He summoned you as well?" Alain asks.

"No. Where's Nathan?"

"Searching the ballroom for you. Augustus insisted I—"

I take off as fast as my heels can carry me past him. Alain returns to my side when I reach the main staircase. "I am sure he is fine. He *can* take care of himself, can he not?"

Not in the bar. Not in the hallway I was in earlier either. *No, no, no, no, no ...* When we reach the ballroom, I can barely breathe from the panic leaking through my crumpling walls. One quick glance, and I can tell he isn't here. No one's tall enough. "You go right, I'll go left. We'll meet back at the bar in five."

Alain moves right as instructed while I veer the opposite way. Nathan's face isn't the only person's I search for. I check every waiter's face to locate my messenger. Alain's right, Nathan can take care of himself. I've seen him take on werewolves, pyrokinetics, even three ghouls at once and come out victorious. He's fine. He *has* to be fine. We will find him. He's fine. He's fine, he's fine, he's fine, he's fine ...

When I end up right back where I started, a few agonizing moments later I notice my hands are trembling. I ball them into fists as I hustle toward the bar. Alain waits at the entrance. "I did not—"

"Go check the men's bathrooms. I'll wait here."

Alain nods before carrying out his task. I'll stay here. Nathan'll search here too. He's probably as worried about me as I am him. We shouldn't have split up. I should have come to the bar with him. Stupid. So stupid. He's fine though. He's fine. He's—

"My, have you aged."

My head jerks to the side where a waitress stands with tray in hand. It takes my addled brain a moment to place her. Thick black framed glasses, platinum blonde hair in a pixie cut, baggy pants and white coat, but that cruel smile affixed to those sensual lips cannot be disguised. I've waited for this moment, chased it over two continents, rehearsed my speech to this bitch for a decade, but now it's here … stinging bile rises into my throat, stopping my powers of speech. "And not well."

Instinct takes over and I begin to raise my finger for a hex, but Christine grabs my wrist, squeezing so tight I moan in pain. "Before you attempt anything else idiotic," Christine whispers, "you should know I just delivered your husband to our Asher. If I fail to return within five minutes, you shall become a widow. And just between us girls, black has never been your shade. So are you going to be a good little girl?" she asks with a sickening saccharine smile. I have no choice but to nod yes. She studies my face, trying to catch my eyes, but they remain downcast. "Excellent. Now, I have been watching you all night. I know Alain aids you, but is he your sole ally? Your husband's life depends on my believing the answer to this next question. Who else have you enlisted? The police? INTERPOL? Byron?"

"No one else. I swear on my children's lives. It's just us. If it wasn't, they'd be advancing on you right now. You are technically assaulting me," I say, nodding to her hand.

Christine scans the room for potential bogies, but of course finds none. Just disinterested aristocracy lost in their own little worlds. "Fair point," she concedes. "However, please note, I wish nothing more than to plunge my fangs deep into your carotid and shower in your blood as death takes you. If you are lying, then Asher would not blame me one iota."

"Then why not kill me now? Lie to him?"

She leans in to whisper, "Because you do not deserve a quick death, little girl. Because I wish to watch as you lose all you love. To watch as your mind cracks while I slaughter your husband, your children, your little dog too before you finally meet with an unfortunate accident when *I* deem your punishment over. I owe you all that and more for what you have done to that magnificent man." She twists my wrist, literally bringing me down to my knees. "But patience is a virtue, no? My only one." She releases me, and I let out the breath I held in a pant. The grin of hers returns, fueled by my misery. "Now, let's not dilly-dally a moment longer. Someone is not getting any younger. You do look dreadful by the way. Perhaps he will not want you anymore."

"You wish," I growl as I rise.

Her grin drops. "Time to go, *hausfrau*." She wraps her arm in mine. "You have kept him waiting long enough."

Christine leads me out of the salon arm in arm as if we were girlfriends strolling down Fifth Avenue on a shopping trip. No one gives us a second glance as we move through the ballroom. Christine maneuvers me into another hallway, then a more isolated, narrow corridor. Two more twists and there's not a soul in sight. Judging from the racks of costumes and props lining the passages, we're backstage, but I can't be sure. It's so dark I can only see a foot or two ahead.

"Your husband is quite handsome, at least up close. Nice eyes. A definite downgrade without a doubt, but I suppose you could have done worse. In my experience, tall men are often hung like elephants. Perhaps I can persuade Asher to spare him, at least until I satiate my curiosity. If memory serves, you always did enjoy a good foursome, or at least pretended to. Does hubby like strange too? He must. Sex with you would be intolerably dull otherwise. I speak from experience."

"And still Asher risked imprisonment and death to find *me* and not you," I point out. "Imagine th—"

Something hard smashes into my stomach with the force of a plane crash. I not only double over, but puke the bile from earlier all over the floor. Shock gives way to intense pain through my muscles, my organs, even back to my spine. I can't breathe. I can't breathe or gasp or hell even blink for a few seconds. "Well, *that* shut you up," says Christine. "I must say I like you far better when you know your place." I manage to take a breath. Another. Fresh tears fall when I attempt to straighten. Too soon. "Oh, you better hurry, little girl," Christine chides in a little girl voice. "Three minutes left and counting. You know the importance Asher places on promptness."

Get up, Anna. Get up. Now! I manage to force myself upright though my abdomen protests with further agony. She may have broken a rib. I know, despite the darkness, she can see my face even if I can barely make out hers. I clench my teeth shut and stare at the bitch with enough contempt and determination to fuel an army trudging to war. I wipe the bile from my chin and spit the rest on her shoe. She didn't break me a decade ago, she sure as hell isn't going to tonight. "Do you feel better now? Why don't you smash my face as well? We both know it wouldn't matter. Not one iota. You can gouge out my eyes, slash my face to ribbons, rip off my jaw, and he would still love me. He would still chose me over you. And you know why, Christine? Why after centuries of chasing him, of sacrificing for him, of being his willing slave, he only feeds you the table scraps of his love? Because you're beneath even him. You're nothing but a pathetic, weak, vindictive, stupid, common whore. To him you're just a mangy dog who follows him around, but he won't allow in his house. He pities you. And in the end, no matter what you do: save him, fuck him, lay down your life for him, nothing can change that because nothing can change what you are. And *you* know it." With my chin up, I take a step ahead of her. "*Your* master awaits. Let's get this over with."

I'm more than a little surprised she doesn't kill me, right here and now. If she had half a brain, she would. Or maybe she gets off on emotional pain. That's all that awaits her up that staircase. But Asher's wishes are her commands. Without a word, she takes point, leading me up to a staircase. Each step is utter agony and the only sound beyond my pants are her chuckles at my pain. I trail her as fast as I can. At least the pain distracts me from the myriad of horrors that may await me at our final destination. A gust of arctic wind assails me when Christine opens the door to the roof.

Ten years. This moment was ten years coming. I'm prepared. I'm strong. Descended from Vikings. Survivor. Federal agent. Wife. Mother. I am the woman who can take care of herself. I am Anna Olmstead Asher West. *I can do this.*

"*Mo chuisle.*"

And there he is. You really can't fight fate.

"Hello, Asher."

Even now, even after all he's done to me and mine, he still takes my breath away, though for an entirely different reason than before. He's so gaunt now, cheeks so hollow his cheekbones could cut glass.

Even here in the dim light I notice the bruised circles under his eyes. Gone is the lustrous, thick curly hair now cut to perhaps an inch and dyed black. The white waiter's coat like Christine's washes his already pale skin to an almost gray hue. A corpse. I'm gazing at nothing more than a corpse. But for a moment, just one tiny moment, it was as if we are back to the beginning where I was just a lost girl and he was this heavenly creature sent to save and love me as I was meant to do for him. How full of hope and promise that moment was. But it's over and this is what remains. I stare at the corpse of my soul mate, but only for a moment before turning my attention to the love of my life.

Above me on the ledge, Nathan stands as still as a nearby gargoyle, staring at nothing, seeing nothing. He's locked inside himself, nothing but a puppet and with one tug, one word, he'll topple like one. I hope Christine took his emotions away, otherwise he has to be scared out of his mind. I'm not even on that ledge, and for a brief second, my own fear paralyzes me. Like a knight wielding a sword against a dragon, something deep within me manages to fight the emotion back. He's helped me find my strength for so long, taken care of me when I was facing the worst.

My turn.

I meet Asher's eyes, my scowl deepening until my lips curl up like a wild animal's. "Let him go," I growl. "This has nothing to do with him. This is between you and me."

"You are still so beautiful," he says breathlessly, completely ignoring my pronouncement.

"Did you hear me? I said let him go, Asher," I order with the sharpness of a razor.

"The most beautiful creature I have ever laid eyes on."

He's not listening. He's lost in his own world where he expects me to run into his waiting arms and shower him with kisses and promises of eternal fidelity from this moment on. Anna Asher would. She begs from her grave for this very action. Anna West banishes her back to hell. I pick up my skirt, and hoist myself the three feet up onto the ledge mere feet from my husband. As I catch sight of just how high we are, almost ten stories with nothing but hard pavement below, I instantly regret this action. One misstep and it's certain death. That doesn't only apply to the fall.

"What are you doing?" Asher cries as he moves toward me.

"Don't come any closer," I warn. He takes another step, and I hold out my hand. This time Christine, probably thinking I'm about to curse him, moves to his side to deflect the attack. I lower it. "Don't. I'll jump. I swear I will."

Both vampires actually listen, stopping where they stand. The gesture does have the desired effect, snapping him back to reality, probably for the first time in years. "Please come down from there, *mo chuisle*," he begs. "It is not safe."

"I come down when my husband does."

"This is madness! Come down at once!" he orders.

"Madness? *Madness*?" I shout, voice echoing over the wind. "*You* dare lecture me on madness? You murdered my friends. You kidnapped me. Raped me. Tried to kill my husband. Terrorized my children. And you expect me to forget it all? Run off into the moonlight to spend an eternity locked up in a house in Jersey with you and your psychopath girlfriend? *That* is madness. I tried to kill you, Asher. I tried to murder you in your sleep. You should hate me."

"I could never hate you. *Never.* I deserved what you did. Without question. What happened … what I did … what *I* did was unpardonable. There was no excuse. *None.* And more nights than not, especially when I recall my offense, I wished Christine had not saved me." He pauses. "Since you left, I have been in hell, exactly where I belong. But I wish to make amends, my Anna, my darling, my blood." Asher moves a pace toward me. "Yes, I am mad. Madness has gripped me since the moment we met. And in that madness I have committed crimes that I never thought myself capable of, but even through the worst, there has been one shining beacon to guide me out of the maelstrom: you. Our love. Anna, I have existed for almost a millennia. I have experienced all this world has to offer thrice over, but when I met you, when you allowed me to love you, when you gave that love back in return, I was reborn. I was *alive, mo chuisle.* And you were happy. So happy. You shone as bright as the sun every moment we spent together. I know because … we are one, Anna. I am yours, and you are mine: body, mind, and soul. Our fates are intertwined, and when you fight against that, nothing but misery follows."

He takes another step. "I know you harbor love for this man. He is the father of the children I could not provide you. But he has imprisoned you in a world of mediocrity. You were meant for more than he can provide, Anna. You are so much better than that."

"But you're wrong. That's what you never understood about me, why we will never work. There is *nothing* better than that. Not for me. I don't want, no I don't *need* the world. I don't need fancy clothes and trips around the globe and constant parties. That is not who I am, and it never was. I need love. I need to wake beside a man who I know fifty years from now will be there, no matter how difficult things get. Who will be as loyal to me as I will be to him. Who respects me and my wishes even when they're inconvenient or he doesn't agree with them. I need more than *you*."

"Whatever you need, I shall give you, I swear I shall."

"You're not listening to me. You *never* listen to me," I snap. "I loved you. I loved you with every fiber of my soul, of my being, and you took advantage of that. You took all I had and left me with barely a grain for myself. And you expect me to let you do that again? What will be different? Nothing, except I'll hate you. You have managed to destroy almost *every* bit of love I still have. I am not in love with you anymore. I'm sorry, but I'm not. But that doesn't mean I haven't forgotten you, or forgotten what we *did* mean to one another.

"But it's over. We cannot get it back. I cannot save you, Asher, and I don't need you to save me. You did your job. You taught me everything I needed to know in this life. I have a good family, good friends, *I'm good*. I'm happy. I am happy, Asher. And if you love me even half as much as you claim to then you would be happy for me, as I would be happy for you if you found peace. And love. Why can't you do the same for me?" It's a risk, I know it's a risk, a grave risk, but I leap from the ledge and walk toward the crumbling vampire, even meeting his red tear rimmed eyes. Even now, his despair moves me, stirring the same within my soul.

"I'll go with you. If you promise to leave my family in peace, I will go with you. I won't flee. I will be by your side until you cast me aside. But it won't be real, my Asher," I say, caressing his frozen cheek. "What we had was real. *It was*. It was real, and beautiful and transcendent. But it's over now, my Asher. And you're tarnishing it.

Sullying it out with acts like this. And if I go with you, every touch, every time I have to play make-believe, it'll be another stab at that love until we're choking on its ashes. And I would rather have ten years of true, pure love that we experienced together than an eternity in its pale shadow." Cradling his face in my hands, I wipe his falling bloody tears with my thumbs as my own fall unabashed. "The greatest thing you'll ever learn is just to love and be loved in return,'" I whisper. "I love you. I will always love you. Please love me back. Let me go. Please, my darling, my blood, *let me go*."

"I ... cannot," he whispers. "I cannot. I ..."

"Then I'm sorry," I whisper. "I'm so sorry, my love." As fast as possible, I reach around to the hidden knife taped to my back and slide it between his ribs straight into his chest. "I'm sorry." He is so shocked at first, mouth opening as if he wishes to speak, but only for a moment. Then just ... relief. Sweet relief. Asher stares into my eyes as I do his. I literally watch as his heart not only crumbles around the blade but under the weight of my truth. I feel it within me, crushing me as well. Yet what's left is understanding. There's no hate, no fear, no doubt. I just see ... *him*. *My* Asher. I knew he was still in there. That I'd find him.

"Anna ..." he whispers.

"I know." I lightly kiss his lips. "I forgive you. Just please forgive me."

"I—" he croaks.

"What ..." Christine says behind us.

As easy as it went in, I pull the knife out at the same time as I raise my free hand, the hex already leaving my lips. "*Placidus!*"

She's too fast. She's vanished by the time the hex reaches the spot she just inhabited. *Merde*. Asher collapses to the ground as a gust of my wind knocks Nathan onto the roof, momentarily out of danger. I'm not. My husband barely lands when I feel arms encircle my torso from behind, tightening like a python. My F.R.E.A.K.S. training, the hours I spent getting walloped by Oliver in those early days, kicks in. A backward head butt loosens her grip while the second assault, complete with sickening crack as I break her cute nose, releases me all together. Without missing a beat, I swing around knife first. She's not so spry this time. The silver dagger slices her cheek, drawing more blood as her nose continues to spew. Christine stumbles back, more from surprise than pain. She stares at me as if I were a stranger. I don't believe it ever crossed her mind that I could and would fight back. Yet, she chuckles.

"Kitten's grown claws."

"Now hear me roar, bitch."

Another gust of wind propels her toward me, toward my blade, but I blink and she's vanished. I'm forced backward by my own wind as well, almost collapsing on Asher. This distraction loses me my tentative upper hand. I blink again and she's beside me, taking a fistful of my hair and flinging me aside. I roll and roll until I hit the wall with the force of a car crash. Pain. Agony everywhere, vibrating down my spine, my arm, especially my head. There's a whole galaxy of twinkling stars before my eyes. What …

"Get up," I hear her say but can't comply. Nothing in my body will function properly. "Climb on the ledge." What is she talking about? I shake the fuzz away enough so I can see through the stars. Panic cuts the rest away.

Nathan.

My husband, still under her power, obeys the command, climbing onto that ledge like the marionette he is. I attempt to raise my finger to hex the bitch, but she's too fast. I feel my arm twisting painfully to the side before I realize she's the one performing the task. She meets my eyes. One look and she's in there, tendrils burrowing through my brain. She locks me inside, locks me away from my power, from my words. All she's left me is my rage. My terror. It continues to wash through me like a tsunami, over and over again. Christine yanks me up by the hair and drags me across the roof toward Nathan.

"I am going to enjoy this so much more than I enjoyed ripping into your witch friends that night," she whispers. We stop two feet from my husband. *Oh, Nathan, I'm so sorry…* "Remove your dagger," Christine orders.

As Nathan pulls out his blade from under his shirt, Christine digs her claws into my lower jaw and chin, forcing me to stare at her slave. "You are doing this to him, not I," she whispers. "You will feel every agony tenfold, you little bitch, and know this is because of you." Louder, she orders, "Slash your face."

It's as if the blade cuts into my own cheek, the flesh stretching open as Nathan draws it across his face. "Again!" I fear my knees may buckle as he slices the other side. "You stole from me the only thing in this wretched disgusting world that I ever loved," she whispers against my ear, voice crumbling. "He was mine. Mine for eons before your father ever squirted you into your mother's rotten womb. *Mine.* And I was his.

"Plunge it into your leg until you hit bone!"

Nathan complies, slamming the knife in almost to the hilt. "In the other one!" It disappears again into his flesh. My legs almost give out, as do Nathan's. He sways on the ledge, and for a second, my pain is overshadowed by terror as the love of my life totters backward, about to fall. "Stand up straight!" Christine orders. Somehow Nathan finds equilibrium and obeys his master. "You do not get off that easy, little girl," she hisses into my ear. "Now throw Anna your dagger!"

I feel his torture as he removes the blade from so deep inside his leg and fear I may vomit again. The knife lands at my feet. "Pick it up." My body obeys, taking the blade in my hands, my husband's blood now literally on my hands. Christine steps in front of me, her eyes and cheeks saturated with blood still falling. She looks so sad, so pathetic, so young just now. That pitiful whore passed around from master to master, used and abused until one pinprick of light found its way into her life. She chased it for centuries, and I stole it from her. Twice. I almost feel sorry for her. Almost.

The rivulets of tears continue to flow as she meets my eyes. "This will not end tonight, Anna. I will leave here and even if it takes me years, know I will find your children, and the tortures you face this night will be lullabies compared to the wrath I shall inflict upon them. Then I shall turn them to continue my retribution for centuries to come, I swear to whomever is listening, I will. Tales of their agony will be legendary. I owe you *that* much and more."

Move your arm, Anna, I will myself. *Move it. Move . . .*

"Join your husband on the ledge, Anna."

My leg moves forward, then the other, completely out of my control. *Please no. Please . . .* I climb on the ledge. *No.*

"Gaze upon your wife, Mr. West." Nathan obeys. Oh, his ravaged face. My poor husband. *I'm so sorry, my sweetheart.* I meet his teary hazel eyes and see his fear. His pain. My fault, all my fault. "Take one last look upon her beautiful face, Mr. West, for it is the last thing you shall ever see." *No. No...* "Pierce his heart, Anna. Kill the love of your life as you did mine. Do it. *Now!*"

No. No, no, no, no, no... don't...

I struggle with all my might but my shaking arm slowly rises. *No. No...* I glance from my arm to Nathan once more. There's no recrimination in his gentle eyes, only sadness. The blade reaches his chest, and he closes his eyes. *Oh, I'm sorry, sweetheart. I love you...*

"Christine..."

Her grip loosens a little inside my brain at the sound of his voice, enough so the knife stops at Nathan's rib. Then it's gone. *She's* gone. The oppression lifts. With a gasp, I drop the blade just as Nathan collapses against me. Both pairs of legs finally able to buckle, we land on the ledge, his bloody cheek resting over my pounding heart. *What the hell...*

"I am sorry, my darling Christine. So sorry."

My discarded blade, the one I used to impale him still in his hand, Asher holds the dying Christine in his lap, petting her hair as blood pours like a river from her slit throat onto his hands, legs, and the ground. She stares up at him in shock as her eyelids flutter and her mouth opens and closes like a fish on dry land. She reaches up to touch his cheek but hasn't the strength. "So sorry, my love." He kisses her forehead. "So sorry." Tenderly, he lays his lips upon hers and begins to weep. This is how she dies, in the arms of the man she loves as his heart breaks for her. Far better than she deserves.

Asher places one more kiss on her still lips before turning my way. We gaze into one another's eyes, each set brimming with heartache. Of sorrow for the other. Without a word uttered, I know. For me. Despite my betrayal, despite my truth, he slit his only friend's throat for me. To save my husband, my children, my life. "Thank you," I mouth as I cling to my husband.

Asher just nods, one reverent nod before vanishing with Christine into the dark night, the only remnants he was ever here a pool of his lovers' blood and a swinging door. No matter. I squeeze my husband as tight as he does me. Nothing else matters but this. *Him.* For now at least.

See you soon, my Asher. I'll be waiting.

———

"I brought you some coffee," Alain whispers as he steps into Nathan's hospital room.

Always the heavy sleeper, Nathan doesn't stir. He needed two dozen stitches and a blood transfusion. They admitted him for the night, but he'll need plastic surgery for his face and may walk with a limp from nerve damage to his left leg. Even when he was waiting for the pain meds to kick in, and I kept apologizing, he just squeezed my hand and reminded me I went through childbirth twice because of him, so he still owes me one. Oh, how I adore this man.

Still holding his hand, I haven't let go since we arrived here, I use my other to take the coffee. "Thank you."

My friend nods. "It is almost dawn. I must go, but Lord Augustus assured me not only will the authorities continue to search but a few of his operatives will as well. Asher shall not get away this time."

"I know," I whisper. I gaze up at him and smile. "Thank you. For everything, thank you."

"We are family after all," he says with a genuine smile. "Try to rest."

"I will." There's simply one more task I must complete.

Alain squeezes my shoulder before departing once more. Now nothing left to do but wait.

He never was one to draw things out. Not five minutes after Alain leaves, a nurse enters but instead of a clipboard, she carries a note and blank expression. The moment the paper leaves her hand, the spell breaks. Her eyelids flutter as she stares at me. "What … why did I come in here?"

"I don't know," I lie with a gentle smile.

"Oh." Shaking her muddled head, the messenger departs.

I open the note.

"*Roof. Please.*"

I never could say no to him, even when I wanted to.

I leave the note on the nightstand, tuck in my husband, and steal a kiss like our first before leaving him in his peaceful state. This I must do alone.

"I adore this city." Asher says with his back to me. I don't blame him for this rude gesture. Vienna is beautiful at dawn. Asher stares across the whole of Vienna at the blue and orange sky where the sun has just begun to rise.

I slowly stroll to his side. "Me too." I nod to the right. "Look." His gaze moves toward the Danube. "Remember the first night we arrived here? You said you wished you could see for yourself that it was blue because it just appeared black at night?"

"So you took your camera out during the day and snapped photos to show me it was," he finishes. "So I could see its beauty. You always were so considerate. Far more than I ever was." We exchange a smile at the memory before he gazes upon it once more. "Now, I do not need you to do that for me. It is ... breathtaking."

Though tears spring from my eyes, I smile again. "I'm glad you get to see it. Finally." We stand in silence, side-by-side, taking in its majesty for a few seconds. "Christine?"

"I buried her underneath a tree in Donaupark. It was her favorite."

"She loved you. She loved you more than anyone."

"I know. I always knew. And in my own way, I loved her as well. Simply ... not enough. But that did not give her the right to ..." He can't finish. He shakes his head to clear his own transgressions from thought. "I have lived too long, *mo chuisle*. It makes you forget."

"Forget what?"

"Humanity. The true beauty of the world, and those who inhabit it. You forget everything but your own darkness, and the quest to find some light in it."

"I was a pale comparison to this, huh?" I ask, nodding at the sun.

"No," he whispers vehemently. "*Never.*"

I nod and wipe my tears away before reaching for his hand. Without hesitation, he takes it. Blood red tears drip from his eyes at this gesture. "You are happy? Truly?"

"Yes. I am."

"I am so sorry. *So sorry.*"

"I know. I forgive you. And I thank you. For my life. For the love we shared. From the bottom of my soul, my Asher, *thank you.*"

Still weeping, he nods. He got what he came for, the only piece of salvation I can provide him. He's ready now. He squeezes my hand and brings it up to his trembling lips, kissing it. "I love you."

"I know. And I love you too."

"I am so frightened."

"I know," I say, voice trembling.

"Do not leave me. Not now. *Please.*"

"I'm not going anywhere. I am with you. I am right here, my Asher. I am yours 'til the close of the dream. 'Til death, I am yours, and you are mine. I promise."

And I remain by his side until all the stars burn out, until the sun rises, and the bedrock beneath his feet is no more. Until he is nothing but dust on the wind.

My darling. My blood.

Good-bye, my Asher.

When I return downstairs, Nathan still slumbers. I climb into the bed beside him, curl up against my husband, and fall asleep in peace.

Let the new dream open.

TWENTY YEARS LATER ...
AGE 49
JULY
GARLAND, TX

I LIKE HER.

Though I *do* have the strongest urge to scoop her into my arms and protect her from this new world she's found herself in. Poor Agent Alexander has no idea what she has gotten herself into. Even with Oliver by her side, the odds are against her. *Oliver.* There's someone I haven't thought of in years. Alain never allows me to bring him up when we chat. Sounds as if he's doing well.

I watch through the window as Joe leans in to say something to the new agent, something flirty judging from how red she becomes and the shy smile streaking across her face. Ah, young love. I do hope Oliver hasn't set his sights on this one, at least for Joe's sake. My son may be the local heartbreaker but Oliver competes on an international level. He best keep her safe from Lord Freddy through, or he'll have to answer to me.

The telephone rings again, and I cut short my spying. I grin when I see the display. "Hello, lover."

"You better know who this is," Nathan says playfully.

"Martin? Peter? Alice?"

"Ha, ha, ha," Nathan deadpans. "So, how'd it go with the freak?"

"Wonderful. She may be our new daughter-in-law if Joe has his way."

"Oh. So, what'd she need the potions for?"

"Vampire glamour. Seems a local cabal have been quite naughty."

"Some things never change, huh?" He pauses. "You're the best, Mrs. West. You know that?"

"I learned it from you, Mr. West."

The front door opens as Joe rushes in again. "Agent Alexander gone?" I ask.

"For now," he says with his father's confident grin.

I raise an eyebrow. "So we'll be seeing more of her?"

His grin grows. "*Maybe*," he chuckles. "I need to borrow Dad's golf clubs. About to close a deal."

"In the garage, sweetie."

"Thanks! Love you, Mom!" he says before bounding down the hall.

Shaking my head, I meander toward the fireplace mantel the agent was snooping before. "Did I hear right? Are all your guests finally leaving, Mrs. West?" Nathan asks seductively. "Will you be having the house all to yourself?"

"I will, Mr. West. And I'm all yours."

"Dang right. Be home in five minutes."

"See you soon, sweetie."

Chuckling, I click off the phone. He is downright irresistible sometimes. Oh. Asher's picture is crooked. "What do you think, Asher? Think Miss Beatrice Alexander can hold her own in our dark, twisted world?" His smile says it all. "You're right. *They* don't stand a chance."

I adjust my Asher so he fits perfectly among the other family photos and stroll upstairs to get ready to greet my husband. Oh, I do so love these days of wine and roses. Dowson was wrong, they can last a lifetime.

And beyond.

ACKNOWLEDGMENTS

First, thanks to all my readers. I adore and appreciate each and every one of you.

Second, to the Prince William, Fairfax County, and Peachtree City libraries for allowing me a place to go that isn't my house. You keep my cabin fever in check.

Third, to all the people at Midnight Ink who helped shepherd this book to publication. You make this whole publishing process seem so easy and it is not.

Finally, thanks to my mother who told me she loved the character Anna. That one spark spawned this entire book.

© Bill Fitz-Patrick

ABOUT THE AUTHOR

Jennifer Harlow (Manassas, VA) earned a BA from the University of Virginia in Psychology. Her eclectic work experience ranges from government investigator to radio DJ to lab assistant. Visit her website www.jenniferharlowbooks.com to read her blog, *Tales From the Darkside*; listen to the soundtrack to this book; and more.